THE COMPOUND

GWENNA McALLIS

ISBN 979-8-9885669-0-8 (paperback)
ISBN 979-8-9885669-1-5 (hardcover)
ISBN 979-8-9885669-2-2 (ebook)

Cover design by: MiblArt

Published by Oracle Hawk Press

Author website: www.gwennamcallis.com
Instagram.com/gwennamcallisauthor
Facebook.com/gwennamcallis

Content Warning

The Compound is a new adult supernatural horror novel. As such, it contains story elements that some readers may find offensive, disturbing, or triggering. A few of these elements include: death and fantasy violence, infant death, profanity, anti-religion, descriptions of medical procedures, and mentions of mental illness and physical abuse.

For all the outsiders.

PROLOGUE

June 2002

Crofton, Tennessee

A TORRENTIAL RAIN TRAPPED Daniel Wester indoors late one June afternoon. Boredom found the ten-year-old boy quickly and beckoned him into rebellion. Though he knew the rule, Daniel dared to amuse himself by sneaking into his father's forbidden bedroom.

He would be in big trouble if he got caught. No doubt about that. But his father was in the kitchen, all the way on the opposite end of their double-wide trailer, completely engrossed in the task of trying his hand at a homemade meatloaf. This seemed like the perfect opportunity to take the risk.

The door to Pete Wester's bedroom stood slightly ajar and provided enough space for Daniel's small frame to slip inside without him ever actually touching the door itself. That somehow made what he was doing seem less criminal. He wriggled carefully through the entrance and peered around at his forbidden surroundings, trying to decide where to explore first.

Few furnishings occupied the small bedroom. A quilted queen-sized bed, a single nightstand, and an old four-drawer dresser with a mirror. The largest piece, the dresser, caught Daniel's attention.

He tiptoed across the carpeted floor toward it, then hesitated.

He glanced back over his shoulder nervously and listened for the recognizable cadence of his father's approaching footsteps. But he heard only raindrops smacking against the metal roof.

His adventure continued. The old dresser had a sweet, woodsy smell, kind of like pine needles. It reminded Daniel of the long walks he and his dad took so often through the woods that encircled their home. His eyes glided gleefully across the top of the piece, from the plastic comb and hairbrush set to some spare nickels and dimes to a bottle of cologne. Honey-gold liquid-filled half of the glass bottle marked *Stetson Original*.

Daniel removed the cap and sniffed the nozzle. It smelled like Dad. Very carefully, he picked up the bottle and gave the back of his neck a single spritz, just the way he had seen people do it on TV. He set the bottle back where he had found it.

His fingers found the brass knob on the top drawer. He slid it open. Feeling the sting of guilt, he peeked over his shoulder a second time, but the coast remained clear. The thrill of his little r overwhelmed his guilty conscience, and he refocused his vision on the contents of the drawer.

Socks. Mostly black, but a few tan and white ones. Daniel boldly reached inside and moved the socks around, just to make sure the drawer held nothing more interesting. It did not. He moved on to the second drawer and did the same. Nothing but underwear. The third drawer held only white cotton undershirts, and the fourth contained the baggy t-shirts and lounge pants his dad wore around the house on the weekends.

Dissatisfied, Daniel crept over to the nightstand. The small bedside table held a lamp, a shiny silver alarm clock that currently read four-thirty, a faded leather King James Version Bible, and a framed four-by-six photograph of his mother.

Pictures of Helen Wester were rare; this was one of only three in their home. He had never known her. She died when he was a baby. Each time he came across her photographed face, he had to stop and admire her, for it was the only way he could ever be with her. He stared at the photo, momentarily mesmerized by her radiant image. Her auburn hair glowed. Her hazel eyes shimmered as they gazed back at him. He could easily see himself in her. Though he shared his father's coloring- fair skin, blue eyes, and thick, black-brown hair- he had inherited his mother's bone structure. He had her rounded chin. Her dimples. Her nose.

He finally tore his gaze away from the picture and jerked open the nightstand's single drawer. Nothing too exciting in here either. Just a roll of Tums, a pair of glasses, and a few copies of *Reader's Digest*. He extracted the glasses and tried them on, but they made everything blurry and gave him a headache. He put them back and closed the drawer. Where next?

The closet.

It almost called out to him. He stole across the room to the closet door and gingerly pulled it open. He cringed, expecting the door hinges to squeak loudly and give him away, but they did not make a sound.

A single light bulb dangled from the ceiling. To turn it on, you had to tug a metal chain attached to the base of the fixture, but Daniel was tall enough to do that now. The bulb glowed to life as he clicked it on.

A steel rod held his father's clothes. Lots of plaid. Flannel. Wrangler jeans. A couple of nice button-downs and khaki slacks that he wore to church. He had a special hanger for ties, even though he only owned five different ones, three of which Daniel had given him for Father's Days past at the suggestion of his babysitter, Miss Priscilla. He also had a special hanger for belts, Daniel observed. Who knew grown-ups had so many kinds of hangers?

On the floor of the closet, his father's shoes lined up neatly, like toy soldiers at attention. Six different pairs of them, all dull blacks and browns and kind of smelly. Behind the shoes, Daniel glimpsed several stacks of dusty old books. They seemed a little misplaced, but he didn't think anything else about it. He didn't even bother reading the titles. He liked to read well enough, but these books all looked long and boring and probably didn't have any pictures.

He glanced up at the top of the closet, where a shelf held an assortment of items. Some ratty shoe boxes, more big books, extra folded blankets and quilts, and, poking out from beneath the bottom quilt, a wooden box.

A really interesting wooden box.

Daniel wanted to get it down. The fact that it was partially hidden beneath the quilts intrigued him. He had to know what was inside it.

At first, he thought it would be out of reach, but when he stood on his toes and stretched up as far as he could, he brushed the rough wood grain with his fingertips. He grasped one of the corners and slid it forward an inch or two. As he attempted to move it around, he realized it was much heavier than he had imagined. He almost dropped it when he finally pulled it out from under the blankets. But he maneuvered it slowly, cautiously, until he held it at last within his hands.

The rectangular box, probably over a foot wide, definitely over a foot long, and several inches deep, looked ancient. In several places, the dark chocolate wood had been scratched or chipped. The fancy metalwork on the corners had rusted. Carved into the sides and top of the box were several round, complicated designs with weird-looking stars and overlapping triangles and maze-like twists and loops winding across them.

He plopped down cross-legged on the closet floor and leveled the box across his thighs. Not wasting any time, he opened it.

Or tried to.

The large rust-corroded metal clasp on the front would not open until a key had been inserted into the lock.

Daniel's excitement deflated. There was no key.

He tried to think. Had he seen an old-timey key in any of the drawers he had just nosed through? No. He would have certainly noticed something like that. He looked down at the lock once more. Maybe he could pry it open. People did that kind of thing on TV all the time. If he could find some kind of-

"Daniel."

At the sound of his father's stern voice, Daniel felt his heart drop into his abdomen.

Using his peripheral vision, he discerned his father's figure standing to his left. He couldn't bring himself to turn and look up at the man.

"What do you think you're doing?"

That tone. Daniel winced at the quiet yet subtly harsh tone of his dad's voice. He didn't hear that voice often; he was normally a well-behaved kid. He didn't usually do things like this. What had gotten into him? He knew the rule. *No going in Dad's bedroom alone.* He knew it wasn't okay to go through other people's things without asking, but that's what he had done. And all for what? He hadn't even been able to open this stupid box.

"Daniel, what are you doing with that box?"

There would be consequences for this. He couldn't even re- member the last time he had gotten in trouble or what kind of punishment he had received. Maybe a time-out? Daniel was ten now, and ten seemed too old for time-outs. What kind of new, age-appropriate consequence would Dad enforce? He might take away his bike. Ground him from TV for a week. Or even-

"Answer me, son."

Daniel gulped. "I-I'm sorry, Dad, I just- I just got bored and..." *Thought I'd go through your private belongings.* He realized how stupid his plan had been. "I don't know." He didn't even try to

think up a lie; he had never been any good at lying. "I don't know. I'm sorry."

"Did you open that box?"

For the first time, Daniel looked at his father. With his wide eyes and unusually pale complexion, Pete Wester appeared more terrified than angry.

"Did you open it?"

"No, sir. It was locked," Daniel said, dumbly admitting that he had tried.

He heard his father release a sigh. Something like relief swept over his features. He rubbed his forehead and looked down at the box. "Give it to me."

Daniel moved so fast, he didn't even remember standing up. He seemed to have teleported from the closet floor to his father's side, arms extending the mysterious wooden box toward the man. He lowered his head in shame as the weight of the object transferred from his hands to those of his father.

"Go to your room and stay there until supper time."

Daniel did as he was told. He sat on his bed for nearly an hour, imagining all sorts of dreadful punishments he might be forced to endure. But at five-thirty, when his father called him to the supper table, nothing happened. He acted like Daniel had spent the entire day minding his own business, playing quietly in his room. The incident was never discussed.

Days passed. Then weeks. Dad never once mentioned what had happened, and Daniel surely didn't bring it up. But he thought about the box all the time.

At night, as he tried to fall asleep, he pictured the strange designs carved into the box's surface. He visualized Dad's pallid complexion and the alarm in his eyes. He could still hear the fear in the man's voice as his question echoed in his thoughts: *Did you open that box?*

The third Saturday of July, Dad decided to build a compost bin.

Daniel rode shotgun as they drove into town. They grabbed sausage biscuits and extra-greasy hashbrown rounds at the Hardee's drive-thru on the way to Benson's Hardware for materials. Daniel liked Benson's. At first. He liked the woodsy smell of the lumber section. But as usual, Dad lingered far too long there, comparing prices of every single thing, and Daniel got bored.

That's when the idea came to him.

When they returned home, Dad went outside and immediately got to work. Daniel heard him hammering away in the yard, focused on his project.

This was it. This was his chance. He had plenty of time to dash into Dad's bedroom and get another peek inside his closet at the wooden box.

Just like that afternoon three weeks ago, he crept into the room, opened the closet door, and clicked on the light. He peered up at the shelf, craning his neck.

Shoe boxes. Books. Blankets.

The box was gone.

The mysterious wooden box became something of a legend. In August, when he returned to school and started fifth grade, Daniel told his best friend, Lena Dillon, about his discovery, and it turned into a recurrent topic of their conversations. They relished the invention of all sorts of theories- some more ridiculous than others- about the box and what it held.

The box held Daniel's real birth certificate and adoption papers and various other things that proved the two of them were actually twins separated at birth. (Although with Lena's white-blonde hair and nearly translucent porcelain skin, they couldn't possibly be related.)

The box contained a disguise kit that Dad sometimes dressed up in and roamed around town wearing. He could be anyone. The mayor. The gangly bow-tie-wearing guy that bagged groceries at Piggly Wiggly. Even Mrs. Driscoll, the dreadful, shriveled old schoolteacher who once made a kid write sentences on the board for burping in class. They'd never seen Dad and Mrs. Driscoll in the same room...

That one was a classic.

In truth, Daniel liked to believe that the box stored his mother's old things. Her diary, personal mementos, items like that. As pleasant as that idea was, he thought the box had a more dangerous feel to it.

That's why the theory that made the most sense was the gun theory. The wooden box most likely held a gun and bullets. Daniel's father kept no weapons in sight, but that didn't rule out the possibility of him owning one. They lived in rural Tennessee. Pretty much everyone had one. If his father did own a gun, he definitely would have kept it wisely hidden away and locked up. That would also explain why he had been more upset over the prospect of Daniel opening the box than him merely finding it, as well as why it had vanished when he had gone looking for it a second time. His father had been forced to find a new hiding spot because he knew his nosy kid would snoop again. He didn't want Daniel to accidentally shoot himself or anyone else.

Still, there was that lingering dream that the box held something way cooler.

A few times, when Lena had come over to the Westers' place to hang out, she and Daniel had set out to look for the box together, but something had always thwarted their mission. His father called them into the living room for snacks, or he suggested they go outside and get some fresh air. Or the door to his bedroom would simply be locked. Dad was always a step ahead of them.

Finally, they gave up.

They grew up and forgot about the box.

Until the day Daniel found the key.

ONE

Eleven Years Later

A DEAFENING THUNDERCLAP JOLTED Daniel from sleep. It shook the walls of his bedroom. Rattled the windows in their frames. His bed even quivered beneath him.

He wasn't just awake now, he was alert. And jumpy. That crack of thunder had sounded like a canon going off outside his window. That would fray anyone's nerves in the middle of the night.

Except it was no longer night, apparently. Faint, gray light slipped around the edges of his curtains, suggesting a dreary morning. He became aware of how abnormally quiet it was in his room. He didn't hear the usual whirring of his window-unit air conditioner. No faint electrical hum in the background. Only silence.

The storm had knocked off the power.

Well, if there was any upside to being a college graduate with no job prospects in sight, Daniel decided this was it. A Monday morning power outage would send most people into panic mode, but since he currently had no job to report to, he could roll over and go back to sleep if he wanted.

But he didn't. He was too awake now to even consider it. Besides, he was roasting underneath his covers, thanks to the powerless air-conditioner, and he needed to pee.

He tapped his iPhone on the nightstand to check the time. *5:32 AM.* Daniel peeled back his sheets and pushed himself up. It felt better with the blankets off, but the almost tangible humid air in his bedroom still pressed against him. His cotton T-shirt and boxer briefs, wet with perspiration, clung to his body like plastic wrap.

He stepped out into the dark hallway where the air felt much cooler. The unusual silence resulting from the power outage followed him. The lack of sound in the place seemed strange, almost eerie. The only audible thing was the pounding clatter of raindrops against the metal roof and the occasional rumble of thunder, which seemed to be growing fainter as the storm moved away.

He started toward the bathroom and passed his father's room on the way. The door was open. Even in the dim light, Daniel noticed the bed was neatly made. Dad was up earlier than usual. In the kitchen, probably, having his coffee and doing his morning Bible study.

He went on to the windowless hall bathroom, where he flicked the light switch on out of habit. No light came, of course. He used the toilet in near-total darkness then set out to join his father in the kitchen.

It was terribly early, but he was wide awake and didn't feel like lying back down. Plus, he was kind of hungry. He'd start his day a few hours earlier and maybe take a nap in the afternoon. No classes, no job. He could take a damn nap if he wanted.

Breakfast would have to be Honey Nut Cheerios in dark, shadowy silence, Daniel realized. Well, probably not silence. Not with Dad up. The man was a morning person and would surely have things to chat about at the table.

Daniel felt a little bummed. He would miss the morning routine he had fallen into since graduation, a lazy custom that consisted of experimental homemade omelets and streaming the next episode of *Doctor Who* on Netflix.

On the bright side, as long as the power was out, he wouldn't have to scroll Indeed for new job openings. He wasn't bummed about that. The keywords *"bachelor's degree in history"* near *"Crofton, TN"* always gleaned a depressing array of food service and retail opportunities. He was already two months into his student loan grace period, which meant he had less than three months to find work before Sallie Mae was up his ass. He didn't want to accept the growing likelihood of having to call up his old manager at the Wendy's on Highway 111, all to earn *just* enough money to make his monthly student loan payment.

He needed to expand his job search to Chattanooga. Maybe Nashville and Memphis. But those last two would require relocating, which would require deposit money upfront and, well, some other big things Daniel wasn't prepared for just yet.

He would be more than happy to procrastinate job hunting for a little while today. He couldn't lose himself in adventures with the Tenth Doctor, though; not with the power outage. Maybe he'd read. It had been a few semesters since he'd read for fun, before the required reading for his history classes had burned him out on the hobby. Reading sounded like a solid plan.

He rounded the corner of the kitchen, already wincing, mentally preparing himself to receive a painfully cheery morning greeting from Dad. But the kitchen was empty.

Except for a shattered coffee mug lying in a brown puddle on the floor.

An unpleasant tingling sensation swept over him as he stared at the broken pieces. "Dad?" he called out. His voice bounced hollowly off the oak cabinets. "Are you okay?" His eyes wandered around, scanning the floor, making sure his father wasn't lying hurt somewhere.

He found no other signs of the man except for his Bible, which lay open on the kitchen table in front of his chair, abandoned.

He stepped into the living room. The outdated rust-colored sofa held no one. Nor did the brown recliner, Dad's recliner, in the corner.

Feeling a bit nervous, he headed to his father's bedroom. Everything appeared to be in order. All neat and tidy, just the way Dad always left it. He moved into the attached master bath. The darkness made it difficult to see in there, but Daniel could tell it, too, was clean and lacking his father.

He sprinted toward the laundry room, the only room in the double-wide he hadn't visited this morning. He found nothing but a washer, dryer, and a box of powdered Tide, its floral-fruity fragrance overpowering the small room.

Daniel just stood there, frozen, staring at the detergent, trying to figure out what to do.

Maybe Dad had left. Maybe after dropping his coffee, he gave up and went to that new little coffee shop out on the highway that was trying its best to make sad, Podunk Crofton a bit hipper. Or maybe Dad had simply gone to work early. But without cleaning up his mess?

He went to the living room and peeked out the window, out at the front yard. His heart slid to his stomach. Dad's pickup sat in its usual spot.

Daniel checked the wooden key rack that hung next to the front door. Dad's key ring hung there- his truck key, house key, and the spare key to Daniel's shitty Saturn SL1- undisturbed.

His father hadn't gone anywhere. So where was he?

Outside? Maybe he had stepped out into the storm for some reason. That was the only other possibility.

He turned the handle of the deadbolt and heard a click as it disengaged. He moved his hand to the top of the door to unfasten the security chain. Then he stopped.

He had just *unlocked* the deadbolt, and the chain bolt was firmly in place.

Dad had not gone this way.

Daniel felt a bit nauseated as he re-locked the deadbolt. There was only one other place he could try, and that was the back door. If it was also locked...

His knees wobbled as he crossed the shaggy brown carpet in the living room and returned to the kitchen. This time, he didn't look down at the broken coffee mug. He didn't want to see it again. It felt too sinister, somehow. He stepped carefully around it and walked to the screen door that led to the backyard.

Dad had to be out there. Maybe he had slipped in the rain. Fallen over a downed pine tree. Gotten struck by lightning. The horrible possibilities came rushing into his mind, one after another.

But none of those scenarios could be true because the back door was locked.

All three security latches- the deadbolt, barrel bolt, and chain lock- were pulled tight, their locks sturdily in place. No way Dad could have done that from the outside.

Daniel looked out the window anyway, hoping to catch a glimpse of his father walking back toward the trailer. But all he saw through the silver curtain of rain was the wide, empty yard, soggy with mud puddles, and the thick semicircle of clustered pine trees that lined the perimeter of their property.

There was one last thing he could try. He raced to his bedroom. Seized his cell phone from the nightstand. He punched Dad's number.

Ring. Ring. Ring. Ring.

After what seemed like ages, his father's calm voice came on with his vague but polite recorded greeting: *"Please leave your name and number. I'll call you back as soon as possible."*

When the beep sounded, Daniel had a hard time getting started. He opened his mouth, but nothing came out.

"Uh, hey, Dad," he finally squeaked. He cleared his throat. He started pacing the floor and wandered out into the hallway. "It's me." He paused again and tried to steady his pathetic-sounding voice. "I, uh, I just want to make sure you're okay. Where are you? Call me back as soon as you get this, okay?"

He hung up.

Daniel raked a hand through the messy brown waves atop his head. What did all this mean, exactly? What was going on? He felt himself starting to panic, and he hated himself for it. He needed to stay calm. Think straight. This would all probably turn out to be nothing, anyway. There was probably some simple, non-catastrophic reason for his dad's disappearance.

But he couldn't think of a single one.

He resumed his pacing. He gnawed on his bottom lip as he roamed the hallway. He ended up back in the kitchen, back with the broken coffee mug. He stared at his gloomy surroundings, trying to get a grip, trying to figure out what to do. There were no neighbors to call. The Westers' trailer stood alone on a secluded, wooded lot at the end of a one-lane dirt road a few miles outside of town.

He considered calling the police, but what good would that do? They didn't care unless the person in question had been missing for at least forty-eight hours, right? At least that was the case on TV. Would they even believe him, with no evidence that Dad had ever left their property? Or worse- would he be blamed?

Something shiny caught his attention and broke his thoughts.

Something on the kitchen table, inside his father's open Bible, reflecting the light coming in through the window. He hadn't noticed it earlier. He wrinkled his forehead as he approached it.

Thunder growled overhead. The sound seemed a bit portentous now. Daniel's breath snagged in his throat when he got close enough to make out the shiny object's shape.

A key.

Balanced across the pages of the First Epistle of Peter, an antique brass key.

His fingers trembled as he picked it up. It was the right size, the right shape. Daniel knew exactly what it unlocked.

But why was it here, left out like this, after all this time?

He turned it over in his hands and ran a shaky fingertip along the edge, tracing the tiny ridges and notches. It was meant for him. This key was a message from Dad, an explanation for his disappearance, a solution for finding him.

Daniel suddenly wondered if the open pages of Dad's Bible were significant, if maybe he had left a note in a margin or underlined specific letters or words in the scriptures to compose some sort of message for him. A too-hopeful, childish thought perhaps, but he peered down at the pages anyway and found a single line marked with yellow highlighter. Fifth chapter, eighth verse:

> *"Be sober, be vigilant; because your adversary the devil, as a roaring lion, walketh about, <u>seeking whom he may devour</u>."*

The latter part of the verse had been underlined with a black pen for emphasis.

Daniel tried to convince himself that the highlighted verse was a coincidence, that Dad had merely dropped the key onto a random page. But he couldn't ignore the heavy, precognitive notion that the verse was important- at least to his father.

Dad had always been a devout Christian, but one of the quiet ones. Though he'd dragged Daniel to church every damn Sunday since forever, he had never been overly pushy or controlling about his faith the way some religious parents were. Because of this, Daniel respected his father's beliefs despite not sharing them.

However, given the strange circumstances of Dad's disappearance and the content of this highlighted passage, a fresh wave of anxiety rushed over his body as new possibilities occurred to him.

Bits and pieces of lectures from the psych class he'd taken a couple of semesters ago came ripping through his thoughts, agitating his nerves with words like *schizophrenia* and *paranoia* and *religious delusions*.

He tore his eyes away from the foreboding text and refocused on the antique key. The key that would unlock the box of secrets his father had hidden in his off-limits bedroom for years.

TWO

E VEN THOUGH HE HAD been waiting to hear it- *longing* to hear it- when the knock at the front door came, Daniel jumped as though he had been electrocuted.

His fingers fumbled as he disengaged the locks. He jerked the door open and found his best friend on the porch. The silvery light of the rainy morning played a creepy effect on her pale skin and hair. She glowed like some kind of otherworldly fairy creature. It was almost unsettling. Her gray-blue eyes stared up at him, impossibly wide, announcing to him without a single word that she was just as terrified as he was.

"Hey." Lena Dillon spoke in an unusually somber voice. "Any updates? Did you try calling the mill?"

"Yeah, I called them right after we hung up. Dad never showed up for work."

She heaved a sigh. "Shit."

"Yeah. Nobody there knew anything else, either. No one's heard from him." He inhaled deeply and blew it back out. "Come on in."

He opened the door wider, giving her space to pass by him. He watched her as she stepped inside, her purple flip-flops squeaking and squelching loudly, soaked from the rain. She wore a pair of stretchy black shorts, the kind cheerleaders wore, though Lena had never been a cheerleader. These same shorts had been looser and longer on her last summer, before the stress of nursing school final exams and state boards and a new job at the hospital. Now they clung tightly to her curves, hugging rounder hips and thicker thighs.

Daniel became aware of his lingering stare and glanced upward at her sky-blue tank top. This garment also stretched to accommodate her plumper frame, particularly around her midsection. The thin fabric was so damp with raindrops, he could make out her floral-print bra underneath. Yellow daisies. He felt his ears growing warm as he noticed this, and he immediately forced his eyes elsewhere. His gaze fixed instead on the patches of black cat fur clinging to her top, evidence of snuggles with her beloved tuxedo cat.

Lena's long, white-blonde hair had been pulled back into a messy braid. Little strands stuck out in an unruly manner, rebelling against the orderly, woven pattern and rubber band.

Once she was inside, Daniel closed the door behind them. Locked it. He turned around to find her staring openly at him the way he had probably just stared at her. Her eyes met his for a split second, then she shifted her gaze away, embarrassed.

That's when Daniel realized his clothing situation. He peered down at his gray TARDIS T-shirt and plaid boxer briefs and felt the tips of his ears blaze even hotter. "Sorry. I, uh, I forgot. Man, I think I'm losing it. I'll go put on some pants."

Her cheeks flushed a pale pink as she absentmindedly fidgeted with the strap of the oversized beige purse slung over her left shoulder.

Daniel suddenly felt awkward. "I'll, uh, I'll be right back." He excused himself, darted into his room, grabbed the nearest pair of jeans from a pile of dirty clothes on the floor, and slid them on over his shorts, feeling like an idiot. Who forgets to put on pants?

He returned to Lena in seconds. He felt his heart jump in his chest when he first glimpsed her standing alone in the shadowy living room. The lighting, again. It made her look weird. Like a disembodied spirit of the dead.

The events of this morning had turned him into a nervous wreck. He determined to pull himself together.

"Your power still hasn't come back on?" she asked, staring up at the lifeless ceiling fixture.

"Nope. I hope it does soon. It's getting stuffy in here."

"Yeah. The same at my apartment. We sure do take air-conditioning for granted, don't we?"

"Oh, yeah. Especially this time of the year."

"Mm-hmm. Summer in Tennessee is no joke."

What the hell were they doing, chatting about air-conditioning? Wasting time. Stalling.

Their eyes met abruptly, almost accidentally. Lena's frightened gaze mirrored his own so candidly, they froze in anxious silence for a moment.

This was bad.

They both knew it.

Whatever had happened to Dad was so dire, he'd found it necessary to make his box of secrets available to his son.

Daniel sucked in a deep breath. He reached down, plucked the antique key from the corner of the coffee table where he had set it, and held it out to Lena.

She took it from him gently, reluctantly. Her eyes gleamed with fascination as she cradled it in her palm. "It was just lying out on the kitchen table?"

"Yeah. On top of his Bible."

She gave a slight grimace, undoubtedly recalling the disturbing details Daniel had already shared when he'd called her half an hour ago. "So, he wanted you to find it," she said. "He wants you to find that old box and open it. Whatever is inside, it may tell us where he is. Or it may help us figure it out."

Or it might contain a gun. That's what they had finally written it off as years ago. Maybe something so terrible had happened, Dad thought Daniel would need the weapon to protect himself.

"It can't be a gun," Lena said, gazing into his eyes as though she were reading his thoughts on tiny projection screens inside his pupils.

"Well," he breathed, "we have to find the thing first."

"Where could he have moved it to?"

"I don't know. I haven't looked for it in, like, ten years. Maybe he put it back in his closet."

"Maybe. Let's start there." She unzipped her huge purse and began digging inside it. "I didn't know if we'd need it or not, but I brought a flashlight."

Of course. Lena always had everything, like a well-prepared soccer mom. She unearthed a compact black flashlight and gave it to him.

"Thanks." He flicked the switch to test it out. Startlingly bright LED beams lit up the living room. Temporarily blinded, he flipped it off. "Very nice."

She set her purse on the couch arm. "You lead the way."

Together, they moved down the hallway, crossed the threshold of his father's bedroom, and approached the closet. He felt like a little kid again as he turned the knob on the closet door and yanked it open.

He reached up to click on the light bulb, then remembered the power was out. He glanced at Lena. "Habit."

"I know. I've been doing it all morning."

Daniel turned on the flashlight. The round beam moved like a stage spotlight, illuminating the cob-webbed corners of the closet. Over a decade had passed since his last visit, but little had changed. Dad had accumulated a few more shoe boxes, more ties, and half a dozen new baseball caps to cover his thinning hair. On the shelf, the old blankets and quilts were exactly where they had been. Daniel lifted them and found nothing.

"Maybe behind the shoe boxes?" Lena suggested.

Daniel passed the flashlight to her. She held it over his shoulder while he moved the shoeboxes around. No wooden box.

Lena sighed. "Underneath the bed?"

"You take the flashlight and check there. I'll look in the dresser."

"Okay."

He went to the dresser and immediately began rummaging through the four drawers. Enough light came through the bedroom window to brighten the area, but his search came up empty. "Any luck?"

"No," her muffled voice replied. "Nothing under here but plastic bins full of coats and winter clothes and stuff."

The only other piece of furniture in the room was the nightstand, and Daniel could tell by looking that the legendary wooden box was too big to fit in its single drawer.

"If it's not in here, where could it be?" Lena asked. She brushed a clingy dust bunny off of her shorts as she stood to her feet.

"I don't know." He glanced up at the ceiling. "I really think it's in here somewhere." His eyes followed the strip of brown wood trim around the top of the room like he expected something to line up wrong. Like the opening to a secret passageway would suddenly reveal itself to him.

Lena looked down at the floor and started shifting her weight around, apparently hoping for the same thing. A loose floorboard, maybe, like in the movies.

"Can I have the flashlight?" he asked.

"Yeah, sure." She handed it to him. "Do you see something?"

"No, I just-" He moved back to the closet, feeling something pulling him to it. "I just wanna look in here again."

Daniel parted the hanging clothes and glided a hand over the wall behind them. No hidden safe or entrance to a secret room. He had seen too much TV.

He squatted down and shined the light around in the bottom of the closet. With all the shoes lying about, it smelled like stinky feet. Daniel felt fairly certain at least half of these shoes were the exact same ones that had been here when he was ten years old. A particular pair of black Rockports sure smelled ripe enough to have been worn for over a decade.

The flashlight beam caught the spines of the dusty old books Daniel had seen down here as a child. He hadn't bothered to read the titles then, but he did now.

Demons: Knowing Your Enemy.

Possessions and Exorcisms.

A History of Demons.

Demonology: Adramelech to Zepar.

"Uh... come here."

"What?" Lena came to his side and crouched next to him. "What is it?"

"The books."

It took her a second to scan over the titles. "What the hell?"

Daniel reached in and removed *Demons: Knowing Your Enemy* by Dr. Clyde Sherman. He opened it and began flipping through the pages. Chapter titles such as, "Guarding Yourself from Demonic Attack" seemed to jump off the page at him. The book featured diagrams of occult symbols, from basic circles of protection to complex hexagrams, that could be drawn around oneself to ward off evil spirits.

Blue ink underlined specific passages. Little notes in Dad's blocky, all-caps penmanship filled the margins. He had taken his time studying these volumes.

Daniel felt sick as he recalled the highlighted scripture he'd discovered next to the key:

> *"Be sober, be vigilant; because your adversary the devil, as a roaring lion, walketh about, <u>seeking whom he may devour.</u>"*

Okay. So. Dad was truly worried about demons and the devil. A psychiatric diagnosis was looking more likely by the minute. Daniel's stomach churned as he wondered for the hundredth time where the man had gone. He feared for his safety more than ever.

"Has... has he always had these?" he heard Lena ask.

"I-I think so. But I didn't pay any attention to them before."

"Why the hell would he have this kind of stuff?"

"I have no clue."

Lena shifted around and planted her backside on the floor. "Do you remember that time in high school? Junior year, I think. We rented *The Exorcism of Emily Rose* on DVD, and your dad kinda lost his shit when he saw it because he *'didn't want that kind of evil in his house.'*"

He looked at her.

Her eyes were huge again, fixed on the disturbing old books. "Isn't this the same kind of 'evil' he was talking about? Weird, creepy, demonic junk? Why would he keep books like this?" Lena paused. "Does he really believe in all this stuff?"

Daniel considered it for a moment. He thought of all the Sunday mornings he had spent sitting on a church pew next to his father. All the sermons he had sat through on *spiritual warfare*. Those were popular Christian buzzwords. Church people loved to bemoan how Satan and his army of demons constantly did battle against God, His angels, and His human followers on Earth.

Anything negative that happened in the life of a Christian was automatically declared an attack from the enemy- the devil and the demons who did his bidding. Anything negative qualified as such. Accidents. Illness. Running late for church. He'd even heard grown adults within the church label things as trivial as misplacing their car keys an "attack from the enemy."

Not today, Satan, and all that ridiculousness.

It was all bullshit. Daniel had never accepted those stories as fact. He viewed those old tales as nothing but that- tales. Stories. Myths. He was a history major, after all. He knew demons were the archaic, ignorant way people of the past rationalized catastrophes like plague and famine. Demonic possession was how they explained bodily disorders that they couldn't understand, things like epilepsy.

Stories like that weren't meant to be taken literally, not in 2013. Society knew better now. Christians just wanted their day-to-day lives to feel special and important.

Wasn't his father smarter than that? Daniel had always assumed so. Sure, the guy believed he had a personal relationship with the

Almighty Creator of the universe, but Daniel could give him a pass on that one. Dad was a lonely widower who found comfort in his benign rituals of prayer and weekly church-going.

He wasn't one of those crazies who went around shoving tracts into strangers' hands, picketing abortion clinics, and burning Harry Potter books. He hadn't painted any of those creepy symbols from *Demons: Knowing Your Enemy* on the floor to protect them from literal demons. Yes, he had been upset about *The Exorcism of Emily Rose*, but plenty of people were. They lived in the fucking Bible Belt. Nearly everyone they knew was scared of the devil. He had friends who weren't allowed to watch *Pokémon* because of its demonic roots. Rebecca Davis from their sixth-grade class couldn't even eat Lucky Charms cereal because her parents believed *all* magic was of the devil.

Still. The questionable stack of books in the back of his father's closet made him wonder.

"I don't know," he finally said. "But we need to find that box."

"Right."

As Daniel slid the book into its place between the others, he felt one of the corners catch on something. "Hang on." He pulled the book out again and shined the flashlight where it had been.

Wood.

His heart leaped with excitement. He moved another book out of the way, reminding himself that the wood he had seen might just be the back of the closet. But when he shoved aside *Principalities, Powers, and Rulers of the Darkness*, he realized his hunch had been correct.

Daniel heard Lena gasp as he pulled the ancient wooden box from its hiding place. The movement caused a small explosion of dust. He coughed.

"Oh my god," Lena breathed. "It's beautiful."

It was. It looked just as enticing and mysterious as it had eleven years ago. He brushed a disgustingly thick layer of dust off its surface and revealed the carved symbols. Intricate occult designs that looked, he realized with dismay, a little too much like the protection symbols he had just seen in that book.

Maybe he would look them up later. If he found the nerve.

Box in hand, he rose to his feet. "Come on. Let's set it down over here." He took it to his father's queen-size bed and sat down, balancing the box across his lap. The mattress squeaked as Lena joined him. She scooted close until their outer thighs were touching. He dug the key out of his pocket and turned to her.

"Well. I'm a little nervous."

Lena didn't say anything, but judging by her wrinkled forehead and unblinking wide eyes, she shared his anxiety.

Daniel held his breath as he forced the key into the rusty lock.

THREE

T HE HINGES CREAKED AS Daniel raised the lid of the box. Inside, he found papers.

Lots of papers, different sizes and textures, most of them faded and yellow. He didn't give them much attention though, because, on top of them, a large, crisp manila envelope had been placed horizontally, face up. Six capital letters had been written across the front with a black Sharpie:

DANIEL

Upon finding his name, Daniel felt his tongue growing heavy and his mouth dry. He felt Lena's eyes on him as he reached inside and removed the envelope.

"Hey, um, Daniel?"

He looked at her.

"Are you, uh," Lena stammered, "are you sure you want me here for this? This might be really... personal or something."

"Yeah." He swallowed. "Don't go. Please."

She nodded.

Daniel refocused on the envelope. He turned it over and un-fastened the little gold clasp. More papers, about three or four of them, all letter-sized printer paper. He slid them out.

The front page was a letter, a few short paragraphs written in Dad's compulsively neat, blocky hand.

Daniel glanced at Lena again and found her staring at him, obviously hesitant to read over his shoulder. He appreciated her trying to give him privacy, but they were in this together. And, well, he didn't want to read it alone. He moved the paper closer to her so they both could read it.

Daniel,

If you're reading this, then I'm in trouble. The most important thing for you to do right now is to get to safety as fast as you can. I've put directions to your Aunt Geri's place inside this envelope. Go straight there. She'll know what to do next. Despite what little you know about her, she loves you, and you can trust her.

No matter what's happened to me, don't call the police or anyone else. Don't tell anyone what's going on. The more people you get involved, the more people you risk getting hurt.

This is very serious, Daniel. You'll need to wear the pendant I put in the envelope for you. Keep it on you at all times. Take the box with you. Take the books in my closet too.

I'm sorry I haven't told you the truth before now. I just wanted to keep you safe. I love you more than my own life.

Dad

When Daniel finished reading the letter, he read it again. Then two more times. He still didn't know what to think.

Lena spoke first. "Aunt Geri. She's your dad's sister, isn't she?"

"Yeah." He gulped. "But I've never met her."

"Where does she live?"

"I don't know. Dad never said."

With trembling fingers, Daniel leafed through the attached pages, the driving directions to Geri Wester's home. Rows and rows of step-by-step instructions, all handwritten by his father. And they filled up two and a half pages. The trip looked very tedious.

"He said 'despite what little you know about her'," Lena said. "What's that? What *do* you know about her?"

Daniel scratched his forehead. "Not much. She's a carpenter. I do remember him saying that once, it stood out. She's older than Dad, I think. The two of them had some big blow-out a long time ago, and they haven't spoken to each other for years."

"Oh."

"I don't know why he wants me to go to her."

"Well, he says you can trust her."

"Yeah."

They both stared at the letter again. *If you're reading this, then I'm in trouble.* What the hell kind of trouble had Dad gotten himself into? *Don't call the police*? Why not? Had he done something illegal? What else would that mean?

Daniel looked at Lena. He wanted to ask what she thought about all these red-flag statements, but he couldn't seem to find his voice.

She fiddled nervously with a loose strand of her hair, then resolutely tucked it behind her ear. "What about the pendant?" she asked. "That part sounded especially weird. It's in the envelope?"

Daniel reached into the envelope and felt around at the bottom until his fingertips closed around a cool chunk of metal. He pulled it out.

A quarter-sized silver medallion etched with symbols hung from a simple leather cord. In the center of the medallion, a five-pointed star surrounded an embedded obsidian stone. Smaller symbols like the ones in Dad's books and on the outside of the old wooden box were situated at each of the star's points, all of them unique and equally foreboding. A circle enclosed all of this, with a ring of words making up the outermost edge.

At least he thought they were words. The language was certainly not English; the alphabet was ancient. Daniel's new history degree hadn't landed him a job yet, but it allowed him to make some educated guesses here. He'd seen images of stone tablets with similar characters in one of his world history classes. Phoenician alphabet, maybe? Or Etruscan? Maybe even older than those. It could be Mesopotamian cuneiform for all he knew. None of his professors had spent much time focusing on the history of the alphabet, so Daniel wasn't sure.

Keep it on you <u>at all times</u>.

Daniel swallowed hard. "God."

"Yeah," Lena breathed. "This is weird."

"Really fucking weird."

The two of them sat there for a while without speaking, just staring at the strangeness in front of them.

Daniel's chest tightened as he ran his fingers back and forth across the engraved metal pendant. He felt something welling up inside of him, something heavy and painful twisting behind his sternum. He thought he was going to cry. Or vomit. He finally mustered the strength to verbalize the question that had been gnawing at him since he'd first found the key.

"You... you don't think Dad's lost it, do you?" He felt his eyes stinging, burning. He blinked urgently. "Like... maybe he's had some kind of psychotic break?"

"Honestly? I don't know." Lena grew quiet, thinking. "He's been sitting on all this for years, apparently. He's had it all at least since we were kids. But he's never had any signs of mental illness. I mean, he doesn't have a history of anything like that, right?"

"No."

"I know he's very religious, and he always has been, but your dad is one of the most grounded, sensible, practical people I know."

"Yeah, but that doesn't always mean much."

She shrugged. "Has he been acting weird lately? Like, has he seemed different? Have you noticed any changes in his behavior at all?"

"No." He took a minute to ponder her question further, replaying all the encounters with his father he could recall from the last few days in his mind. "Nothing."

"Has he been taking any new medications?"

Asked like a true registered nurse. She sounded so professional. "Not that I know of. I mean, he's healthy. I'm pretty sure all he takes is baby aspirin and a multivitamin."

Lena nodded. "Okay. For now, let's assume he's lucid and just go along with it. Maybe your aunt will know what's going on. I'll drive. We can take my car."

Daniel felt nauseous again. A certain part of the letter came into his thoughts.

Don't tell anyone what's going on. The more people you get involved, the more people you risk getting hurt.

"I don't think it's a good idea for you to go," he said.

"What?"

"You said to assume he's lucid, right? You read what he wrote about getting other people involved. He said not to tell anyone."

"Yeah, but it's kinda too late for that. Have you told anyone else?"

"No. Well, I did talk to the secretary at the mill when I called to see if Dad had shown up today, but I didn't give her any details. Look, if Dad's lucid and he thinks you could get hurt-"

"It doesn't matter. You can't go alone."

"The letter says I have to."

"Listen, I already know he's missing. I know he's in trouble. And according to that letter, *you're* not safe until you get to your aunt. If I don't go with you, I'll just be sitting around here on pins and needles, worried about you and your dad both." She grasped his forearm with her left hand. Her fingers felt like popsicles. "Please let me go with you."

"What about work?"

"I'm off today."

"Well, what about tomorrow?"

She bit her lip. "I'll call in."

Lena had never called in to work. Ever. Not even when they worked part-time fast food jobs in high school. She rarely got sick and was far too responsible to blow off a shift for anything else. She'd only been working at the hospital for a few weeks. She was still new, fresh out of nursing school, trying to assert herself and find her way there.

"Are you… are you sure?"

"You're family, Daniel, this is an emergency."

"Do you even have PTO yet? You've only been there for-"

"It's okay. We're not worrying about all that stuff right now. This. Is. An. Emergency."

He sighed. "What about Mr. Darcy?"

"Oh, he's fine. He has food and water to last him a couple of days. Even if he didn't, he could get by on his own fat stores. Or maybe he could make himself useful and actually catch a freaking mouse for dinner."

Daniel smirked at that.

"I'll just have my mom come by and feed him while we're gone."

"And what the hell will you tell her?"

"Ugh, I don't know, Daniel, I'll think of something. I'm not letting you go by yourself."

"You're not 'letting' me?"

"Nope."

He scoffed and peered down at his lap, at the pentagram medallion, at the envelope, considering everything for a moment. "Okay," he exhaled at last. He lifted his eyes to hers and stared meaningfully into them. "Thank you."

Lena smiled and gave his arm a gentle squeeze. "We should hurry. He said to take the books. I can start loading them in my car while you pack a suitcase. And I think you better put on that necklace."

"Really?"

"That's what he said to do."

Daniel brushed his fingertips across the black gemstone and the ancient engravings. *Assume he's lucid.* He couldn't grasp the full weight of what his father's lucidity would mean. Where had Dad even gotten this thing?

Lena stared at him, waiting.

This was absurd. It was all absurd. Daniel sucked in a sharp breath and slipped the leather strap over his head. The medallion dangled against his chest.

Lena was still staring.

"What?" he asked.

"Do you... feel... anything?"

He almost laughed. "Um. Gaudy. That's about it."

"Huh."

Though he had to admit, as silly as it was, he was semi-expecting to feel *something* when he put it on. He'd sort of imagined being bathed in a warm glow as the medallion imbued him with magical powers.

But no. He hadn't felt so much as a tingle.

"Yeah. Not really your style," she agreed with a small smile. "Maybe tuck it in your shirt."

He tugged the collar of his T-shirt and dropped the pendant inside. The medallion fell into place, resting against his heart. The coolness of the metal felt surprisingly nice against his skin in the humid summer air. He actually shivered.

Lena didn't notice. She was already on her feet and headed to the closet to begin removing Dad's creepy old books.

FOUR

D ANIEL THREW SOME CLOTHES and toiletries in a duffel bag, and they loaded Dad's book collection- about a dozen tomes altogether- into Lena's Camry. They took Highway 111 into Crofton, where they made a quick stop at Pinewood Village Apartments.

Pinewood Village was one of exactly two apartment complexes in Crofton; in all of Jamison County, actually. Of the two options, Pinewood Village was the nicer one. Their sole competitor, Riverview Court, was on the rougher side of town near two vape shops and the mobile home park (and there was no river in sight). Pinewood Village was clean and recently updated on the inside, though they had retained their out-of-place beige stucco from the eighties on the exterior. The single-level complex offered two-bedroom villas with patios, and Lena lived in unit D6.

Daniel and Lena stood together in her kitchen at present, illuminated by only the bleak, gray daylight that streamed through the window panes. The power was still out here, too.

Neither of them knew what or how much to pack. They didn't know where they were going or how long they would be there. Yet somehow, always-prepared Lena had managed to fill up a backpack, a rolling suitcase, and a green duffel bag of her own in well under fifteen minutes. Daniel could only guess what she had decided to bring along. He watched her now, tossing road snacks into a reusable shopping bag from T.J. Maxx, while he held Mr. Darcy.

The short-haired tuxedo cat purred contentedly as Daniel scratched the silky fur between his ears.

"You're being abnormally sweet today," Lena said to the cat as she grabbed a couple of Honeycrisp apples from a decorative wooden bowl on her counter.

It was true. Mr. Darcy had a special fondness for Daniel and always harassed him for pets the moment he saw him, but today, he was being particularly clingy. He tilted his feline chin back, exposing the white fur of his neck and chest (his *cravat*, Lena called it), begging for scratches. Daniel appeased him. Mr. Darcy's shrewd golden eyes stared into Daniel's for a moment, then he flopped his head against Daniel's chest and rubbed affectionately.

Lena's mouth fell open as she watched this. "Aww! He must be able to sense something's wrong."

Daniel nodded and squeezed the cat a little tighter.

Lena opened the fridge and removed a couple of generic store-brand bottled waters. Daniel knew she hated the plastic waste, but the tap water in Crofton was truly horrendous and she couldn't afford a filter yet. She slipped the bottles into her T.J. Maxx bag. "Okay. I'm all set. I just need to leave my mom a note."

She rushed off down the dark hallway.

Daniel remained in the kitchen, Mr. Darcy growing heavy in his arms. He stared at the refrigerator door as he waited, his eyes scanning the handful of magnets Lena had collected. A black-and-white cat butt that Lena's mom said was 'vulgar'. A square with a vintage painting of a waterfall and the words *Ruby Falls*. She'd purchased it from the Ruby Falls gift shop when they'd visited a couple of years ago.

A larger, round, dusty-pink magnet featured a woman's facial profile in silhouette with the overlaid text: *Obstinate Headstrong Girl.* He'd bought it for Lena last fall after she'd lost her mind over it at Winder Binder bookstore in Chattanooga. The magnet held up the most recent photo of them, a Polaroid snapshot from a photo booth at a high school classmate's wedding last month. Daniel cut a goofy face as he held a cardboard monocle over one eye. A black cardboard mustache on a stick obscured the top half of Lena's big, open-mouthed smile. The photographer had caught her mid-laugh.

Daniel loved it.

Thunder rumbled outside as Lena returned with a piece of paper and a pen. She set both on the beige laminate countertop, clicked the pen top, and stared at the blank paper. Except it wasn't entirely blank. A tacky border of bright yellow roses lined the edges. Actual stationery. A gift from her mother, no doubt. An old-fashioned Southern lady like Carol Dillon most certainly would have made sure her daughter had proper stationery.

Daniel watched Lena as she fiddled with the ink pen, clicking its top repeatedly, compulsively. Her eyes stared off toward the living room at nothing. He could see the wheels turning in her head. At last, she put pen to paper. She wrote quickly, but she still produced a lovely cursive her hypercritical mother *might* approve of. Her cheeks reddened as she penned her letter, and Daniel wondered what lie she was concocting to excuse her absence. He glanced away, trying hard to not read over her shoulder.

"Done." Lena clicked the pen top a final time and dropped it on the counter. "Now." She grabbed her iPhone from its spot by the stove and lit up the screen. "It's seven-fifty-three. Mom will be heading into her eight o'clock Pilates class, so it'll be a good time to text her. She'll be too distracted to see it, so we won't have to worry about her responding for at least an hour and a half. Maybe longer if she decides to get smoothies with Barbara." She rolled her eyes as she said this.

"Okay. What are you gonna tell her?"

Lena sighed. "Something vague to buy us a little time. Ideas?"

They brainstormed quickly and settled on:

> *Sorry it's last minute but can you feed Mr. Darcy for a couple days? More details later. He's good for today but will need food tomorrow. Thanks!!! :)*

Lena's phone chirped as she hit send. "Alright. Let's go."

"Bye, Mr. Darcy," Daniel said, giving the cat a final scratch on the head. He set him down on the carpet.

Mr. Darcy threw himself against Daniel's shins, rubbing back and forth across the bottom of his jeans.

"I'm sorry, buddy," Lena told him, squatting to give him a back rub. "We gotta go."

A great peal of thunder, the loudest one yet, boomed around them. The floor shuddered under their feet. The windows vibrated.

"Jeez," Lena said. She stood up and slung her purse strap over her head. "That's gonna be fun to drive in."

Mr. Darcy crouched down close to the carpet, his ears flattening against his skull. The fur along his back bristled and stood on end as he stared at the front door.

Daniel and Lena heard a fierce, low, throaty growl.

"Oh my god," Lena breathed. "That's *him*."

"Since when does he get like this during thunderstorms?"

"Since today. He's never done this before."

Daniel felt uneasy as he watched Mr. Darcy's tail swat back and forth, back and forth, his golden eyes dilated and fixed on the entrance to the apartment.

"I-I think we need to go," Daniel said, grabbing Lena's duffel.

She nodded.

Mr. Darcy crept a few inches toward the door and released a ghastly hiss.

"What is it?" Lena asked her pet, wide-eyed. She heaved her backpack onto her shoulder. Hesitantly, she added, "Do you... see something?"

The silver medallion from Dad felt heavy and cold against Daniel's chest. A rising sense of dread engulfed him. He seized the handle of Lena's rolling suitcase and lifted it off the floor, not wanting to make a bunch of noise. "We need to go, now," he whispered, moving into the living area. "But not out the front."

Lena kept quiet as she followed him past the chocolate brown couch, around the oval-shaped mahogany coffee table that held a terrarium of succulents (artificial, because of Mr. Darcy) and a stack of pretty books. They congregated at the pair of French doors leading to the patio and stared outside.

The rain was even heavier now. A jagged streak of lightning shot down from the sky, striking way too close for comfort.

"Shit," Daniel breathed. The air around him suddenly felt so cold, he expected his breath to form a misty cloud. His scalp prickled as Mr. Darcy hissed again behind them. "Ready?"

Lena grimaced as thunder rocked the apartment. She was clearly *not* ready, but she nodded anyway.

Daniel jerked open the door on the right and out they ran, into the downpour. The cement patio was slippery beneath Daniel's sneakers, and he did a harrowing slide once, but he willed himself steady as they hurried around the side of the building, taking the back way to the parking lot.

The run to the car was clunky and awkward, thanks to Lena's stupid amount of bags. Daniel knew the way, but the deluge made it hard to see where they were going. The rain looked like static on a TV screen, a filter blurring reality. He felt a surge of panic as he realized they probably wouldn't be able to see an attacker if they crossed paths.

That is if the attacker was even visible to begin with.

A blast of cold air nearly knocked the breath out of him. It was July, how the hell was it this cold? His blood felt like it was freezing inside his veins. The pendant burned like a chip of ice against his chest.

He quickened his pace, propelled onward by an overwhelming sense of urgency. Up ahead, he could make out the familiar lines of Lena's silver Toyota Camry. They were almost there. His legs felt wobbly and weak, but he pushed himself harder.

Daniel saw Lena's car keys flopping around in her hand. The Camry's trunk popped open. They reached the rear of the vehicle and began throwing bags inside.

Daniel's spine tingled as they worked. The eerie, unmistakable sensation of being watched rushed over him. He slammed the compartment shut, and they hastened toward the doors.

As he slid into the passenger's seat, Daniel caught a glimpse of a figure through the windshield. A dark, human-like shape lurking in front of the apartment complex. The thick veil of rain obscured any other details.

Lena cranked the Camry, thrust it into reverse, and left the shadowy figure behind them.

FIVE

Lena guided the Camry onto the southbound ramp of Interstate 75. Daniel rode shotgun, the handwritten directions to Aunt Geri's house and the old wooden box in his lap.

For the first thirty or so miles, both of them had checked the car's mirrors repeatedly, convinced they were being followed. But they never saw anything to indicate such, and after a while, they relaxed a little and focused on the journey ahead of them.

The morning thunderstorm had moved on, and the rain had eased up quite a bit over the past hour. Lena barely needed the windshield wipers now. She kept her eyes focused on the four gray lanes of interstate before them as Daniel skimmed over the directions.

"This says you keep straight on I-75 for about sixty miles," he told her.

Lena clicked on the cruise control. "Okay."

Since they wouldn't need them again for a while, Daniel tucked away the directions. He shifted around in his seat and tried to calm down. He was on edge. If he wasn't checking the mirrors, he was checking his phone for new calls or texts from Dad. If he wasn't checking his phone, he was staring at Lena's phone in the cup holder, expecting the screen to light up with an incoming call from Carol Dillon.

The text they'd worked together to compose wouldn't contain enough information for Carol. She'd be calling any time now with a barrage of invasive questions they couldn't answer yet. *Where are you going? How long do you want me to feed this cat? Did you ask one of your nurse friends first? What about Daniel, he has lots of free time, did you ask him? You do realize I have quite a lot of responsibilities on my plate, don't you?*

Daniel winced at the thought of having a conversation about this with the tiresome woman. Lena put her phone on silent mode and assured him they would ignore any calls from her mother. At least for a while, until they knew more about Dad's situation.

The car went quiet except for the Steel Firesign song playing on the radio. No one spoke for a couple of miles.

"Do you think Mr. Darcy's okay?" Lena finally asked. There was a noticeable tremor in her voice. "I feel like maybe we shouldn't have left him."

Daniel didn't know what to say. He shared her concern for their feline friend, but he had the distinct and worrisome feeling that the shadowy figure outside her apartment had left when they did.

"And I just sent my mom over there." She shook her head regretfully. "Who was that in the parking lot? *What* was that? What the hell is happening?"

He gulped. Before he could formulate a reply, Lena spoke again.

"Okay, so, let's work through this. When you woke up this morning, your dad was already gone?"

He could answer that one, as painful as it was to discuss. "Yes."

"Did you hear any weird noises during the night?"

"No." He drew in a deep breath and blew it back out. "Whatever happened, I slept right through it."

She glanced over at him for a moment. Daniel wondered if he looked as miserable as he felt. As guilty. How could he have slept through it? Dad's coffee mug had somehow crashed onto the floor, so one could assume there had been some kind of struggle (even if it involved hallucinations). And the entire time, Daniel lay snoozing away in the other room, totally unaware. It sickened him.

"The doors were all locked from the inside," Daniel continued. He'd already told her this, but he needed to say it again. "His truck was in the driveway. It's like he just... vanished into thin air."

"It makes no sense."

"None of this does."

"Hopefully your aunt can help us put some pieces together. If your dad is sending you to her, she must know some things."

Daniel placed his right elbow on the armrest. "I wish I knew more about her. Like, at least her phone number. It'd be nice to call and make sure she's home before we drive halfway across America to see her. You know?"

"Yeah. But let's not worry about that yet, okay? I think we already have enough to worry about."

Daniel sighed.

"Why don't you see what else is in there?" Lena suggested, bobbing her head toward the box in his lap. "Maybe there's more about your aunt. Or something else that can help."

He looked down at the wooden container. On their way out the door, he had wrapped it in a clean bath towel to protect it from the rain and the humid summer air. Apart from the items it held, the box itself was precious. Definitely antique, at least a century, maybe even two centuries, old. Daniel thought the thing belonged in a museum somewhere.

His fingers moved carefully as they peeled away the towel and lifted the lid. He swept his eyes over the contents, trying to decide where to start. The papers looked totally different when illuminated by the bright natural lighting inside the car. A small leather journal. Faded newspaper clippings. A stack of old mail bundled by a rubber band.

He picked up a newspaper clipping at random. An obituary. July 1988.

Crider, Jedediah.

Funeral services for infant Jedediah Bryce Crider of Tulsa will be held on July 5, 1988, at Cole Funeral Home. Burial will be in the Roosevelt Hill Cemetery. Jedediah was the only child of Edward and Marion Crider.

"Is that an obituary?" Lena asked.

"Yeah. For a baby named Jedediah Crider. In Tulsa."

"What? Do you recognize that name?"

"No." None of the Criders' names rang any bells. "I know Dad lived in Tulsa for a while when he was young. He went to college there." He glanced down at the date on the obit again. 1988. "He would have been there during the eighties. I guess this was the baby of someone he met at the university."

"How sad."

Daniel placed the obituary back inside the box. He pulled out another one. September 1988.

Garrison, Abigail.

Another unfamiliar name.

The funeral for Abigail Joy Garrison, aged ten months, will be held at 10:00 AM on Friday, September 9, 1988, at Cole Funeral Home in Tulsa. Burial will be-

What the hell? *This* is what Dad's mysterious box contained? Infant obituaries? From Tulsa, Oklahoma? Why did Dad have these?

"It's... another one," his voice shook. "Another obituary. For a baby."

Lena looked away from the road for a brief moment to meet his gaze, her eyes wide with alarm. She didn't say anything.

He slipped the paper back into the box and fought the urge to close it. A new sense of dread swelled inside him, twisting his guts.

Whatever reason Dad had for holding onto these clippings for so long, for hiding them in this locked box in the back of his closet for decades, it couldn't be good. He didn't want to see any more.

But he needed to.

He redirected his attention to the stack of unopened mail. About twenty or so different-colored envelopes containing greeting cards, by the looks of them, all stamped, addressed, postmarked, and sealed. He lifted the stack and nearly dropped it when he read the address on the front of one:

Daniel Wester
119 Martin's Gap Road
Crofton, Tennessee 37300

No return address. The postmark date was six months ago, two days before his twenty-first birthday. He loosened the rubber band that held the envelopes together.

"What are all those?" Lena asked him.

"I don't know," he said, flipping through them. "They're all addressed to me."

"Really?"

"Yeah. No return address on any of them."

Each had been mailed either around Christmas time or his birthday, and the postmarks dated all the way back to January 1996. Daniel couldn't decide which one to open- the most recent one or the oldest.

He finally picked the most recent one. January 17 of this year.

Daniel ripped it open slowly, being careful not to damage whatever might be inside. He slid out a simple black and white card with the number *21* printed across the front. He opened it.

There was no printed message, only a brief handwritten one:

> *Now you can drink root beer without the root. Happy 21st Birthday.*
>
> *All my love,*
> *Aunt Geri*

"It's... a birthday card. From Aunt Geri."

"In *there*?"

Daniel opened the next one, from last Christmas. Another simple design that looked handmade. Just red card stock with a green cutout of a Christmas tree adorning the front. Inside, only a handwritten line:

> *Merry Christmas, Daniel. I hope you have a very happy holiday.*
>
> *All my love,*
> *Aunt Geri*

"This one's from her too. A Christmas card."

"God, there's tons of them."

"Yeah. The postmarks go all the way back to 1996."

Lena turned to him for a second. "You're kidding."

Daniel shook his head.

"So, your aunt has been sending you cards for nearly twenty years, and your dad hid them all, still sealed, in this box?"

He swallowed hard. "That's what it looks like."

"Why would he do that?"

He glanced at the Christmas card. At the stack of two dozen or more unopened ones just like it. Why *did* Dad do this?

Daniel knew zero details about the conflict that had transpired between the two siblings all those years ago, but whatever had happened, Dad always made it sound like Geri Wester was a heartless bitch who had somehow hurt him so deeply, they had severed ties and cut off all communication forever. Daniel had figured his aunt didn't even know he existed. Or if she did know, she didn't care about him.

His entire life, Dad had let him believe it was just the two of them, that no other family members wanted to be a part of their lives, yet evidently, Aunt Geri did.

The cards raised far more questions than they answered. If his aunt's attempts at making contact with him were truly unwelcome, why hadn't Dad just thrown the cards away upon receiving them? Why did he keep them? *All* of them? Every birthday, every Christmas, for two decades?

And if Aunt Geri wasn't such a heartless bitch after all, why didn't Dad just give Daniel the cards at the time? Why did he not allow his son to have a relationship with their only other living relative?

Daniel felt his chest growing tight. "I don't get it. Why'd he hide these from me?" He tossed the stack of cards back into the box and slammed it shut. "If he didn't want me to know she actually gave a shit about me, why didn't he just throw them all in the trash?"

He could hear the bitterness in his voice. He hated the way it sounded, and he knew it probably made Lena uncomfortable. But he didn't care.

"Maybe he was waiting to give them to you when the time was right," Lena offered softly.

"And that's today? When he randomly disappears without a trace?"

Lena didn't say anything.

Daniel sighed. He grabbed a corner of the bath towel and jerked it over the box. He was tired of looking at it.

SIX

W HEN THEY REACHED CHATTANOOGA, Daniel pulled the directions out again and guided them off of I-75 and onto I-24 West. They followed the Interstate across the Georgia state line, then back into southern Tennessee, where after another hour or so, they exited onto a two-lane highway. They followed this road for an hour and a half, then took a rural back road.

Then another.

And another.

As they rode, Lena advised him to eat something. They shared a meal of peanut butter crackers, apples, and bottled water.

Just after one-thirty in the afternoon, they crossed the Arkansas state line. They soon found themselves in the midst of another heavy thunderstorm. Pounding rain made the winding two-lane highway slippery and difficult to see. This, plus the fact that the Camry's gas tank was swiftly approaching empty, led to a pit stop.

They pulled into the empty lot of a grimy little roadside store called Al's Gas 'N' Go, the only service station they had seen for miles.

Daniel and Lena stood together at the fuel pump next to her car, bickering over who should be the one to pay for the tank fill-up.

Both felt obligated to assume responsibility for payment. Daniel had no current income, of course, but he was listed as a joint owner on Dad's checking account. He carried a debit card for emergency use, and this definitely qualified as an emergency expense. But he finally gave in and let Lena pay, with the understanding that he would replenish her snack bag with plenty of refreshments from inside the convenience store.

Daniel paced slowly around the gas pump, eager to stretch his legs for a bit while Lena operated the fuel nozzle. As he moved, he took in their unfamiliar, seemingly lifeless surroundings. The place was eerily silent aside from rain pelting against the store's roof and periodic grumbles of thunder. He saw no other cars parked at Al's, neither by the building nor next to the only other pump the station offered. No cars whizzed by on the road. The only other sight to behold was a clump of trees across the empty two-lane highway.

Despite the July date, Daniel felt chilly again. The storm had drastically cooled the air. He returned to the car and fished around inside for a jacket, knowing Lena would most certainly have one somewhere. And she did. He grabbed a gray oversized hoodie from the backseat and tugged it on.

Lena watched him over the roof of the car and made a face. "You're cold?"

"A little bit."

"*How?* It's ninety degrees out here."

He shrugged.

"Do you have a fever?"

"I'm okay, just feeling chilled."

She narrowed her eyes at him, suspicious, until the gas pump clicked off. She returned the nozzle, collected her receipt, and joined his side.

The two of them stared reluctantly at the convenience store. They both needed to pee and grab some groceries, and this looked like the worst possible place to do either of those things. But they didn't exactly have any other options.

Daniel cringed as they approached the place, unable to over-look the dirt and grime that covered just about every inch of the building's crumbling exterior. He gripped the door handle, trying not to imagine the thousands of microscopic organisms that likely resided on it. A rusty old cowbell hanging from the door jangled as he pulled open the door.

The silver medallion felt frigid against his chest as he crossed the threshold. He shivered.

Inside, the air smelled of hot dog water and dirty mop ends, with subtle notes of mildew and cigarettes. The Eagles crooned from an old stereo boombox behind the cash register, which was, at present, unmanned. No people in sight.

"This place is freaking creepy," Lena whispered to him.

"Yeah. Let's hurry."

Lena walked noticeably close to him as they passed the store's two aisles of surprisingly well-stocked shelves on the way to the restrooms.

Al's toileting facilities were just as filthy as one would have ex-pected. They did their business as quickly as possible, washed their hands with nothing but water because the soap dispensers were empty, and reunited by the soda fountain.

"Here," Lena said softly, reaching into her purse. She extracted a small bottle of hand sanitizer and squirted a generous dollop of gel into his palm, then hers.

The cold alcohol stung Daniel's skin as he rubbed his hands together. "Thanks."

"Let's grab some snacks and get out of here."

They moved hastily, collecting beef jerky, candy, and little bags of flavored peanuts from the shelves. From the cooler, they got a citrus energy drink for Daniel and a bottled coffee beverage for Lena. Despite all the driving they had already done, they were only one page through Dad's handwritten directions. They needed caffeine and sugar to stay alert.

They carried their provisions to the register and placed everything on the counter.

Still no sign of any employees.

Lena rang the little bell next to the cash register.

DING!

No response.

They exchanged worried glances, then Daniel called out, "Hello?"

Still nothing.

The Eagles song on the radio ended abruptly.

Silence.

Daniel felt the same sensation he'd experienced during their hurried escape from Lena's apartment. The distinct, troubling feeling of being watched, only now the feeling was twice as intense.

Lena gripped his forearm. "Daniel," she breathed.

He glanced at her and followed her gaze behind the counter to the floor.

Boots.

Gray cowboy boots on the floor, toes pointed up at the ceiling, scuffed and caked with dried mud. A pair of denim-clad legs were attached, the rest of the body hidden from view.

Daniel shivered again.

Lena whipped around the counter to survey the scene, evidently in nurse mode. Daniel followed her apprehensively, keeping an eye on their surroundings.

She screamed.

On the floor behind the cash register, a man lay motionless on his back, spreadeagle, in a crimson pool. Trails of blood flowed from his ears and nostrils. Empty black caverns gaped open where his eyes should have been.

A clap of thunder boomed overhead and around them, rattling the building's foundation beneath their shoes.

"My apologies," a voice said from behind. A woman's voice with a thick Southern drawl dripping with the sugariness of sweet tea. "Are y'all ready to check out?"

They turned.

A heavyset white woman with a bleached-blonde perm leftover from the eighties stood next to a rack of Little Debbie cakes. She wore muddy brown cowboy boots, acid-washed mom jeans, and a fuchsia T-shirt with *Jesus Loves This Hot Mess* printed in sparkly gold letters across her large bosom. A name tag pinned to her shirt identified her as *Mindy*.

Daniel was freezing. The pendant around his neck had grown intolerably cold against his chest. His entire body trembled from the chill- and probably terror as well.

Something was "off" about this woman. He couldn't tell what, exactly, but something in her eyes was all wrong.

In her hands, she held a once-white cloth stained with red blotches. She guided the fabric in between her fingers, wiping more of the red stuff onto it.

"Aw, y'all look scared." *'Scared'* sounded like *skeered*. She tilted her head to one side and frowned. "Musta found Al. My poor husband." Her bottom lip poked out in an exaggerated pout. "Well. *Mindy's* poor husband."

Daniel gulped.

Her not-quite-right hazel eyes met his, and her lips parted into a big smile, revealing a set of teeth yellowed from years of tobacco use. "We've been waitin' for you, Daniel."

His stomach turned a cartwheel.

"We've been waitin' for you for a *loooong* time."

He felt Lena's hand in his. Her palm was clammy but warm. He was grateful for the heat. He interlocked his fingers tightly with hers.

Mindy glanced down at this and smiled even wider. "Aww. Look at y'all holdin' hands. Ain't that precious? You make a cute couple." She tapped her chin with a finger as if in thought, then clicked her tongue. "You know what? I bet Pete would be over-the-moon happy to see y'all get together. He's always loved you like a daughter, Lena. Mm-hmm. Pete would be thrilled. If he wasn't dead as a doornail."

Daniel's heart raced at the casual drop of their names, especially his father's name alongside the word *dead.* They needed to get to the car, fast. He scanned the space between them and the door and tried to estimate how quickly they could run to it.

Mindy seemed aware of his assessment. "Sorry, darlin', I can't let you leave."

She raised her left hand toward the entrance, twisted her wrist, and the locks on the double glass doors inexplicably clicked into place.

His heart jumped into his throat. Lena squeezed his hand so hard, it hurt. Things were happening like a movie scene playing out before him, like he was watching it all in slow-motion. None of this felt real.

Mindy took a step closer, still smiling. "You're gonna stay put for a while."

Her hand shot up in their direction, blood-stained palm aimed at them. She did that magic twist of her wrist again. This time, nothing happened.

Mindy's eyes widened in surprise. Something had gone wrong. Her gaze shifted to her arm, which remained stretched outward in midair, unmoving. She grunted and snarled with frustration.

"HOW?" she growled at him in a terrifying guttural voice that wasn't Mindy's.

Then Daniel saw it. Only for a second.

Her eyes changed. The pupils, irises, and scleras dissolved into translucent chunks of glass. A soulless translucence that chilled him to the bone.

Not glass. *Ice.*

Then the empty frigid pools flickered back to hazel.

GO.

Everything within him screamed that now was the time to move. He didn't hesitate. He tugged Lena's hand and together, they bolted for the exit. As quickly as he could manage, he unlocked and pushed open the door. The cowbell jangled wildly.

"Damn you!" Not-Mindy shrieked at them. "*Damn you both!*"

They sprinted to the car and climbed inside. Lena swore under her breath half a dozen times as her trembling fingers fumbled with her key ring, struggling to find the correct key to start the car. She finally grasped the right one and shoved it into the ignition. The engine came to life. Lena slammed the gear shift into 'drive' and pounded the accelerator, still whisper-cursing.

The tires skidded across the rain-slicked highway as they sped out of the parking lot. Daniel kept his eyes fixed on the convenience store. From his passenger seat view, he could see the woman standing inside, arm still outstretched, frozen in place. She grew smaller and smaller until the distance between them made her impossible to see.

Giant raindrops battered the windshield as they zipped down the highway.

Daniel closed his eyes. Flopped his head against the headrest. He sucked in a sharp breath and slowly released it. "What the hell?" he finally heard himself say.

"What the hell?" Lena echoed in a strained voice he didn't recognize.

He looked at her. She was crying.

"I know," he said. "I know."

"What... what just happened?"

He had no idea what to say. No idea what to think. He felt queasy. His chest ached. His brain hurt. Too many thoughts, questions, and images darting back and forth around inside his skull at once.

His dad. Missing.

The box. The books. The silver medallion.

The shadowy figure outside Lena's apartment.

The dead man without his eyes.

The woman with the ice eyes.

A demon.

Dad was right about demons.

Dad was dead as a doornail.

No. That thing possessing Mindy was lying, fucking with him. That's what demons did, right? They twisted the truth to confuse people, to torment them. It had worked. Daniel felt confused and tormented. Reality seemed to be dissolving into nonsensical fragments all around him.

What if that creature wasn't lying? What if Dad was dead?

He couldn't think about that yet. He would not.

Daniel focused on the only lead they had, the only truth they could trust. The letter his father had left behind. Dead or alive, Dad was in trouble. They needed to get to safety as quickly as possible. They needed answers.

They rocketed down the highway, racing toward Geri Wester.

SEVEN

NIGHTFALL CAME, AND LENA had to turn on the headlights. Another hour passed. Two hours. Three.

The roads grew bumpier. The power lines grew scarcer. Eventually, they were surrounded by nothing but sprawling corn fields and cotton fields and patches of forest. With no streetlamps to be seen, the dark was nearly impenetrable. At least the thunderstorms were behind them. Rainfall would have made visibility impossible.

Daniel was sure they were lost, for they were, truly, in the middle of nowhere. He couldn't remember the last business or house he had seen. All signs of civilization had disappeared an hour ago.

Then the directions led them down another road, a dirt road lined thickly with trees. They went a few slow miles, then made another turn. By this point, they had made so many twists and turns, he wasn't even sure which state they were in. He was almost convinced they were going in a giant circle.

That's when the directions got weird.

Daniel squinted in the light of the overhead reading lamp to make sure he had read his father's words correctly. "Uh... he says there'll be a large red sign on the right that says 'Restricted Area:

No Unauthorized Vehicles Beyond This Point.' He says to drive past it and stop for the guard at the front gate."

Lena looked at him, clearly terrified. "*What?*"

"That's what it says."

"Are you *sure* your aunt is a *carpenter*?"

No. In fact, Daniel wasn't sure of anything anymore.

"There's the sign," he said, peering through the windshield.

The headlights of the Camry lit up the reflective metal sign, highlighting its warning: *Restricted Area: No Unauthorized Vehicles Beyond This Point*. It had a distinct military look to it that gave off Area 51 vibes.

"Daniel, I don't like the looks of this."

Neither did he, but he tried not to let on.

He stared up ahead and saw nothing but darkness. "Do you see the gate yet?"

"No. I don't think-"

Lena stopped mid-sentence and jammed the brakes. She flicked on the left turn signal for absolutely no one.

Daniel eyed the left side of the road, trying to make out where she could possibly be about to turn. Then he saw it.

A tall, threatening, chain link security fence with iron posts and what looked like barbed wire strung across the top. Something you might find lining the perimeter of a prison.

It was the only place to go. The road ahead of them dead-ended abruptly into dense forest.

The fence glowed menacingly in the amber light of an attached floodlight. A row of untamed, overgrown bushes formed a wall inside the fortress, obscuring whatever waited for them on the other side.

This could not be right.

They had to be outside some kind of military base. Some top-secret government facility, miles and miles away from the edges of society.

That's what it looked like from the road, anyway.

Aunt Geri couldn't possibly live here.

As Lena made the turn, the dark figure of a man appeared. Even in the darkness, Daniel could see the outline of an enormous black rifle that looked like something only military personnel would be licensed to carry.

"Oh, shit," Lena breathed, stopping the car at the closed gate. The man began to approach them. "What do I do?" she asked in a panicked whisper. "What do I say?"

"I don't know. Dad doesn't say anything except 'pass through the gate'."

"Dammit, Pete Wester. Look at that gun, Daniel. He has a gun. A giant gun!"

The armed guard reached her door.

"Roll down the window," Daniel whispered.

Lena groaned softly and pressed the button to lower her window.

"Can I help you?" the guard asked in a gruff voice. Shadows concealed all details of his face.

Daniel cleared his throat and leaned forward, placing his shoulders slightly over Lena's lap. "Um, yes, sir, hello. We're here to see Geri Wester."

"Geri Wester?" the guard repeated. "Let's see some ID."

"Oh, um, sure." Daniel dropped Dad's directions to the floorboard and began digging in his back pocket for his wallet. He removed his driver's license and passed it to Lena.

Lena had fished her own license from her purse. She extended the cards out the window.

The guard examined their identification for a couple of seconds, glancing back and forth from their DMV photos to their real-life faces. "Visitors of Ms. Wester, you say?"

"Yes, sir," they replied in unison.

The guard stooped over a bit and looked into the car. The interior dome light over their heads cast a warm glow onto his face, illuminating his features. Square jaw. Brown skin. Neatly-trimmed black goatee around thin lips pulled taut into a permanent grimace. Dark eyes fixed intensely on Daniel.

He stared for a few uncomfortable seconds, then stood upright. "I'll be right back with your cards."

The man walked away, grinding gravel with his heavy boots. They watched as he disappeared into the shadows.

Just inside the gate, they could see an aluminum shack with several windows. A guard shack, from the looks of it. He must have gone in there.

Lena turned to Daniel. Very quietly, she asked, "What is this place?"

"I don't know."

"I feel like we're at Fort Knox or something. What do the rest of the directions say?"

"That's it. That's all the directions."

"What?"

"Yeah."

"Is this a prison? Is your aunt an inmate?"

"I hope not."

Lena heaved a sigh. "I really don't like this. God. Did you see his gun? He had a gun."

"Yeah. I noticed."

"Who would need a gun like that? I've never even seen a gun that big before. And where did he go with our licenses?"

Lena rambled on nervously for a minute or so until she ran out of things to say, then they sat in silence, waiting for the guard to return. The longer they waited, the higher their anxiety levels climbed. Lena kept drumming her fingernails on the steering wheel. Daniel's right knee bounced uncontrollably.

After about ten excruciating minutes had passed, the guard returned. He gave Lena their identification cards. "Mr. Wester, you're clear to enter. Miss Dillon, you'll need to go back the way you came."

Daniel's stomach flopped.

Lena gasped.

His heart pounding in his ears, Daniel swallowed hard, then spoke up, "Sir, she's with me." He hoped his voice didn't sound as shaky as he thought it did.

"My instructions say just you, Mr. Wester. I can't make allowances for additional visitors due to safety concerns."

"But, sir, please. We've come so far and-"

"No additional visitors," he interjected firmly.

Daniel didn't know what to do. After their experience at Al's Gas 'N' Go, after Mr. Darcy's behavior and the figure lurking outside her apartment, he feared for Lena's safety as much as his father's. But how could he argue with this security guard and his massive weapon?

The words from Dad's letter echoed in his head. *Don't tell anyone what's going on. The more people you get involved, the more people you risk getting hurt.* What was he supposed to do?

"Sir," Daniel cleared his throat and sat up a little taller, "I'm afraid my friend here is in danger. I'm worried about what might happen to her if she doesn't get to safety. We... we've been through a lot today."

The guard looked back and forth between them, studying their faces for a moment. "I don't make the rules. I'm sorry."

Daniel swallowed hard. "Do you know my aunt?"

The guard hesitated, then said, "I do."

"Is there any way I could talk to her? If we could just tell her what's going on, I think she would want Lena to come with me."

The man heaved a sigh. "I can arrange safe lodgings for Miss Dillon for the night. With any luck, I'll get clearance approved for her by tomorrow morning. But for now, only Mr. Wester is permitted into the compound."

"It's okay, Daniel," Lena said, turning to him. She gave his arm a gentle squeeze. "Go ahead."

"No way."

"I'll be fine."

"You don't know that."

"What *do* we know anymore?"

He looked at her apologetically.

"Go ahead," she urged.

"I have transport to your aunt's cabin waiting for you on the other side of this gate. You're free to exit this vehicle now and gather any personal belongings," the guard told him. He shifted his focus to Lena. "Miss Dillon, please remain seated. Place your vehicle in 'park' and shut off the engine. I'll need to hold your keys temporarily until your accommodations have been finalized."

Lena did as she was told. The engine went silent. Her keys jingled as she passed them off to the guard.

Daniel reached for her hand and clasped it tightly. "I'm so sorry."

"It's okay." She mustered up a small smile. "It'll be okay."

He let go of her, opened the car door, and stepped out, collecting the towel-wrapped wooden box on his way. Gravel crunched under his sneakers as he joined the guard at the rear of the Camry.

"I, um, I have a *lot* of personal belongings in the trunk."

The guard raised a brow.

From within the car, Lena pushed the button to open the rear compartment.

A flashlight appeared in the guard's hand and clicked on, casting a blueish spotlight on the trunks' contents. Daniel watched the man's face as he scanned over his father's books. His unchanging expression was unreadable.

"Nice library," he said.

Daniel couldn't tell if he was being sarcastic or not.

His flashlight clicked off. "Wait here. I'll be back with some boxes and some extra hands."

He disappeared into the shadows once again.

Daniel felt nauseous and sweaty in the warmth of the summer night air. He set Dad's box down in the trunk so he could unzip the gray hoodie. He slipped out of it, which helped a lot, and tossed it into the trunk. A gentle breeze drifted through the trees around him. It cooled the damp areas of his shirt and his skin pleasantly.

While he was alone, he decided to stash the precious box in his duffel bag. It seemed wise to handle it discreetly around these strangers. Hastily, he rearranged his clothing inside the bag to create a protective nest for the box.

The guard returned with a second man, each of them carrying sturdy black plastic milk crates.

"This is Bear Solomon," the guard said, gesturing toward the new man. "He'll be escorting you to your aunt. Go ahead and unload. We'll be opening the gate up momentarily."

Bear Solomon. Is that what he'd said? An unusual name, but an apt one, for this man was beefy and hairy enough to be of the Ursidae family. A wooly beard that must have taken years to grow covered half of his face. His tight-fitting crew neck tee showcased his broad shoulders and exposed thick, muscular arms covered in a forest of hair. He towered over Daniel by at least half a foot.

Daniel took the crate from the unnamed guard and began transferring Dad's books into it. The giant called Bear reached into the trunk, grabbed *An Encyclopaedia of Witchcraft and Demons,* and placed it in the other crate. He worked quickly, not stopping to ponder the curious titles, not once meeting Daniel's eyes.

A loud metal clattering filled their ears. Up ahead, the security gate parted like slow-moving automatic doors. On the other side of it sat an idling dark-colored pickup truck beneath the light of a single lamppost. A narrow gravel road shrouded in darkness stretched forward into the unknown.

"The bags too?" Bear asked, now that all the books had been collected. His deep, gravelly voice matched his appearance.

"Just the black duffel. The rest belong to my friend."

The unnamed guard leaned in, seized the bag for him, then closed the trunk. "Follow us."

Daniel carried the heavy crate behind the two men, making uncomfortable eye contact with Lena as he passed by her car window. He dreaded leaving her. Without her comfortable, familiar presence, he felt lost. Vulnerable. Afraid.

Not to mention guilty.

The guilt made his stomach hurt. Guilt for involving her in this, for letting her drive him halfway across the country, for their terrifying experience at the gas station, and now for getting separated, for her having to stay alone only God knew where. She acted bravely, but he knew she was just as scared as he was.

The guilt was torture. He *never* should have called her. Something told him he would regret that phone call forever.

Bear placed the crate of books onto the truck bed, and the other guard loaded Daniel's duffel bag. Daniel set his crate on the bed as well, staring at his duffel, picturing the wooden box inside it. It was probably safe wrapped in the towel, buried in the layers of his extra clothing, but he still hoped the ride wouldn't jostle it around too much.

The guard who had greeted them initially at the gate pulled open the passenger door to the truck and stepped aside for Daniel to enter. "You're all set," he said.

Under the lamppost, adequate yellowish light illumined him enough to reveal that, although he carried a military-grade weapon, he wore no uniform. His green collared shirt was just an ordinary button-down designed for outdoor adventuring. Mustard-colored cargo pants and basic hiking boots covered his bottom half.

His stern features softened ever so slightly. "My name's Malai, by the way. You're safe here, Mr. Wester. And we'll make sure your friend is too." He dipped his chin. "Goodnight."

Malai disappeared into the guard shack.

Bear was already behind the steering wheel when Daniel climbed into the cab. The man remained silent as he shifted gears and guided the truck forward into the darkness.

EIGHT

T HE GRAVEL PATH WOUND into a dense grove of trees, and Daniel was instantly reminded of the driveway flanked with pines that led to his and Dad's trailer back in Tennessee. It felt eerily familiar, like *déjà vu*.

After a few more yards, a white two-story antique farmhouse came into view. A rusty old Chevy Suburban sat out front. No prison. No secret government facility. Just a single, private residence.

A *very* private residence.

Daniel recalled the guard saying he was being transported to his aunt's "cabin." He wouldn't call this farmhouse a cabin.

But Bear Solomon didn't stop at the farmhouse. He steered to the right, following a new branch of gravel road.

Daniel saw a second house off to the right side, a smaller, more modern-looking one-level home with a minivan in the yard. A few of the lights were on inside the house. They didn't stop here either.

The road curved to the left and revealed another house, one almost identical to the small one-level. And another house stood next to it.

This was a hidden neighborhood, locked within the confines of a prison gate.

The M. Night Shyamalan film *The Village* popped into Daniel's mind.

He didn't know how he felt about this place.

They continued on, passed a few more houses, and came to the end of the road. On the right, a small, rustic log cabin with a rock chimney sat a little further away from the road than the rest of the homes. A gray Jeep Cherokee sat in front. Bear parked the truck alongside it and got out without turning off the engine or saying a word.

Daniel opened the passenger door and climbed out, his legs feeling a bit weak and unsteady.

He sucked in a lungful of air, determined to quell his anxiety. The night air smelled fresh and pure. It felt cool against his skin. Crickets chirped loudly, their synchronized melodies surrounding him from all sides. Overhead, the stars blazed even more brilliantly than they did at home.

As uncomfortable as he felt in this creepy gated community, he couldn't ignore the quiet peacefulness of the place. He found his new surroundings unexpectedly consoling as he collected his duffel from the back and slung it over his shoulder.

Bear lifted one of the crates full of books and carried it silently across the yard.

Daniel grabbed the other crate and followed.

They reached the porch. A simple split-log bench leaned against the cabin wall. At the far end of the bench sat an assortment of different-sized clay pots filled with robust plants, a few green fern-like things and several kinds of colorful flowers.

Before they had a chance to knock, the porch light clicked on and bathed them in a warm orange glow. The front door opened. A woman appeared at the threshold.

Although he had never seen her in person, never even seen a photograph, Daniel knew this was Aunt Geri. She looked so much like Dad, it was unsettling.

Even in the shadows, he recognized the same round face shape, the same high cheekbones, and the same thick, coffee-colored hair, though hers was long and streaked heavily with white. She wore it slicked back and wound into a large bun at the nape of her neck.

Geri Wester stepped out onto the porch, into the orange light, allowing Daniel to take a long look at her. She was tall, almost exactly his height, but her layers of baggy clothing obscured any other physical attributes. She wore loose-fitting jeans and an oversized plaid button-down that hung open over a roomy blue T-shirt. A sprinkling of sandy powder covered her from head to toe. Sawdust. She'd been working.

Daniel wasn't sure about the age gap between his father and aunt, but the deep lines set into her face made her look quite a few years older than her brother, and her tanned, weathered skin suggested she spent a lot of time outdoors.

Beneath a dense canopy of salt and pepper bangs, pale blue eyes the same color and shape as Daniel's stared heavily at him. Undisguised fear swept over her face when they locked eyes.

"Daniel," she breathed.

He couldn't find his voice. The family resemblance was so un-canny, all he could do was stare.

For his entire twenty-one years of life, Dad had been his only family. It was too strange, too surreal, to encounter for the first time, as an adult, another human being who so clearly belonged within that unit.

Aunt Geri seemed to be having similar thoughts. She remained silent as her eerily similar eyes traveled up and down Daniel's body, giving him a thorough once-over.

Bear cleared his throat and set his crate of books on the porch.

"Oh, hey, Bear. Thank you," Aunt Geri said to him. Her voice was pleasant. Soft and a little husky. She'd have made a good radio DJ.

Bear nodded. "Goodnight, Ms. Wester."

"Goodnight, hon."

The bear-man headed back to the truck.

Aunt Geri's face bore honest concern as she looked down at the crate of books Daniel still held in his arms. "I'll, um, I'll grab the other one." She lifted the crate Bear had left behind. "Come on in."

Daniel followed his aunt across the threshold.

Inside, the little cabin smelled of pine and cedar, of the forest. Daniel liked it. The log walls emanated a natural, earthy warmth that he found comforting. Directly adjacent to the porch, the quaint living area held a plaid loveseat, a simple wooden coffee table that looked hand-built, an antique mahogany rocking chair, and a lovely stone fireplace with a mantel covered in framed family photographs.

Daniel was surprised to spot himself in one of those old photos. He was about five or six months old, with curious blue eyes, a toothless grin, lots of chunky rolls, and a head full of dark curls. His beaming young parents held his tiny body between them.

He forced his eyes to the other photographs on the mantel. A few of them depicted Aunt Geri and Daniel's father at various ages. Fishing at a lake as kids. Posing with a vintage Mustang convertible as teenagers. And there was one photo of them with their parents, Daniel's grandparents, whom he also had never met.

"Here, let me get that for you," Aunt Geri said, taking the heavy crate from his arms. The sleeves of her baggy plaid shirt slid back, revealing sculpted forearm muscles that hardened when she took on the weight of the books. Daniel watched her as she surveyed the titles. "Damn. I haven't seen these in a long time. Some of these, never." She set the crate on the floor behind the loveseat. "You can put your bag down wherever you want to, hon. Make yourself at home."

Daniel placed the duffel bag next to the fireplace.

They stared at each other.

"Well," Aunt Geri finally sighed. "I-I don't know what to say." Her lips curved into a small smile that faded quickly. "It's good to see you, Daniel. I know you don't remember me. Last time I saw you, you'd just started solid foods."

Daniel couldn't think of a response to that, so he said nothing and gave her an awkward smile.

"Well, uh, please, sit down," Aunt Geri said, gesturing toward the plaid loveseat. She pulled the antique rocking chair over and sat down in it. "Tell me what's going on."

Apprehensively, Daniel lowered himself to the loveseat. "My dad's in trouble," he said. "He left a letter for me, with instructions to find you."

A heavy pause.

"What happened?" Aunt Geri asked, leaning forward in the rocker. She propped her elbows on her knees and waited with anticipation.

Daniel drew in a deep breath and filled her in on the details. Waking up to an empty home. Doors locked. Dad's truck in the driveway. Finding the key to the box. Calling Lena. Opening the box. He recapped everything that took place before they set out on their cross-country drive.

When he finished, Aunt Geri just sat there for a while, staring at the floor, turning it all over in her mind. "Okay," she said at last. She wet her lips with her tongue. "When you woke up this morning, Pete- your dad- was already gone."

"Yes."

"Did you hear any weird noises during the night?"

"No. I didn't hear anything. Except for the thunder."

Aunt Geri's eyes widened. "Thunder? It was storming?"

To Daniel, his aunt's question seemed irrelevant. Why did the weather matter? Yet Daniel's mention of thunder seemed to have been the most disturbing detail Aunt Geri had heard this whole time. "Yeah. It was."

The woman heaved a sigh. Rubbed her forehead. "Has your dad been acting different lately?"

"No."

"He hasn't seemed upset or worried about anything?"

"No. Not that I could tell."

"And you said all his things were left behind. His truck. His keys. What about his cell phone?"

"I never found his phone. I think he has it with him, wherever he is. He usually keeps it with him all the time, in a, uh, a belt clip."

"And you called his number?"

"Yeah. I got his voicemail."

Aunt Geri sucked in a deep breath. Blew it back out. "Okay. Any other details you can think of?"

Daniel stared at the wood planks beneath his feet, trying to concentrate, to tame his thoughts. They were darting through his mind so quickly, one after another, he couldn't grasp a single one of them. The image of his father's broken coffee mug suddenly popped into his mind. The ceramic fragments had looked so ominous lying there, amidst the pool of coffee. A mangled corpse lying in its blood. But would it mean anything to Aunt Geri?

The insignificant detail of thunder had meant something to his aunt. He decided to go for it. "I found his favorite coffee mug on the kitchen floor." Hearing the sudden shakiness of his voice surprised him. And it bothered him. "It was completely shattered. Coffee everywhere. It seemed like... there had been some kind of struggle."

Aunt Geri's brow furrowed with concern. Possibly sadness. Or sympathy. Daniel didn't know what to make of her facial expression.

Neither spoke for what felt like several minutes but was probably only a few painful seconds.

There was something else Daniel needed to tell his aunt, but he didn't know how to talk about it.

The gas station.

His and Lena's encounter with the eyeless dead man and his demon-possessed wife felt like the hazy recollection of a strange nightmare. He hadn't fully processed it. He *couldn't*. The woman's actions had defied the rules of nature. The way they'd managed to escape... it made no sense. He'd been quietly ruminating on it during the drive here, and there was only one explanation for their survival.

The silver medallion pendant.

Dad's letter said to wear it at all times. Back in his father's bedroom, when he'd first laid eyes on the strange relic, he knew it was meant for protection. Dad had given him a "magic" necklace to protect him from demons. It seemed ludicrous at the time, of course, but after what they had experienced at the gas station, Daniel felt with increasing certainty that the medallion was indeed imbued with some protective- *ugh, he still didn't want to think it-* magic that had saved his life and Lena's.

He couldn't explain why, exactly, but Daniel felt an overwhelming need to keep this information to himself. He was glad he'd kept the medallion inside his shirt, where it remained against his sternum, hidden from his aunt's line of sight.

"Were you followed?" Aunt Geri asked suddenly, interrupting his thoughts.

"Um... I don't think so."

"You said your girlfriend came with you. Where is she now?"

"Friend," Daniel said gently, feeling a little embarrassed about making the correction. "The guard at the front gate wouldn't let her in. He said he would arrange somewhere for her to spend the night. I don't know. I'm really worried about her. After, um, after everything that's happened, I think she's in danger."

"Yeah," Aunt Geri agreed. "But I can assure you, she's in good hands here. You both are."

He gulped. "What is this place?"

"Some place safe." Aunt Geri must have realized her answer was unsatisfactory, for she added, "Listen, I know to outsiders, this place is... weird. As hell. But we'll do everything we can to protect you two."

Hesitantly, Daniel asked, "Protect us from what?" He already knew the answer, but he wanted to hear it verified by his aunt.

Aunt Geri shifted in her seat. "Well, now, that part's gonna sound a little crazy."

"Okay."

"Dammit, Pete," she muttered to herself, frowning. She crossed her arms over her chest, then immediately uncrossed them. "Daniel, honey, I'm not the one who should be telling you this."

The knot in Daniel's abdomen clenched tighter. Sweat began collecting on his palms.

Aunt Geri drew in an extra-long breath. Blew it back out. Her blue eyes, remarkably identical to Daniel's and his father's, stared heavily at him. Her lips parted slowly, and at last, she spoke. "I think a demon came for your father today."

NINE

I THINK A DEMON came for your father today.

Aunt Geri offered nothing else. She seemed to be waiting for Daniel to speak next.

"Um... so... what makes you think that?" he finally found his voice. "Exactly?"

"Well, the thunderstorm, really. Demonic activity causes a fluctuation in atmospheric pressure, which usually results in thunderstorms."

His aunt's sentence sounded like it had been memorized word-for-word from some crazy Wikipedia article in dire need of professional review. Daniel stared at her for a long time, for what felt like hours, trying to think of a reply.

He could not.

"Listen, Daniel," she said, looking him directly in the eyes again. "Most people, when they hear the word *demon*, they think of Linda Blair in *The Exorcist*. They think of stories from Sunday School. Like Jesus casting Legion into the herd of pigs." She stopped. "None of that stuff is even close to the truth."

Daniel's spine felt prickly and cold.

"What most people in these parts think they know about demons? About hell? None of that shit is even in the damn Bible. It was all just made up in the first couple of centuries A.D. by some early Christians. It wasn't canon. It wasn't doctrine. Just a bunch of men sittin' around, makin' up stuff. Now that's a *whooooole* rant for another day, but what I'm trying to say is, you'll have to set aside pretty much everything you think you know about this stuff so far, 'cause it's just not accurate."

A dramatic pause.

"The truth is, Daniel, there are evil creatures out there. We call them *demons* here because that's what the dominant Western religions tell us to call them, but all religions and cultures around the world have lore about these creatures. Every single one. In Japan, they're called *yokai*. In India, *asuras*. *Daevas* in Iran. Different people have given them different names, and they've created different stories about them, about where they come from. But honestly, no one really knows the truth."

Aunt Geri paused again and swallowed. She drew in a sharp breath before she continued.

"What we do know, Daniel, is that these things are *real*. And they're bad. They can hurt you, physically hurt you. Your dad knew that. And he knew, dammit-" her trembling voice broke off. She dabbed at her suddenly misty eyes with the back of her hand. "He didn't wanna believe it, but *he knew* that son of a bitch was coming back. That's why he left that key out for you. Why he wrote you that letter in the first place. He had a plan to get you here to me, to the Compound, to keep you safe."

"Dad knew *who* was coming back? A demon? What are you talking about?"

The cabin went silent.

Aunt Geri stared at him for a painfully long time, her eyes taking on that sad, sympathetic look again that made Daniel feel like an object of pity. "He really hasn't told you anything."

That statement set off an unexpected surge of anger within Daniel. No. Dad hadn't told him shit. He could no longer look at his aunt. He fixed his gaze on his lap, studying the weave of his blue jeans. He didn't know his own father anymore. Maybe he never had. He was beginning to feel like his entire life was a lie.

Aunt Geri rose from the rocking chair.

Daniel glanced up and watched her go to the corner of the living area where an old wooden trunk sat beneath a couple of neatly-folded crocheted blankets. She transferred the blankets to the floor and slid the trunk from its resting place. It squeaked against the planks as she pulled it to the center of the room and parked it in front of the loveseat at Daniel's feet.

He hadn't noticed this item earlier. Like almost everything else his aunt owned, the trunk looked handmade. Dents and scratches marred the distressed wood. The leather handles were barely intact. It looked maybe a century old.

Aunt Geri sank onto the loveseat next to Daniel. She smelled like sawdust and sweat with a faint undertone of some essential oil he couldn't name. She leaned forward, snapped open the gold clasp, and raised the lid gingerly. The sweet, earthy scent of cedar met Daniel's nostrils.

"Maybe this'll answer some questions for you." Aunt Geri reached inside the trunk's parted jaws and removed a bulky black book. Leather-bound and worn, about eight by eleven inches across, maybe an inch or two thick. Some of the pages were barely hanging on. They stuck out sloppily and crinkled at the edges.

A scrapbook.

"Here," she said, extending it out to him.

Daniel took it. Opened it. On the first page, Daniel saw a faded newspaper clipping from *The Tulsa World*. Tuesday, April 5, 1988. The headline:

*6 KILLED IN MYSTERIOUS
RESTAURANT MASSACRE.*

Below, a photograph of a squatty square building surrounded by policemen, paramedics, and a crowd of onlookers. A retro neon sign identified the building as The Rattlesnake Diner.

Aunt Geri glanced up at Daniel. She wore a solemn new expression. "Back in nineteen eighty-eight, your dad and I were one of the few people to walk out of that diner alive."

Daniel gulped. "You were there? When that happened?"

"There was a group of us. We went out for dinner and a movie. *Beetlejuice* was playing and none of us had seen it yet. We met up at the diner with Pete's friend Ted and his girlfriend, Jenny." She hesitated. "I was, as usual, the fifth wheel. Your dad was there with Helen Brown."

"My mom."

Aunt Geri gave a small nod. "They'd been dating about six months by then. Anyway. The five of us were sitting at a table close to the door." Her blue eyes glazed over as they unfocused, as she drifted back into memory. "We were just hanging out, goofing off, when this... man... in an old-timey black suit walked in. Everyone noticed him. He stood out, like a character in a period costume. He came in and just stood there, right inside the door, looking around at everybody, with this awful grin on his face. Then he turned and locked the door behind him. Without ever touching the lock."

Daniel thought of Mindy- well, Not-Mindy- and the way she had somehow telekinetically locked them inside the gas station.

"Ted spoke to him, asked what he was doing locking the door like that. That's when the man killed him."

Daniel's heart lurched. His aunt, his mother, and his father had witnessed the death of their young friend in the middle of a fun night out. How terrible. And traumatic. No wonder Dad had never spoken about it.

"There was a guy sitting at the bar," Aunt Geri went on. "He lost it. Seeing someone killed like that, it stirred something up inside him. He jumped down off his bar stool and went charging after the man. Ended up getting killed in the process."

Daniel was starting to feel sick.

"Six people were killed that day," she said. "Innocent people."

"That's horrible."

After a pause, Aunt Geri added, "The weirdest thing, the worst thing, was the way they died."

A dreadful silence took over the room. Daniel wasn't sure he wanted to know more. He didn't want to ask, but he finally did, if for no other reason than to end the silence. "How did they die?"

"It doesn't make any sense. The man just raised up his arm and pointed the palm of his hand at them. And they dropped dead. Eyes exploded in their sockets."

Daniel felt a fresh surge of iciness crawling up his spine. Al's eyeless corpse behind the cash register and the actions of Not-Mindy matched the details of Aunt Geri's story exactly, confirming the impossible and eradicating any doubts that lingered in his mind.

"When it was all over," she said, "the man's eyes changed. Just for a second, but I saw it. It was like they were made of thick, clear glass. For a second. Then back to normal. Then he disappeared. Literally disappeared, right in front of us. He was just gone."

She waited for Daniel to say something, but he couldn't utter a sound. His stomach churned wildly, threatening vomit. Things were beginning to make sense. Horrible, irrational sense.

Aunt Geri sighed. "I know it sounds insane. But it's the truth."

Once again, Daniel didn't know what to say.

"After going through something like that together, none of us were the same," she said. "The other people that made it out? We weren't strangers anymore. We needed each other, we had to sort out what had happened. We had to figure out what we'd seen."

"A demon."

She nodded.

Daniel got lost in his thoughts for a while before he spoke again. He kept picturing Not-Mindy and her split-second glass-like eyes. "How do you know the man was a demon?"

"We did research," Aunt Geri replied. "For years, we talked to people from all over, experts on the supernatural. People like Dr. Melrose." She said the name like it would mean something to Daniel.

It didn't. "Dr. Melrose?"

"Damn, I thought Pete would have at least mentioned *him*. He taught theology at the university, and he specialized in demonology. He knew your dad very well, they were close. He taught all of us a lot about demons. Like how to protect ourselves from them. How to hunt them, track them, know when they're around. How to fight. All of us diner survivors, we teamed up." She glanced around the room. "And we made this place our headquarters. The Compound."

Things started clicking into place. The secrecy, the paranoia. The little homes tucked away behind a tall iron gate guarded by armed sentries.

This was why Aunt Geri had never listed a return address on any of those birthday cards. These traumatized people were hiding. From *demons.* With time, they had constructed this bizarre supernatural fantasy to mask the pain of seeing their friends brutally murdered in a Tulsa diner. Surely that was why his dad had left Aunt Geri and the others behind, why he had abandoned this cult-like neighborhood and moved to Tennessee. Pete, unlike the other diner survivors, had realized the insanity of it all, and he had escaped.

Daniel wished he could believe that. But Pete was the one who had led him here.

Pete Wester, with his box full of secrets, his collection of do-geared, note-filled demonology books, and the engraved occult necklace he'd instructed Daniel to wear, so obviously believed all of this too.

Only a few hours ago, Daniel would have called it all crazy. And he had. Hadn't schizophrenia or a psychotic break been his first assumption? But what he witnessed in the gas station changed everything. He knew now, he'd known all afternoon, that the woman at Al's Gas 'N' Go was no ordinary woman. He'd met a demon.

Lena was right. Dad was lucid.

This was all really happening.

"That's not all, though," Aunt Geri's voice intruded.

Daniel's stomach flopped. *That's not all?* He wasn't sure he could handle any more.

She exhaled loudly. "The man who came into the diner and killed those six people, the *demon*, he wasn't finished there." Her eyes bored into Daniel. "He came back for the people who made it out alive."

Daniel unconsciously held his breath as he waited for her to go on.

"He started attacking their families," Aunt Geri said. She hesitated before continuing. "He, um, he killed several of our loved ones." She blinked, looked down at the floor for a moment, then back into Daniel's eyes. "He killed your mom, Daniel."

His mouth went dry. Had his brain been capable of stringing together a sentence at that moment, his throat would not have cooperated to get it out.

"Helen was the last victim," Aunt Geri said. "It all stopped after everyone moved in here close together and started protecting themselves."

"Then... why did Dad leave?" Daniel asked at last. "If this is all true, why would he move away? Didn't he think the demon would follow him? Why did he risk getting us killed?"

Aunt Geri's eyes welled with tears. "Because he was an ass. He wouldn't listen to reason. I fought him, believe me. I fought him hard. But he was so damn stubborn. And so angry." A tear slipped down her cheek. "Losing your mother pushed him over the edge. I think he lost it for a while." She wiped her face dry with her shirt sleeve. "He said he couldn't take it here anymore. He was sick of living in fear, and he didn't want you growing up afraid. That's when he took you to Tennessee. Started a new life for himself and for you, away from all of this."

Daniel sat quietly.

"Thing was, we were *all* sick of living in fear. But tough shit, that was our reality. I thought he was a reckless, irresponsible fool to take a six-month-old out of the safety of the Compound. But what could I do? He was the parent, not me. I tried to reach out, tried to help him. But he didn't want my help. He made that quite clear. I suppose all I was to Pete by then was a painful reminder of the past. A past he was trying to erase.”

A past that, as of this morning, seemed to have finally caught up to him.

“So, I stayed here with the rest of the survivors. We put up more houses and turned this place into a community. We’ve all been here ever since, trying to stay safe, waiting for the demon to come back for someone else.”

“And you think that just happened. To Dad.”

Aunt Geri nodded. “I’m afraid so.”

A sudden image of Dad’s lifeless body lying in some nondescript location invaded his thoughts. Blood seeping from his ears and nose. Eyes missing. That’s what the woman at the gas station- the demon- had said; Pete was *deader than a doornail.*

Daniel ran a sweaty hand over his face, feeling once again that he might be sick.

“Well, why now?” he breathed. “After all this time?”

“I don’t know. That’s eatin’ at me too. I really don’t know.”

The demon’s words spoken through the woman’s thick Southern drawl played and replayed on an ominous loop in Daniel’s mind: *We’ve been waitin’ for you, Daniel. We’ve been waitin’ for you for a loooong time.*

“Um, okay, so, there’s something I need to tell you,” Daniel stammered, rubbing his forehead nervously. “On the drive here... Lena and I... from the sound of things, we met a demon.”

Aunt Geri’s eyes widened with shock as Daniel described the encounter at the gas station.

"How the hell did you get out of there?" Aunt Geri asked, incredulous.

"That's kind of the weirdest part. She locked the doors, uh, telekinetically, I guess, and she told us we were staying put for a while. Then she held up her hand at us, like you said the man in the diner did, but nothing happened. She was surprised- and mad- that whatever she was trying to do to us didn't work. And she couldn't move. It was like she was frozen in place. She was still stuck like that, with her arm out, when we made a run for it."

"That's not possible."

Daniel agreed. It wasn't possible, not without the medallion necklace. *Don't tell her about the necklace.* Why was this internal voice so insistent on hiding the pendant? Wouldn't this be helpful information to share with his aunt? "I don't understand any of it, but that's what happened."

Aunt Geri's eyes intensified on him, scrutinizing him. The shift in her gaze made him uncomfortable. He suddenly felt exposed and self-conscious, like maybe something was wrong with him that his aunt was trying to pin down. Like she detected a falsehood.

"Um, she told me..." Daniel's voice faltered. He fixed his eyes on the cedar trunk, unable to meet his aunt's intense stare. "She said Dad was dead."

A beat.

"Did she say anything else about him?"

Daniel reddened as he recalled and recounted her words. "She just said Dad would've liked to see Lena and me together as a couple because he loved her like a daughter, but he wouldn't get a chance because he was…'deader than a doornail'."

Aunt Geri huffed. "Well, demons lie. So that doesn't mean shit. It was probably just toying with you."

He felt a sense of relief at that and let himself relax ever so slightly. He hoped with all his might Aunt Geri was correct. On the other hand, "If he's alive… then where is he?"

"That's what we're going to find out." She clapped the scrapbook shut and returned it to the antique trunk. She eased back into the loveseat. Thought for a moment. Drew in a deep breath and let it out. "Okay. Here's the plan. I'm gonna arrange a meeting first thing in the morning. We can go over everything that's happened, start connecting the pieces, and hopefully, we can come up with some theories. Then we'll know what action to take next."

"Who all will be at the meeting?"

"I'm not sure, but I expect there'll be a big crowd. Once everybody at the Compound has heard about what's happened, they'll wanna do something to help out." Aunt Geri's lips curved into a small smile. "Everyone who was living here when your dad left loved him. Him and your mom. It broke everyone's heart when he left."

Daniel found this somewhat difficult to believe. If they all loved his dad so much, why hadn't they ever visited? Or called? Was the Compound that disconnected from the rest of the world?

And that went both ways. If these people used to be so close to him, why had Dad never, not even once, mentioned them?

"But Daniel, you need to get some rest. You've been through a lot today."

That was an understatement.

Aunt Geri rose to her feet. "It looks like you'll be staying here with me for a while, so I want you to make yourself at home, okay? I've got a spare room that's all yours. If you want anything to eat, just help yourself. I've got all kinda stuff in the kitchen. Anything is up for grabs."

"Okay. Thank you."

"I mean it, Daniel. We're family. Now that you're here, if you need anything, don't you hesitate."

Something about the way she said *we're family* warmed Daniel's insides and relaxed him. Daniel dipped his chin in acknowledgment and stood up. "Lena," he said softly. "My friend. Can't she come here too?"

"Of course. Tomorrow."

Daniel stared.

"Don't worry, she's safe."

"Why can't she just come here?"

"You'll see her at the meeting, Daniel. It's late, and you need to rest."

Daniel didn't like the way she avoided his question, but he was afraid to push it. Afraid and a little too exhausted.

Aunt Geri lingered in the middle of the living area, looking awkward. She seemed to be wavering between her next actions, perhaps searching for the right words to say. She bit her quivering bottom lip as she looked at him. Without warning, she launched herself toward him and pulled him into a tight hug.

The embrace took Daniel by surprise and nearly knocked him over, but after a couple of uncomfortable seconds, he let himself relax into his aunt's arms.

"I'm glad you're here," she said into his shoulder. "You're safe now. I know all this is a lot, but we're gonna figure things out, okay? We'll find your dad." She gave him a final squeeze and took a step back.

Having just met the woman, Daniel had no real reason to trust her. But Aunt Geri's earnestness made itself evident. *Despite what little you know about her, she loves you, and you can trust her.* It was clear she cared deeply for her brother, and for her nephew. In that moment, it seemed they'd known each other far longer than the past hour.

She gave him a warm smile. "Come on, hon. I'll help you with your things."

His aunt's spare room was as minimal and subdued as her living area. A full-sized bed covered in a blue patchwork quilt sat pushed against one wall beneath a curtained window. At the bedside, a simple table held a glowing antique oil lamp. An oak writing desk and chair filled the farthest corner, the desktop barren except for a glass pint jar full of ink pens and highlighters. Next to this stood a small bookcase packed with volumes. Daniel expected to find titles about demons, but instead, he discovered the works of authors like George Orwell, Kurt Vonnegut, and Ursula K. Le Guin.

The two crates full of Dad's books sat on the floor next to Daniel's duffel bag, just inside the door, where his aunt had helped move them before bidding him goodnight.

Daniel kicked off his shoes, sank onto the bed, and stretched out his legs. Despite how weak and tired his body felt, he felt certain that sleep would be impossible tonight.

He lay supine, arms folded beneath his head, watching the flickering shadows cast on the wall by the oil lamp's flame. He liked the simplicity of the house. He really did. And the log walls were nothing but beautiful. He reached out and slid his fingers over the exposed logs, feeling the roughness of the wood grain. Like sandpaper, almost.

He could see himself living in a house like this one day.

Outside that prison-like gate, though.

He peered at the window and wondered where Lena was out there. His stomach panged with guilt as he thought of her.

Daniel reached for his cell phone, which he had left on the bedside table. He lit up the screen. *12:19 AM*. He wanted to call Lena, to check on her, but the lack of bars in the upper corner of the phone screen wouldn't allow that. *No service*. Not that he had expected anything different out here in the middle of nowhere.

He rolled onto his back and sighed as he stared up at the ceiling. He chose to imagine Lena sleeping peacefully in a cozy cabin bedroom just like this one. He'd have to wait until later to know what she was really doing.

His thoughts circled back to his father. He wondered, for the thousandth time today, where Dad was. What he was doing right now. If he was okay. If he was even still alive.

He didn't want to think about this, but he couldn't stop. His thoughts were so jumbled, so anxious, so dark, so filled with images of bloodied empty eye sockets, relaxation was impossible.

Daniel rose to his feet and paced around the room for a bit, eventually deciding to try one of the novels on Aunt Geri's bookcase, in hopes of distracting his brain for a while. He selected the small paperback copy of Le Guin's *A Wizard of Earthsea* and returned to the bed. He'd read the Earthsea books as a young boy and thoroughly enjoyed them. Perhaps he'd find some temporary comfort by losing himself in Ged's world now.

Unable to focus on the text, Daniel gave up after the first two pages.

He set the book on the table, got up again, and stripped off the jeans he'd been wearing all day. Feeling infinitely more comfortable in only his T-shirt and underwear, he slid beneath the bed covers. He dimmed the oil lamp until darkness filled the room.

He closed his eyes, willing his mind and body to relax, to rest.

But in his uncooperative mind's eye, a woman appeared.

Bleached-blonde perm. Hot pink T-shirt with sparkly letters. Employee name tag: *Mindy*. Bloody hands smearing more blood onto a blood-stained cloth. Hazel eyes that morphed into translucent chunks of ice.

A shiver ran from his scalp to his heels, the cells of his body reliving the painful, burning cold he'd felt in the demon's presence. His blood froze in his veins as he imagined her in the room with him now, watching him from the shadows. He could feel her hiding in the corner, concealed by darkness, grinning at him. Waiting.

He reined in his imagination before it got the better of him. He felt like a little kid again, lying awake in bed, fearing what lurked in the dark corners of his bedroom. Daniel forced Not-Mindy's image from his brain and resolved to be brave.

He was safe here. That's what the guard at the gate had told him. Aunt Geri had said the same. So had Dad, in the letter that had directed him to this place.

This demon, this evil, lying creature, wasn't going to win. Dad *was* alive. It wasn't just wishful thinking; Daniel could feel it. Dad was alive, and he was going to find him and get him back. He wasn't sure how, but he was going to do it.

His right hand slipped beneath the collar of his T-shirt and followed the thin leather strap to the medallion. It wasn't icy like it had been earlier. The temperature of the metal matched that of his body now. He clutched the pendant in the darkness and rubbed his thumb across the hard stone in the center. It was raw, not polished and smooth. He traced the ridges and bumps in the stone with the pad of his thumb. He found the mysterious engravings and stroked them, wondering again what they meant. Beneath his touch, the object thrummed with palpable energy, with power.

A power that had saved his life.

Dad had given him this necklace because he had known the journey to finding him would require it. He had equipped him to face dangers like Not-Mindy in the gas station. He'd battled a demon once, accidentally, and with the aid of this pendant, he knew he could do it again.

Yes. He could do this.

He *would* do this.

He would save his father. He would keep Lena safe.

Whatever it took.

TEN

A T SOME POINT DURING the night, Daniel must have drifted off to sleep, because the next time his eyes parted, he
found brilliant golden sunlight streaming through the window.
The gleaming rays poured into the room like fire, igniting the log
walls in a heavenly yellow glow and enveloping Daniel's body in
warmth.

For a moment, he lay still, taking it in. He felt completely relaxed. At peace.

But one glance down at the blue quilt that cocooned him was all
it took.

He remembered.

He was at his aunt's cabin. Inside a weird place called the Compound. Dad was missing. Demons were real. He'd met one. One
upsetting memory from yesterday came after another, flooding his
mind painfully.

Daniel squeezed his eyes shut in a futile attempt to block out
reality. His suddenly confusing reality. He didn't want to deal with
it right now. But images of Mindy's ice-eyes kept bombarding his
thoughts.

With a weary sigh, Daniel opened his eyes and sat up. Everything ached. Muscles throbbed from head to toe. He groaned as he stood to his feet.

His stomach grumbled with hunger. A nervous, nauseated hunger. Aunt Geri had welcomed him to her food stores, he recalled. He pulled on the jeans he'd worn yesterday and wandered out of the bedroom into the front of the tiny cabin.

With such an open floor plan, the kitchen stood practically in the living area. Only about two feet of open space separated the stove from the plaid loveseat he'd sat on last night. Seemed like a bit of a fire hazard to Daniel.

Aunt Geri stood at the kitchen counter- the one, single counter- pouring coffee from an old-fashioned percolator into a brown earthenware mug. She heard Daniel's footsteps and glanced up at him.

"Good morning," she greeted him with a weak smile. The woman looked especially tired, like she hadn't slept at all. She wore the same clothes from last night. A long strand of wavy gray hair had escaped her bun and hung limply to her shoulders.

"Morning," Daniel replied.

Aunt Geri raised the percolator slightly for emphasis and asked, "Wanna cup?"

"Yes, please."

"Cream or sugar?"

"Just cream. Thanks."

"Sure thing." She pulled a second mug from an open wood wall shelf above her. She filled it with steaming coffee. "We'll have to get going soon, so we don't have time for anything but a quick bite. I've got blueberry scones. They're fresh and homemade."

"Wow. That sounds great."

"Don't worry, I didn't make them," she said with a sly grin. "They're from a friend. Baking isn't exactly my forte. My creative skills end with woodworking, trust me."

Daniel returned her grin. He appreciated the lighthearted small talk this morning. Polite, slightly awkward chitchat that did not involve the word *demon* was a welcome, albeit temporary, return to normalcy.

"Oh yeah, that's right, Dad said you were a carpenter."

She nodded, stirring cream into the coffee mug. "Mm-hmm. I like to make furniture and things."

"Did you make any of this?"

"Well, actually, I made almost everything in here," Aunt Geri said. Daniel could tell she was trying to be modest about it, but her eyes lit up as she spoke. She peered up at the exposed beams that ran over their heads. "I built this place, too. With your parents' help."

"Seriously?" Daniel's eyes scanned the cabin, appreciating it even more deeply. "It's beautiful."

"Thank you."

"Really beautiful."

With a hot mug of coffee in each hand, Aunt Geri moved to the dining table- a round surface made of oak, most likely her own craftsmanship, littered with newspapers, notebooks, and loose pages. She set down the mugs and tidied the papers enough to make room for their breakfast.

"Go ahead, hon, have a seat."

Daniel did as he was told.

Aunt Geri returned to her kitchen counter to collect two small plates and a basket of scones. An actual basket, with a handle curved over the top, like Little Red Riding Hood would've carried to Grandma's house. A thick piece of woven fabric in a delicate shade of ivory lined the basket and made a picturesque little nest for the scones.

His aunt took the empty chair across from him and grabbed a scone for herself. Daniel followed suit. The scone was surprisingly warm, as though it had been pulled from the oven only minutes ago. He took a bite. It was dense yet pillowy soft, covered in a sweet, sticky glaze that gave a tiny, subtle crunch with each bite. A blueberry burst on his tongue, filling his mouth with delightfully tart juice.

Daniel had barely eaten the previous day and now his hunger suddenly caught up to him. He could easily have eaten the entire basket of scones. "These are incredible," he said.

"Have another," Aunt Geri said, sipping her coffee. "I know you've gotta be starving."

"Thanks."

It grew quiet as they ate.

"Your dad must be real proud of you," Aunt Geri said, smiling. "You've grown up well. Right handsome."

Daniel could feel an annoying heat spreading across his cheeks. "Thank you."

"I bet you're taller than him now, aren't you?"

"Yes, ma'am. A little bit."

"Oh, you don't have to do all that *ma'am* business with me." She kept smiling as she returned her attention to her coffee.

Daniel stared at his plate awkwardly, munching his scone, trying to think of something to say. There were so many questions he wanted to ask, but right now, he couldn't think of a single one.

Just as the silence grew from slightly uncomfortable to almost unbearable, Aunt Geri spoke up again. "What are you doing these days, Daniel? Are you in school?"

"I just graduated actually, from Hamilton University."

"Oh, yeah? That's great. What'd you major in?"

"History."

She beamed. "Just like your mother."

Her statement took him by surprise. "What?"

"You didn't know your mother majored in history?"

His heart kicked in his chest. He shook his head. Why the hell had Dad never told him that he had followed in his mother's footsteps? He knew Dad struggled to talk about his late wife, but jeez, this was pretty special. This one little fact pulled Daniel and his mother so much closer together.

"I'm sorry," Aunt Geri said.

He couldn't tell if she was sorry she'd brought it up or sorry her brother was, as she'd put it earlier, an ass.

She shifted in her seat and moved on. "Well, tell me, have you found a job yet?"

Daniel released a deflated sigh. That damn question always made him feel like a failure. He'd applied to every single job opening for which his new bachelor's degree qualified him, landed exactly three interviews, and received zero callbacks. Meanwhile, Lena had been hired as a nurse at the hospital before she'd taken her finals. Her job even came with a $3,000 sign-on bonus paid out in its entirety upon completion of the hiring paperwork. The healthcare field was desperate for help. He should've been a nurse.

Not really. He'd heard enough of Lena's stories to know he would be a horrible nurse.

"No. No job. I guess it wasn't exactly the best choice as far as the job market goes."

"What do you want to do?"

Another painful question. Truth be told, Daniel had no clue what he wanted to do. He never had. Lena had always wanted to be a nurse, as far back as he could remember. She'd worked her ass off throughout high school to maintain a 4.0 GPA that would ensure her acceptance into the RN program at Hamilton. Daniel enjoyed school and excelled at it, so much that he actually skipped a grade and graduated a year early, but he was never driven and focused like Lena. He had no end goal. He just liked learning stuff, and he was good at memorization. His 3.7 GPA made going to college a no-brainer, but he really should've given it some brains. He'd merely selected the history program because he thought he would enjoy those classes the most, never really considering how he would use the very expensive piece of paper when he was thrust into the real world four years later. That had felt so far away at the time.

Now graduation was two months behind him, and he was just as lost and clueless as ever.

"Um, well, I don't know, really," Daniel said at last. "I think I'd like to work in a museum. Maybe be a curator one day. I don't know. I've kinda been thinking about trying for grad school."

"Yeah? Wow, that'd be great."

Daniel shrugged. "A master's degree would open up more job options." And it would buy him another two years. Maybe in 2015, he'd have his shit figured out. He doubted it.

"Definitely," Aunt Geri remained upbeat and encouraging, oblivious to Daniel's internal plight. Everyone was always like that. "Well, I can tell you're a very smart young man. I say go for it."

The uncomfortable silence returned.

"So, what about your friend?" Aunt Geri asked. "The one who came here with you?"

Daniel could almost hear the quotation marks around the word *friend*. He swallowed some coffee. "She's a nurse."

"Oh, good for her."

"Do you know when I'll be able to see her or hear from her? You said she'll be at the meeting. I wanted to call her last night to check on her, but there's no cell service here."

"Yeah, sorry about that. We're pretty far from any cell towers. But yes, she'll be at the meeting today. Speaking of which, we really need to head on out."

Relief rushed over him. He hastily downed the last bite of scone. "Sounds good."

Aunt Geri upturned her coffee mug and finished it off in a couple of quick gulps. She got to her feet, cleared their dishes, and led the way to the door, leaving behind the paper mess on the table without offering an explanation as to why it was there in the first place.

Daniel followed his aunt outside.

The place looked quite different in the daylight. Everything was green, from the abundant oak and maple trees to the lush emerald grass to the little patches of gardens in between the houses.

There were six of them, the tiny houses, lined up in a slightly curved row. Aunt Geri's cabin was at the far end, at the edge of a thick forest. Her home was the only one with a wooded backyard. The rest of them had flat, cleared yards with plenty of open, tall grass dotted with wildflowers.

Daniel started toward his aunt's Jeep, but Aunt Geri kept walking. He had assumed they would be driving to the meeting, wherever it was going to be held, but apparently, she had other plans.

"Where are we going, exactly?" he asked.

Aunt Geri pointed toward the narrow gravel road Bear Solomon had driven him in on last night. "There's a place around back we use for meetings."

Daniel tried to tell where the road ended up, but beyond the houses, it hooked to the left and disappeared from view.

As they walked on, he noticed again how quiet the place was. How peaceful. The only sounds came from chirping birds flying overhead and the gravel crunching beneath their feet.

They followed the road around the curve and for the first time, Daniel could see where they were going. The sight up ahead took his breath away.

When Aunt Geri said there was a place out back they used for meetings, Daniel had envisioned a converted garage or an old barn with rows of fold-up chairs inside.

He never expected this.

The Compound was more than just a neighborhood.

It was a miniature town.

The gravel road had suddenly become Main Street. It intersected with smaller dirt paths lined with unassuming rectangular buildings adorned in painted clapboard. The place looked like an old Western film set, with modern solar arrays instead of covered wagons and tumbleweeds. Some of these buildings looked like more private dwellings, but many of them appeared to be businesses. One structure surrounded by six or seven outdoor picnic tables featured a handmade sign marking it as *Pearl's Cafe*. The beige building across the road from it had a wide storefront glass window with *Smith's Store* painted across it. A white building nearby bore a red cross and the single word *Clinic*.

"I-I had no idea all this was back here," he stammered, dumbfounded. He glanced at his aunt and observed a satisfied grin on the woman's face.

"That's kinda the point."

"Wow. This is insane." Daniel shook his head. "You have a store? And a restaurant?"

"Well, now, it's not really as formal as that. Mr. Smith keeps a stock of basic necessities if anyone should need them. And Pearl just cooks enough food at mealtimes to share with anyone who wants it."

"What are the rest of the buildings for?"

"Well, uh, these three here are used for storage," Aunt Geri said, gesturing toward a cluster of smaller, identical edifices with white siding as they passed by. "The first one is for miscellaneous supplies, the second is for food, and the third is the armory."

The armory. Daniel swallowed. Did these people have so many weapons that a building was necessary to store them?

A fourth building stood alongside the other three.

"What's that last one for?" Daniel asked reluctantly.

Aunt Geri looked at him with a flicker of excitement in her eyes. "That is one of the entrances to the underground shelter."

Daniel assumed she was joking. Then when no laughter or alternative answer came, he realized his aunt was being serious.

This place really was insane.

"So, uh, where's the meeting gonna be?" Daniel asked, trying to steer the conversation away from crazy.

"Over there, in the assembly hall. The big white building." Aunt Geri pointed to the largest of all the buildings, a rectangular structure overlaid with white clapboard. It looked like a historic one-room schoolhouse. "We use the assembly hall for a lot of different things. School for the kids, church services, meetings like this one."

They reached the entrance to the building and climbed the three cement steps to the door. Aunt Geri entered first. Daniel followed closely behind.

The place was packed. Rows of metal folding chairs filled with people stretched from wall to wall across the spacious room, all facing a podium and a large projector screen at the front. A pasty-skinned man with gel-slicked black hair stood near the projector at a plastic wheeled cart that held a laptop computer. He connected a cable and mashed some buttons, seemingly preparing for some kind of presentation.

Daniel couldn't help but notice the stares, the whispers, as he moved down the center aisle behind his aunt. Though he recognized no one, he got the feeling everyone there knew him.

Aunt Geri stopped at the end of the second row from the front. Two empty seats, the only ones Daniel had seen, remained next to a tall woman with flawless ochre skin. She wore a sleeveless pink button-down top paired with denim shorts, a breezy summer outfit that revealed impressively sculpted, muscular arms and legs.

"Thanks for saving these for us," Aunt Geri told her.

The woman smiled at her, and when she did, her whole face lit up pleasantly. "Of course." The tight coils of raven hair that framed her face bounced as she shifted over into the outer aisle seat. Aunt Geri plopped down in the chair next to her.

"Daniel!"

Lena.

She occupied the chair next to the only empty one left, the seat reserved for him. The sight of one another was so welcome, so relieving, they hugged.

"God, I'm glad to see you," she breathed in his ear as they embraced.

The sensation of Lena's breath against his ear lobe flooded him with a tingly warmth. He relaxed against her soft, abundant form. "You too."

They let go of each other and took their seats.

Lena looked better than when he'd seen her last. She was visibly calmer, her eyes looked well-rested. She had changed into a wrinkled yet pretty maroon sleeveless blouse and jeans. Her pale blonde hair fell in loose beachy waves past her shoulders, freshly washed. She smelled like peaches.

Daniel became painfully aware of his grossness. He still wore yesterday's outfit. He hadn't even thought to freshen up his deodorant or brush his teeth. He eased into the chair between Lena and Aunt Geri, staying as far from each of them as possible, just in case he reeked.

Aunt Geri tapped Daniel's knee briefly to get his attention. "Daniel, this is Marion Crider," she said, gesturing toward the muscular woman at her side.

Marion Crider. The name sounded familiar, but Daniel couldn't place it.

Marion leaned around Aunt Geri. Her deep-set brown eyes sparkled as they locked on him. The warm smile she had given Aunt Geri upon their entrance hadn't left her features and now it only widened as she met Daniel's gaze. "It's *so* nice to see you, Daniel. I just can't believe it. You're all grown up."

Daniel studied Marion's smooth, radiant face and found the faintest hints of wrinkles in the corners of her eyes and mouth. He guessed she was about the same age as his father, but she seemed a decade or two younger. The woman exuded youth and fitness.

"I'm sorry to hear about your dad," Marion told him, her smile fading. "But all of us are so thankful you've made it back here safely. We'll figure out what's happened."

"You know Dad?" Daniel heard himself ask.

Marion nodded. "We go way back."

"Marion and her husband, Eddie, were in the diner in eighty-eight," Aunt Geri told him solemnly.

"Oh. I'm sorry," he said to Marion, not knowing what else to say.

Before Marion could reply, a bald man walked up and began talking to her, effectively ending their chat.

Daniel turned to Lena. Her wide eyes were busily darting across the room, taking in all of the unfamiliar faces gathered around them.

The way Aunt Geri had so casually described the meeting had not prepared him for something of this magnitude. He had a feeling Lena felt the same way.

"Are you doing okay?" Daniel whispered, wishing he had cleaned his damn teeth. His mouth tasted sour and rotten. It was embarrassing.

"Yeah. You?"

"Yeah. How was last night? I wanted to call you-"

"I know, no cell service. I wanted to call you too. But really, last night was fine for me. I stayed with Marion at this tiny little cabin by the gate. She was super nice and friendly. Really, it wasn't bad at all. She was very kind and made sure I was taken care of."

"That's good."

"How about you? Were you able to get any rest?"

"Yeah, a bit."

"Good." She drew in a long breath and blew it back out. "So. *Demons*."

He swallowed. "Yeah."

"I'm guessing your aunt talked to you about the diner massacre?"

"Yeah, she did."

"Marion filled me in last night. How awful. Your poor dad. But it explains that woman at the gas station, right? And the box and your dad's letter. Everything makes sense now."

He nodded. She seemed surprisingly nonchalant about all this.

"Can you believe all these people live here?" Lena asked him, her eyes scanning the rows of full seats. "All these houses and everything back here, I couldn't believe it."

"I know."

"I'm not sure what to think about this place."

"Me neither."

"You know what it makes me think of? It kinda reminds me of the prison in *The Walking Dead*. Just without zombies. Well, *so far*, no zombies. Who even knows anymore? Honestly, zombies could show up any second and it wouldn't really be that shocking, would it?"

Daniel paused to ponder this for a moment and found her remark startlingly accurate.

Lena rambled on, speaking a little too loudly now. "Okay, but for now, no zombies, just demons. *God.* 'Just demons.' Who even am I? But yeah, so, we're in a demonic version of *The Village.* But honestly, demons or not, why would anyone choose to live hidden out here like this, cut off from reality?"

"Shh."

"I wonder how many people live here."

"Fifty-six," an unidentifiable male voice answered.

Daniel glanced past Lena to see the person filling the chair next to her. He locked eyes with a beefy young guy with tanned skin and a grown-out buzz cut. With his thick neck and ripped biceps, which he obnoxiously accentuated with a too-tight T-shirt, he could have been a professional athlete. An offensive lineman, maybe.

"Fifty-eight, as of last night," the guy continued.

Lena's pale skin flushed a deep shade of pink. Daniel wasn't sure if she was embarrassed about being overheard or if she was overtaken by the attractiveness of their newly discovered companion.

"You must be Fifty-Seven and Fifty-Eight," he said. His hazel eyes stayed glued to Daniel's. "You really Pete Wester's kid?"

The way he said it, like his dad was a celebrity, made Daniel feel strange. "Yes."

The guy stared at him for a little too long, then gave a respectful nod and turned away.

"I-I'm sorry if I offended you," Lena said to the guy. "We're not moving in. Just staying with Daniel's aunt until we find his dad. Do you live here?"

"We *all* live here." He made it sound like she had asked the dumbest question in the world.

Lena's face turned even redder. "Oh. Sorry."

The guy shrugged his brawny shoulders. "I guess it does seem kinda weird to outsiders. Fifty-six people sharing a lot, inside a gate, *cut off from reality*."

Lena winced as he quoted her. "I'm sorry. But, I mean, it *is* a little culty."

"We're not a cult," he said, sounding defensive. "It's a good place to live. A real community. Everyone looks out for each other."

"How... how did you all come to live here? I'm sorry if that's too much. I just... I mean, how did you all find this place?"

A valid question. Surely *all* these people- all fifty-six of them- hadn't been in that diner back in 1988. This guy certainly hadn't. He was close to their age; he probably hadn't been born yet.

"We all have our own reasons for being here." He stared at Daniel. "Everyone has a story."

Daniel gulped. *Everyone has a story*. He wondered what those stories were. What this guy's story was. What histories the people scattered around him had. What they were like. Had his dad really known them? Had he actually survived the diner attack with some of them and gone on to study demons alongside them?

He still could not picture Dad in a place like this. Being friends with people like this.

Daniel had almost mustered up the guts to ask this guy if he had known his father when a hush suddenly fell across the room. He glanced up at the front of the room, where the man with the gel-slicked black hair was still fiddling with the projector.

A second man had joined him. This man, a distinguished-looking older white guy with neat gray hair and a well-groomed beard, gave the first man a pat on the back before stepping up to the podium himself. Despite his casual getup of a short-sleeve charcoal-colored chambray shirt and khaki cargo pants, he had the air of a respected politician. The way his presence had brought silence upon the crowd told Daniel he was the one in charge here.

"Good morning," the leader announced from behind the wooden stand. His deep voice bellowed throughout the spacious room so clearly he didn't need a microphone.

Aunt Geri leaned over and whispered to Daniel, "That's Walter Garrison. He's the one that started this place."

Walter Garrison grasped both sides of the wooden podium with his hands and propped his weight against it. "The reason for today's gathering is not one I am eager to share with you." He cast his gaze downward. "Some of you have already heard about what has happened."

Daniel scanned the assembly hall to observe the audience's reactions. Some of the faces appeared expressionless as they waited for Walter Garrison to give them the details. Others bore looks of sadness and concern. Yet most of them, he noticed, wore their fear plain across their features.

"As of yesterday, our friend and former comrade, Pete Wester, has been reported missing," he announced somberly.

A few audible gasps echoed across the room.

Daniel felt himself growing hot. The air was getting stuffy in this room packed full of people.

"His status and whereabouts remain, at this point, unknown." Walter Garrison spoke like the director of the FBI holding a press conference. "We have confirmed thunderstorm activity around the time of his disappearance, early yesterday morning. As Eddie will show you, the details do seem to indicate the presence of a demonic entity."

The pale man with the gel-slicked black hair at the projector must have been Eddie- *Marion's husband, Eddie?-* and that must have been his cue to take over.

He clicked on the projector, and a map of Tennessee appeared on the whiteboard behind him. "Late Sunday evenin', a thunderstorm came outta nowhere and hovered over the town of Crofton, Tennessee," Eddie told them. He seemed to speak out of one side of his mouth and had a lazy, Deep-Southern twang. Even from here, Daniel could see the glistening wetness of his oily skin. Eddie clicked a button and a digital representation of a thunderstorm popped up onscreen over the small black dot that marked Daniel's hometown. He suddenly looked like the weatherman on channel six. "And when I say over Crofton, I mean *directly* over Crofton. No storms anywhere else across the region all weekend long."

Daniel stole a glance at his aunt. Her eyes stared unblinking at the projector screen, her face impossible to read.

Beyond her, Marion focused on Eddie. Was this pasty, oily guy with the tacky, goop-filled hair really her husband?

"This is how it suddenly looked a little after eight o'clock Monday morning." Eddie pressed the clicker a second time. The swirly gray image of the thunderstorm vanished. "All clear. Just like that."

Eight o'clock. That was around the time they had left Lena's apartment. Lena had texted her mom just before her eight o'clock Pilates class. He tried to remember when the storm had stopped yesterday. He wasn't sure, but he knew it had not lasted long. The sky had been clear and sunny during most of their drive. Not that he had been paying much attention. Though he did recall the massive rainstorm that forced them to stop at Al's Gas 'N' Go.

"I spent the night combin' weather reports, checkin' to see where another freak storm like this one mighta popped up. Thought that might tip us off as to where this thing went next." Eddie clicked the button and pulled up a map of central Arkansas. A red circle emphasized an area on Highway 8 in the middle of expansive green that represented forest. "Right here. A little gas station in Middle-of-Freakin'-Nowhere, Arkansas."

Eddie's dark eyes met Daniel's.

"Just so happens, Pete's son, Daniel, stopped for fuel at this gas station on his drive here yesterday."

Beads of sweat crawled across Daniel's skin as he felt more eyes turning to him.

"See, Pete left behind a note with directions for Daniel to find us. He feared he'd need our protection. He and his young lady friend here, Lena Dillon, came to us last night. They barely made it out of that gas station alive, but somehow, they did, and they're safe with us here today. But we all know they might not get so lucky again."

A pause.

"The storm stayed right here over this spot for a couple hours, then disappeared. Nothing else since then, anywhere." Eddie clicked off the projector. "Seems this demon don't wanna be found."

Daniel heard his aunt release a sigh.

"Thank you, Eddie," Walter Garrison said. He had remained at his perch behind the podium throughout Eddie's presentation. "Many of you are worried that the demon might come this way next. That's understandable, of course, as it does seem to be following Daniel. As a precaution, several folks spent the dark hours of this morning placing additional warding sigils on the perimeter gates. We have also increased the number of guards at each post. But we don't want you to worry. We all know this place is safe, and you have all been trained thoroughly and would know what to do in the event of an attack." The speaker's eyes caught Daniel's. "At this time, our concern is finding Pete. And protecting his son."

Cheeks warm, Daniel stared down at his lap.

"As Eddie said, Pete's son, Daniel, returned to us last night. He and his friend are staying here for the time being. I ask that you all do everything you can to make them feel welcome. This is a difficult and confusing time for them, and they need our support."

Aunt Geri reached over and gave Daniel's forearm a small squeeze.

"In the meantime, rest assured that we are doing our best to find this demon and to find Pete."

"Our best?" someone close by spoke up, challenging Mr. Garrison.

Daniel turned to his left. It was the beefy athletic guy next to Lena, sitting on the edge of his seat, looking ready to explode.

"So, sitting around here on our asses, waiting for something else to happen, that's doing our best?"

Walter Garrison's expression did not change, nor did his gaze falter. "For now, yes, it is."

"Anybody out there could be next in the line of fire. You're really gonna wait around until somebody else gets killed before you do something?"

Somebody else gets killed. Daniel felt his heart sink. Had these people already written his father off as dead?

"No one has been killed," Mr. Garrison replied sharply. "And I would like to keep it that way. That's why no one goes anywhere or does anything until we find out more information about what's happened to Pete."

"What about his house?" The brawny hothead shot back at him. "Wasn't he taken from inside his own house? Isn't anybody gonna check the place out, look for clues?"

"No one is leaving. Not yet."

"Heath has a point," a bald man in the front row chimed in. "Wouldn't it be wise to look the place over? To examine the scene of the crime? Eddie just said the storm moved on. The place ought to be clear."

The muscley guy- whose name was apparently Heath- threw up a hand. "Exactly. Thank you."

"Yes," Mr. Garrison said. "Eddie did say that. But-"

"But I also said that the storm came outta nowhere," Eddie spoke up. "What we're dealin' with here, there's no warnin'. It could come back at any time. That thing knows what we'll do next. In fact, it expects us to go over to Pete's place and look for clues. Walkin' in there could be suicide."

"Sure, it'd be dangerous," Heath said. "It'd be a risk. But it's one we have to take if we're gonna find Pete and put an end to this thing before something else happens."

Mr. Garrison stared at him in silence.

"We're all trained, we all know what to do if something happens. You just said that yourself not two minutes ago. I say we get a handful of our best people together and head out this morning."

The assembly hall went quiet. Everyone seemed to be waiting on Walter Garrison to make the call.

The leader's eyes swept away from Heath to Daniel. "What do you think?"

Daniel's heart leaped in his chest. What the hell? Surely, Walter Garrison wasn't leaving this decision up to *him*. Returning to the site where this had started was the only lead he could think of too, but he didn't know enough about all the variables to declare it the best choice. He didn't know with any certainty what they should do next, he just wanted his dad back. When his aunt beside him cleared her throat and shifted in her seat to sit up straighter, Daniel realized with great relief that he had been mistaken. Mr. Garrison had spoken to Aunt Geri.

"I, um-" Aunt Geri stopped to clear her throat again. "I think they're right. I don't know how else we're gonna find my brother if we don't start there."

Mr. Garrison nodded. "Alright then. We'll do this on a volunteer basis. I want five of you headed to Crofton within the hour. The rest of you will stay here and keep this place safe." A pause. "Those who stay will meet here every morning at eight o'clock to share updates." Mr. Garrison released his grip of the podium and stepped back. "Meeting adjourned."

Immediately, noise filled the air as people began standing up and talking amongst themselves.

Daniel turned to Lena, whom he could tell felt just as lost and helpless as he did. What now? Would they join the search party in Crofton, or would they be forced to stay here?

As Aunt Geri rose to her feet, so did they. Daniel glanced behind Lena to catch Heath's eye, to talk to him about the excursion, but he was gone. He had already disappeared into the crowd.

Daniel felt a hand on his shoulder and turned. It was his aunt's. "Come on, hon," she told him. "Let's get back to the cabin."

Unsure of what would happen next, Daniel and Lena followed Aunt Geri out the door.

ELEVEN

P EOPLE CONTINUED TO STARE at Daniel as everyone filed out of the assembly hall and went their separate ways along the various paths throughout the Compound. All the attention people were giving him, all because they apparently used to know his father, bothered him. They all knew him, but he knew no one. Even though nearly all of them offered friendly nods and empathetic smiles, the attention unnerved him.

He trudged along in silence, between Lena and his aunt, passing the numerous clapboard-covered outbuildings that formed the main street. Once they were beyond the last of the storage buildings, the one Aunt Geri had said was for *miscellaneous supplies,* whatever that consisted of (probably something more intriguing than toilet paper and extra batteries), Daniel could take the quiet no longer. "So, what's the plan?"

Aunt Geri looked at him.

"Going back to Crofton," he said. "How are we going to do this?"

His aunt cleared her throat and glanced down at the gravel path. "*We* won't be going anywhere. You two are staying put, with me, here at the Compound."

Daniel had expected as much, but it still pissed him off. "Then what the hell can we do? How can we help find Dad?"

Aunt Geri blew out a sigh. "Honestly? I don't know."

"Well, there has to be something," Lena said.

"Look, this isn't a normal missing person situation," Aunt Geri told them, halting mid-stride. The three of them stopped and faced each other in the center of the path. A gentle breeze made Aunt Geri's big plaid shirt billow around behind her like a cape. "We can't talk to the cops. We can't go around town hanging up posters with Pete's face on them. Trust me, I don't like it any more than you do, but we'll have to sit tight here and wait for the others to get back."

"But back there, in the meeting, you said you don't know how else we're gonna find my dad if we don't start at the trailer."

"Yes, I did, but I wasn't talking about the three of us specifically. Listen, Daniel, your dad sent you here for protection. Why the hell would you leave and go back where you came from the second you get here? That doesn't make a lick of sense. We know they're after you. You already had one run-in with a demon." Her eyes narrowed, and she planted her hands on her hips. "And you know what, we need to talk about that. I've been thinking about it all morning, and I'm convinced you shouldn't have made it out of there alive. What am I missing? There's gotta be something you're not telling me."

A surge of anxiety swept through Daniel's body. He knew he needed to tell his aunt about the medallion necklace, but that internal voice kept nagging him to stay quiet.

His eyes met Lena's. They had not discussed their miraculous escape from Al's Gas 'N' Go. They were too shocked and terrified to rehash it in the car, and they hadn't had a chance to talk since they'd arrived here. He wondered if Lena had come to the same conclusion regarding the necklace. He searched her gaze and decided she had. Her gray-blue eyes prodded him, urging him to speak up. Would Lena tell his aunt about the necklace if he didn't? He was pretty sure she would.

Daniel's heart raced. He needed to tell her.

Despite what little you know about her, she loves you, and you can trust her.

"There, uh, there was a necklace," he said at last. "In the envelope from Dad, with the directions to the Compound. He said for me to wear it at all times."

He watched as his aunt's fierce stare dropped to his neck, taking in the leather cord that disappeared beneath his shirt. Aunt Geri wet her lips with her tongue before she asked, in a quiet, hesitant voice, "May I see it?"

Daniel's hands grew damp with nervous sweat as he reached toward his shirt collar. Fighting the nearly overpowering compulsion to hide the pendant, he grasped the leather band resolutely and pulled the medallion from its resting place against his sternum. He didn't remove it. He wouldn't. Couldn't. He let it hang on the outside of his T-shirt so his aunt could view it from a safe distance.

Aunt Geri's jaw went slack. "My god," she breathed.

"Do you recognize it?" Lena asked her.

"No, I haven't seen it before, but it's an amulet. And from the looks of those symbols, a very powerful one." Her eyes widened. "I've never seen anything like this in person, but I've read about them. It's a shield. Holy hell. It shielded you from that demon's powers and rebounded the spell."

Daniel visualized Mindy frozen in place, arm outstretched, cursing at him. She'd told them they were going to 'stay put' for a while, but nothing happened to them. She, however, stood locked in place.

Her spell ricocheted.

"That's the only explanation," Aunt Geri said, "This thing is incredibly powerful. Where the hell did Pete find it?"

Good question. And if this shield's protective magic was so damn great, why wasn't Pete wearing it? Why had he kept it locked away in a dusty box in the back of his closet all this time? Maybe he had a second one, another amulet he was wearing right now, wherever he was.

Gravel crunched behind them as a young couple approached. A shaggy-haired man and vibrantly-tattooed woman, neither of them much older than Daniel and Lena.

Hastily, Daniel grabbed the medallion and stowed it inside his shirt.

The couple acknowledged them with polite smiles as they passed by, continuing along the path toward the houses. Once they were out of earshot, Daniel spoke again. "Okay, well, if this necklace is so powerful, then it should be alright for me to go to Crofton and help with the search."

Aunt Geri heaved a sigh. "Daniel. Think about this. If demons are after *you*, and you go along with the others, you're increasing the chances of an attack. You're the only one with protection. The demons won't hesitate to wipe us all out to get to you. If you're not worried about yourself, then worry about everyone else you'd be putting in danger. Innocent people who are out there volunteering their time, risking everything, to help you find your dad."

That was a gut punch.

He knew his aunt was right. And in actuality, Daniel had searched the trailer quite thoroughly before leaving it. He had passed from room to room several times, scanning the place, looking for signs of his father. He and Lena had certainly combed every inch of Dad's bedroom during their search for the hidden box. Was there a chance they had missed something that would help them find Dad? Possibly. But not likely, he admitted. He wasn't sure it was worth the risk.

"Demons are looking for you, Daniel. They've gotta know Pete sent you to me, and they've gotta be pissed about what went down with you guys in that gas station. Now, I'll do everything in my power to protect you, both of you. Anybody here will do the same. But. We all agree that you two won't be going anywhere for a while, not until you learn more about what we're up against."

We all agree?

Clearly, at some point before the big town meeting, Aunt Geri had spoken with Mr. Garrison and Eddie and Marion and whoever the other higher-ups were around here. Daniel wondered what else they had all agreed on.

"So. Here's what's gonna happen. The team of volunteers will go to your house and look for clues. The three of us will stay here. Lena, we're gonna go get your stuff to bring to my place. Then I think we should go through Pete's books and see if we can find anything useful. Maybe something about that amulet."

"Okay," Daniel gave in.

Lena nodded in agreement as well.

Aunt Geri stepped forward, leading the way back toward the main entrance of the Compound. Daniel and Lena fell into step beside her. It was late morning now and the sun was almost directly above them. There were no trees here in the clearing to filter the sun's rays. The mid-July sunlight beat down harshly upon them as they moved, and Daniel began to sweat.

They passed a livestock fence to which he had paid no attention earlier. A couple of floppy-eared brown goats stared at them, munching on grass.

"Is anybody *really* safe here, then?" Lena asked, her voice soft and timid. "What makes this place any safer than Daniel's house?"

"Well, the posts and the top rails of the perimeter fence are made of iron, which repels demons. We've also got cloaking and warding sigils carved into the posts. You might've heard Walter mention those in the meeting. They added several more this morning for extra reinforcement. They keep demons out, make this place impossible for them to find."

Daniel and Lena exchanged uncomfortable glances. Magic and folklore were the only things keeping them safe here. They knew the amulet from Dad fell into this category. Despite seeing the relic in action, it still required some hefty suspension of disbelief to trust the things Aunt Geri was telling them.

"I know how batshit it sounds," Aunt Geri said, sounding apologetic. "Believe me. I've been in your shoes. I didn't wanna believe it either."

"It's... a lot," Lena said.

"It is," Aunt Geri agreed. "I just need for you kids to trust me. Trust all of us."

They would. It would take some effort, but they would. What other options did they have?

Dad's dog-eared copy of *Demons: Knowing Your Enemy* by Dr. Clyde Sherman, Ph.D., lay open before Daniel and Lena as they huddled around Aunt Geri's kitchen table. Dad's handwritten notes in the margins leaped off the page at them:

> *Black salt- circle around self, lines across entrances*
> <u>*COLD IRON*</u> *– extremely powerful against super-natural entities, stopped even God himself??? - Judges 1:19*
> *Protective gemstones- black onyx; agate for children*
> *Tibetan incense- burn for protection*

Daniel knew this was his father's writing. He knew this book had come from the depths of the man's bedroom closet; he was the one who had removed it. But the words his father had jotted down so carefully still blew his mind.

Aunt Geri placed two mugs of freshly made coffee in front of them before sitting down next to Daniel with her own cup. "Find anything interesting?"

"Thanks," Lena said, lifting her mug from the table. "Do all of these things really work?"

"Which things?"

"Tibetan incense. Black salt. Protective gemstones."

Daniel studied his aunt's face as he reached for his coffee, eager for the caffeine.

"Well, they're all good precautions," Aunt Geri told them. "I keep a line of black salt on the lintels above all the doorways and windowsills here. I also carved warding sigils into the wood above each doorway."

"Really?" Lena asked, sweeping her eyes around the little cabin to catch a glimpse of one.

"You can't see them from here. They're small. I didn't want them to be obvious."

Daniel suddenly wondered if Dad had done the same to their trailer in Crofton. He tried to conjure mental images of the doorways and windowsills in their home but found it nearly impossible. How often had he *really* looked at them? The doors and windows were always there, but always in the background. It was entirely conceivable that he'd been oblivious to small, inconspicuous carvings in the frames for years.

The idea made him uncomfortable.

Had he overlooked lines of black salt, assuming it was dust or dirt resulting from a working single father's less-than-perfect housekeeping? Did Dad have a magical gemstone collection somewhere in plain sight? Had he burned Tibetan incense for protection without Daniel knowing what it was? He wanted to go back home and do a *different* kind of search with his new knowledge.

"But really," Aunt Geri said, pausing to take a sip of coffee, "those things only work on the lower-ranking demons. The ones with fewer abilities."

"They have different ranks?" Lena asked her. She leaned forward in her seat a little, listening keenly for more details.

"Mm-hmm."

"What about the one from the diner?" Daniel asked. "The one you think came back for my dad. What is his rank?"

"Pretty high up on the totem pole, unfortunately."

"So, these things wouldn't work against him?"

"All that stuff, no. But some things would. Like, iron seems to be a pretty universal problem for demons, even if only for a moment."

"What do you mean?" Daniel asked.

"Well, for instance, you can attack a demon with iron weapons. Iron blades. Iron bullets. Hell, theoretically, you could whack 'em with an iron skillet. Iron won't actually *kill* a demon, but the impact will put it out of commission for a little while. It can buy you some time."

"How much time?" Lena inquired.

Aunt Geri raised her eyebrows. "That depends, too. It can take the weaker ones a day or two to remanifest. But the higher-ups? Sometimes only minutes."

"When you say remanifest, how do you mean?" Lena asked.

"The way they appear to people. See, demons can appear in any form they want. They can change from shape to shape because they're incorporeal beings."

Daniel's mouth felt impossibly dry. He took another sip of coffee. "Is that why they possess people?"

"Only the weak ones. The stronger ones don't have to possess anyone. They can make themselves appear human at will."

"So, basically, what you're saying is," Lena said, "anybody out there could actually be a demon disguising itself as a person."

Aunt Geri nodded. "Basically."

The natural milky-white tone of Lena's skin had gone even paler. Daniel watched as she swallowed an extra-long gulp of coffee.

He thought of Mindy. The heavyset blonde with a name badge pinned to her pink T-shirt. *Jesus Loves This Hot Mess.* She'd said Al, the dead man behind the cash register, was her husband. Was the woman with the outdated perm possessed? Was that a real woman, named Mindy, married to Al, her body hijacked for use as a vessel for a demon?

Or had they encountered a fully demonic creature, presenting itself- *manifesting*- as an invented character called Mindy?

The dull throb that had remained in Daniel's head since yesterday morning suddenly seemed worse. He rubbed his forehead. "Is there a way to tell the difference?"

"Usually not until it's too late."

Daniel shivered despite himself.

"So," Aunt Geri sighed. "Iron weapons can buy you time. Do either of you know how to shoot? Are you comfortable with guns?"

Comfortable with guns? What the hell kind of question was that?

"No," they answered in unison.

Lena, looking terrified, added, "Not at all."

"Okay, well, we could work on that."

Lena frowned.

"Hey. I don't like guns either, sweetie," Aunt Geri said, eyeing her, "but iron bullets are a much safer bet than, say, a dagger. You gotta be pretty damn close to a demon to do any damage with a knife, and you better hope to hell you don't ever get that close."

An uneasy silence filled the cabin.

Daniel watched Lena as she blinked and lowered her gaze to the open book before them, her irises shifting left to right as she scanned the text. He thought he detected tears forming in the corners of her eyes and knew he should change the subject quickly.

"Do you think the stone in the amulet is black onyx?" Daniel asked. "I see Dad made a note about black onyx in the margin there."

Aunt Geri leaned closer to read Dad's handwriting. "Oh yeah. Probably so. Black onyx does have strong protective and shielding properties on its own."

"Really? Could we use it to make more of these?" Daniel gestured toward his chest, to the amulet hidden beneath his shirt. "To protect everyone here?"

"If we can figure out all the components used to create that one, sure. But it didn't just protect you; it was somehow able to ricochet the demon's abilities, to make the demon the victim of their own magic. That would take a lot more elements than just black onyx and some symbols. That's some complicated spellwork."

Daniel didn't know what to say.

"But maybe it's in one of these books," Aunt Geri said. "Pete wouldn't have told you to bring them all with you if he didn't think they were important. We just have to look."

That in itself sounded like a Herculean task. Eleven weighty volumes composed Pete Wester's occult library, the smallest of them over four-hundred pages long. Most of the content was written in a dry, formal, academic style that was difficult to read despite the fascinating subject matter. A couple of tomes were quite old, too, penned in archaic English that would require additional effort and concentration.

Lena stared at the two milk crates overflowing with giant books and appeared equally overwhelmed by the daunting prospect.

"Ms. Wester," she said, correcting her posture so she sat up a bit taller in her chair. "Has this ever happened before? Has anyone ever gone missing because of a demon?"

Aunt Geri hesitated before answering. "No." She swallowed hard. "In all our past experiences, when they show up, they kill on sight."

Daniel's stomach clenched upon hearing that statement. Of all the things that had been said about his father's current predicament, this one struck him as the most discomforting.

Dead as a doornail.

"But that doesn't mean that's what happened this time," Aunt Geri added. "Look, if there's anything in your house, Daniel, our people will find it. They'll let us know if any leads turn up."

His aunt's repeated use of *if* wasn't too reassuring either.

Lena took another long drink from her mug. Then another. She set the empty mug onto the tabletop with a clink. "Well, just tell us what we need to do to help in the meantime."

"The best thing you can do is stay calm. And be patient," she told them. "But I know those are also the hardest things to do."

"Yeah," Daniel said.

"And you know what? Pete thought prayer was good, too. A lot of people here believe in that. Prayer. Manifesting. Maybe we all need to be praying that your dad is alive and safe, and that we'll find him quickly."

A possibility suddenly revealed itself to Daniel. If evil was real, if these malevolent incorporeal entities were an actual, tangible threat to humanity, perhaps there were benevolent spiritual beings out there too. Something like angels or positive deities. Maybe they were every bit as present in the daily lives of humans. Dad believed in all of that. Why couldn't it be true?

It was a nice thought. One he desperately needed. Nice thoughts were few and far between lately.

Secretly, he wanted to get his aunt's opinion on the subject. To see if she'd had any angelic encounters as well. But something kept him from asking.

Hope, he realized later.

Hope that there was a good side to all of this held his tongue.

Hope, and a distinct, crushing fear that his hope for goodness would be in vain.

TWELVE

A FTER A COUPLE OF tiresome hours spent fruitlessly slogging through Dad's books, Aunt Geri put together a lunch of garden vegetable sandwiches for the three of them. It was a simple recipe- mayo, cucumbers, butter lettuce, and heirloom tomatoes, but it was perhaps the freshest, tastiest sandwich Daniel had eaten in his life. His aunt had grown the vegetables herself in a raised bed behind her cabin. Her friend Pearl had baked the bread, a delicious, chewy sourdough. Exquisitely sweet peaches harvested from the Compound orchard followed for dessert.

They consumed the meal outside on Aunt Geri's front porch. They hadn't wanted to clear the kitchen table and interrupt their progress; several of Dad's books lay there, open to the pages where they'd left off. Daniel and Lena sat together on the rustic split-log bench, balancing their plates across their laps. Aunt Geri sat on the porch steps doing the same.

From their spot on the porch, Daniel surveyed the area. Not much of the Compound was visible from Aunt Geri's place. He could see a bit of her neighbor's house to the left, a small bungalow-style place with a chicken coop in the back. To the right, untouched woods edged up to the side of the cabin. Daniel wondered how deep the forest went and how much of it was contained within the fence.

"How big is this place?" he asked his aunt.

She swallowed the bite she was chewing before she answered. "A little over three hundred acres."

"Seriously?" Lena gasped. "That's... impressive." She glanced around, taking in their surroundings. "How did you all make this place? Like, how did you start? How did you get all this land?"

"The guy with the gray beard that led the meeting this morning, Walter Garrison? This used to be his daddy's farm."

Daniel recalled the old white farmhouse he had seen on the way inside the previous night. All the rest of the neighborhood- the homes, assembly hall, various outbuildings- had clearly been constructed in much more recent years on the land behind the original 19th-century farmhouse.

"Walter and his family were living in Tulsa when the demon attacked us in the diner. His wife was one of the ones murdered that night," Aunt Geri told them. "Like I said before, all of us who survived bonded afterward. When the demon came back and more of our loved ones were killed, Walter told us about this big piece of land he had inherited out here in the country. He invited everyone to move here. He fixed up the farmhouse for him and his son. The rest of us started building our own places out back."

"Wow," Lena said.

"After a while, other people came. Extended relatives. Others who had survived demon attacks. Everyone had their own reasons for moving in. As we grew, we pooled together our abilities and resources and did what we could to turn this place into a self-sufficient little community."

Daniel took a bite from the peach. Juice dribbled down his chin. "Do you ever leave?" he asked, wiping his face with the cloth napkin his aunt had provided. "I mean, what do you do when you run out of food or somebody gets sick?"

"A few of us do go on supply runs every now and then. But most of our food is grown inside the gates. And you saw our medical clinic. Maeve Lewis, she's a nurse practitioner. She moved in a few years back after her husband was murdered and set up the clinic for us."

Heath's words came to Daniel's mind: *We all have our own reasons for being here. Everyone has a story.*

"That's really wonderful," Lena said. "That you have onsite medical care, I mean."

Aunt Geri nodded. "Maeve takes good care of us."

The conversation lulled as they finished the last of their lunch. Daniel allowed himself to relax a bit as he listened to the birdsong echoing around the woods next to them. He felt rejuvenated from the meal. He'd been hungrier than he'd realized, and the food had eased the growing headache he had developed while studying Dad's dusty old books.

The sound of an approaching vehicle caught everyone's attention. A clunky, rusted, nineteen-seventies-model Chevy Suburban rumbled down the road and came to a stop in front of Aunt Geri's cabin. The grumbling engine shut off, leaving Daniel's ears ringing. The driver's door opened, and Heath climbed out.

It shocked Daniel that Heath was still here. Of all the people who had been in this morning's meeting, he was certain this guy would have volunteered to go to Crofton to search the trailer. It had been his suggestion, after all. But it was one o'clock in the afternoon. The team had been gone for hours.

Heath shoved his hands in the pockets of his sand-colored cargo pants and walked around the hood of the Suburban toward them.

"Well, hey there," Aunt Geri greeted him, rising to her feet. She glanced over her shoulder at Daniel and Lena. "Kids, this is Heath Garrison."

Garrison. Like Walter Garrison. This guy and Mr. Garrison seemed pretty opposed to each other in the meeting, but they had to be related. Aunt Geri had just told them Walter moved into his old family farmhouse years ago with his son. Heath was the right age to fit the bill. Daniel really wanted to know if his deduction was correct.

Heath Garrison dipped his stubble-covered chin at them. "We met already." He sounded just as gruff and surly as he had at the meeting.

"What brings you by, hon?" Aunt Geri asked him. "Is there any news?"

Heath cleared his throat. "No news. I just wanted to see if there's maybe something I can do to help." He paused and cleared his throat again. It seemed like a nervous tic, but maybe he had allergies. "Surely there's something to do besides sitting around here on our asses, waiting on word from Eddie and the others."

Aunt Geri brightened at this. "There is, thank you. Pete sent about a dozen books with Daniel. We've been trying to go through them, but it's a hell of a job. Why don't you come in?"

Heath nodded and ascended the porch steps, his heavy-duty brown boots thudding against the wooden planks.

Daniel gathered his lunch dishes and raised himself from the bench. He was of average height and build, but he felt stubby and frail as he stood next to Heath. Broad-shouldered and solid as stone, the guy was even more intimidating at full height. He towered over the three of them like the Incredible Hulk.

He wondered again why Heath was not headed to Crofton.

Daniel decided to be a gentleman and carry Lena's dirty dishes for her. She didn't seem to notice. Her gaze was fixed on Heath, and like before in the assembly hall, she was blushing. Deeply.

Daniel found this unreasonably irritating.

Aunt Geri held open the front door to her home, allowing everyone inside. Daniel trailed behind Heath as he crossed the threshold. For the first time, he noticed a mahogany belt slung around the guy's waist. An ivory knife handle protruded from a leather sheath hanging from it.

"I'm surprised you stayed behind," Daniel finally said aloud. "I thought you'd have been the first to volunteer."

Heath turned to him. He looked even more gigantic inside Aunt Geri's meager living room. With a sneer, he replied, "Oh, I was."

Daniel stared.

"My dad's an asshole."

"Your dad is... Walter?"

"Our self-appointed leader." Heath rolled his eyes. "He always knows best. To him, I'm a fucking twelve-year-old."

Aunt Geri scratched her left ear. "Well, dads are like that sometimes."

An uncomfortable silence filled the cabin.

"Um, speaking of dads," Daniel ventured, "why don't we get back to work?" He slid a chair away from the table and sank into it, returning to page 78 of *Possessions and Exorcisms,* co-authored by husband-and-wife demon-hunting team Harry and Hilda Birch. Both the blurb and author bio on the back cover were laughable. It had been published in the seventies, at the height of America's *The Exorcist*-induced demon hysteria. *Possessions and Exorcisms* seemed like utter bullshit, concocted by a desperate married couple trying to cash in on Satan's revival. But Dad had included it in his collection, so it was worth a closer look.

Before fully diving back into it, Daniel watched as Heath's eyes- honey-brown irises with flecks of mossy green situated beneath a canopy of long, sweeping lashes- scanned the titles Dad owned.

"Damn," Heath remarked appreciatively. "Quite the library."

"Isn't it?" Aunt Geri said, returning to her seat next to Daniel. "Pete left a letter behind for Daniel that said to bring all these with him. We're going through them all, hoping there's something helpful to be found."

"Okay."

"Just grab one and have a seat."

Heath squatted down and selected *An Overview of Protective Symbols.* He strode to the remaining empty chair, the one between

Aunt Geri and Lena, and sat down. Daniel watched as Heath's stupidly pretty eyes met Lena's. Her already-pink cheeks deepened to crimson. Daniel could almost feel the heat radiating from her. He would've been embarrassed for her if he weren't so annoyed.

He forced his attention to the open pages before him, to see what advice Harry and Hilda were peddling. A bold text heading read *Exorcism Rites.* Full paragraphs beneath this heading stood out, highlighted in neon yellow. Rows and rows of Dad's notes filled the margins. Clearly, he had spent a lot of time on this page.

"Looks like Pete was really focused on exorcisms," Aunt Geri commented.

Daniel glanced at her, then at the pages of the book in front of her. Whatever she was looking at was also heavily highlighted and annotated. Daniel could make out enough to tell that the text was in Latin.

Aunt Geri gestured from her book to Daniel's. "It looks like he put in a lot of work trying to memorize all these long Latin incantations to expel demons." She heaved a sigh and sat back in her chair. "Unfortunately, he wasted his time."

"What do you mean?" Daniel asked.

"Exorcisms are bullshit," Heath chimed in. "Just a buncha showy, Catholic, pomp-and-circumstance shit."

Daniel couldn't argue with him there.

"Right," Aunt Geri said. "Daniel, do you remember when I said to throw out everything you know about demons?"

Daniel nodded.

Aunt Geri brushed her sweaty bangs out of her eyes, and Daniel saw deep creases in her forehead. "Well, like I said, we call them *demons* because of Western religions. But these things aren't 'fallen angels' who serve Satan. None of these exorcism rituals are gonna send them back to Hell, because they're not from Hell. There is no Hell. There's no Satan. That's all Christian mythology. These creatures are ancient, far older than Christianity or any other Abrahamic religion."

No one said anything.

A lump had formed in Daniel's throat, making it somewhat painful to swallow. He glanced at Lena. The blush had vanished from her skin. Her mouth hung open slightly as her wide eyes stayed glued to his aunt.

Daniel's eyes met Heath's for a second. The guy was watching him, assessing him, waiting to observe his reaction to what Aunt Geri was saying. Daniel pushed his shoulders back, straightened his spine, and turned to his aunt, determined to suppress the terror growing inside him.

"Okay, so," Daniel began, willing his voice to be steady, "if all of that isn't real, if they're not from Hell, then where are these things from?"

"That's the big question," she said. "They've plagued the earth for all of recorded history. I mean, we've got lore and protective amulets from cultures all over the world, going as far back as ancient Mesopotamia. But in all those thousands of years, nobody- *nobody-* has figured out much of anything about them."

Daniel swallowed hard, eyeing the book before him. He doubted Harry and Hilda Birch, with their feathered hair and bell bottoms, knew any more about these ancient beings than he did.

"Sure, there's lots of stories, lots of writers peddling their theories," Aunt Geri said, gesturing at the books. "But very little is concrete."

"That's not very comforting," Lena said.

Daniel agreed. "Are we wasting our time here, then? Reading all this?"

She shook her head. "At the very least, reading your dad's notes helps us understand *him* better. We can see what *he* thought was important, which could give us an idea about what was going on."

"If he thought exorcisms were this important," Heath said, "maybe he knew somebody who was possessed. Maybe he was getting ready to face them right before this happened."

That was an intriguing idea. Daniel mentally took inventory of everyone they had encountered in the days leading up to Dad's disappearance. The cashier and other shoppers at Piggly Wiggly on Saturday. Their server at Cracker Barrel. The entire congregation of Bethesda Christian Church on Sunday. Could *any* of them have been possessed by the demon from the diner, watching them, waiting for the right moment to strike?

Aunt Geri had indicated that the demon from their past was strong enough to manifest itself as a person. It didn't require a human vessel. If she was right, if Dad knew *the* demon was coming for him, he should've known an exorcism would be useless.

"Could be," Aunt Geri said to Heath. "I think he probably just wanted to be prepared in case he came across someone who was possessed. We gotta remember it's been twenty years since Pete left the Compound. We've all learned a lot here in that time, but Pete hasn't been here to learn with us. He doesn't know some of the stuff we do. Like, Latin exorcisms are bullshit."

Heath bobbed his head. "Good point."

Aunt Geri stared at the kitchenette behind Heath for so long without blinking, Daniel followed her gaze to see what had captured her attention. Their dirty lunch dishes sat on the counter, but everything else was in order. He realized his aunt stared at nothing, lost in her thoughts.

The room grew quiet.

Assuming the conversation was over, Daniel glanced back down at *Possessions and Exorcisms* and picked up where he'd left off:

Exorcism Rites

The ministry of our Lord Jesus Christ provides the foundation for what is today known as the rite of exorcism. The many miracles He performed throughout His thirty-three years on Earth included the expulsion of devils or 'unclean spirits' from at least twelve demon-possessed individuals. While the formal rite of exorcism used by the Catholic Church has no basis in Scripture-

Daniel smirked at that last line. *No basis in Scripture.* Even the Birches could admit the contradiction there.

His aunt's voice interrupted his thoughts. "If Pete had never left, this wouldn't have happened," Aunt Geri said, her voice filled with bitterness. With regret. "I should've tried harder to convince him to stay."

Daniel didn't know how to respond. No one did. The four of them sat around the table in unpleasant silence, avoiding each other's eyes.

What was there to say? Daniel couldn't understand why his father had placed them both at risk by leaving the safety of the Compound all those years ago. Aunt Geri had said he was angry, grieving, and sick of living in fear, but those were nothing but crappy excuses for irresponsible behavior that could've easily gotten them both killed. It was a miracle nothing had happened until now.

Yeah, maybe Aunt Geri *should've* tried harder to make him stay.

He wondered what his life would've been like if Dad hadn't left. What would his childhood have been like, growing up inside the gates of the Compound? He wouldn't have met Lena. He winced at the thought. She'd always been there. He couldn't imagine life without her in it. Would Heath have been his best friend instead?

One thing was certain: Dad would be here right now.

They wouldn't be huddled around this table trying to figure out what the hell had happened to him, hopelessly scouring his books for clues.

Hopelessly. Did he really believe that?

The silence within the cabin had grown tense. Unbearably so. Daniel wanted to say something to ease things, but he couldn't think of a damn thing. There were no reassurances for his aunt, for any of them. Nothing he could say would change that.

Because of his own carelessness, Pete Wester had finally met the fate that had always been coming for him. Daniel knew this now. He only hoped they could find him before it was too late.

THIRTEEN

Hours passed. Daniel finished *Possessions and Exorcisms* and moved on to *Power Over Demons* by A. R. Maxwell. It sounded like a cheesy self-help book, a guide to confronting and overcoming one's inner conflict. But no, A. R. Maxwell meant literal demons, and he had devoted four hundred fifty-two pages to explaining various ways to fight them.

> *Evocation, derived from the Latin term 'evocatio' meaning 'invitation, calling', is the deliberate act of calling forth or summoning a supernatural entity into one's personal vicinity. It should be noted that within dominant religions such as Christianity and Islam, evoking spirits is regarded as morally wrong, associated with wickedness, and highly frowned upon.*

Daniel laughed, a bit hysterically due to exhaustion. No shit, Maxwell. He read on, skimming the paragraphs, struggling to focus.

-cause harm to people- enter their servitude- must first know the entity's true name- might call forth a demon in order to obtain spiritual insight or information- the bidding of the practitioner-

His head swam as the text on the pages ran together into strings of nonsense. He'd been reading this stuff for way too long. His neck and shoulders throbbed with tension. His back ached and his butt cheeks were numb from sitting on the same hard wooden chair for hours.

He gave up. Flopped back into the seat and rubbed his tired, watery eyes. A quick glance at Lena told him she felt the same. He caught her squeezing her eyes shut, then forcing them open wide again in an effort to focus. Her scleras were red with fatigue. She'd looked exactly like this a few weeks ago when she'd spent hours studying lecture notes, giant nursing textbooks, and homemade flash cards, tirelessly preparing to sit for the NCLEX.

A growl filled the room.

Someone's empty stomach. He was pretty sure it was Heath.

That was it. He was calling it. "I need a break," Daniel announced.

Lena nodded gratefully. "That sounds like a good idea."

Heath stretched his chiseled arms overhead for a few moments, yawned, and eased back into his seat. He threw a glance at his wristwatch. "Damn. It's nearly six. No wonder I'm starving."

"Why don't we step away from this for a while and grab a bite at Pearl's?" Aunt Geri suggested. Her blue eyes glittered brightly as she added, "She's doing Mexican food tonight."

Daniel felt his own stomach grumbling at the mention of Mexican food. That was his favorite. Lena's too. It was kind of their thing.

Back in Crofton, no matter how busy Lena got with nursing school or, more recently, work, they had a standing Thursday night meetup at La Frontera downtown. Thursday night was half-off burritos, which was the primary feature that made La Frontera their go-to place. They'd claim their usual booth in the back corner and update each other on the last week's events over tortilla chips, salsa, and discount burritos.

Lately, these weekly updates consisted of Daniel's job search challenges and Lena's unbelievable patient encounters. Those normal conversations felt so far behind them now. Were those days over? Would they ever spend another Thursday evening at La Frontera, where the only horrors to be discussed were no job offers and a patient's enema gone wrong?

It seemed like a very distant prospect.

"There'll be a crowd," Daniel heard Heath say. "Maybe we can talk to some people, see if anyone's heard back from the team that went out this morning."

"Sounds great," Lena said, scooting her chair away from the table.

Daniel stood and stretched his left arm across his chest, then the right, trying to bring some relief to his muscles. Joints popped audibly as he moved. He felt far older than twenty-one at present. He seemed to have aged at least a decade in the last twenty-four hours. Uncovering a lifetime of secrets and having deadly primordial beings on your tail would do that to you, he supposed.

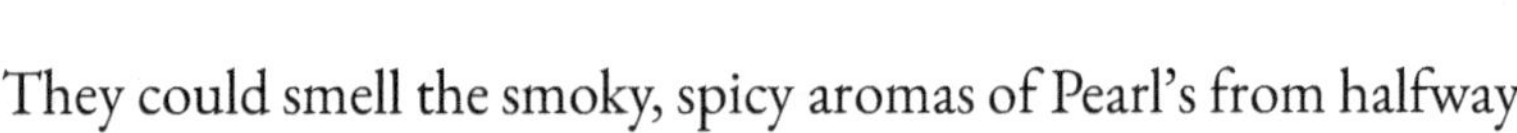

They could smell the smoky, spicy aromas of Pearl's from halfway across the Compound.

Daniel's stomach rumbled with anticipation as he, Lena, Heath, and Aunt Geri strode along the gravel path that led to the central square. But as his mouth watered longingly, he felt a twinge of guilt. Dad was still missing, status unknown, possibly dead, and Daniel was thinking about burritos and salsa.

The day had felt so pointless. So unproductive. Sure, he had learned a lot from Dad's books. He'd gained a lot of new knowledge about demons that might come in handy at some point. But was he any closer to finding his dad? Had he done *anything* to look for him?

A fiery, bitter anger replaced the hunger in his belly. How could he keep doing this? How could he keep doing nothing?

He forced himself to focus on Aunt Geri's words for the hundredth time. He *couldn't* do anything right now. Dad had told him to come here. Go to the Compound. Take the books and look at them. Trust Aunt Geri. As frustrating as it was, he was already doing all he could do.

But it didn't feel like it. Everything felt wrong. Not getting out there and actively searching for Dad felt wrong. Sitting down and enjoying Pearl's Mexican feast felt wrong.

He trailed slightly behind the others, trudging onward down the path in angsty silence.

The sun dipped below the horizon and left the Compound in a hazy purple glow. Enough light remained to illuminate the pathway, but the outbuildings were in shadows. Crickets chirped all around them as they strolled toward Pearl's.

Warm lights appeared up ahead, glowing like stars against the darkening indigo sky. He heard music drifting faintly from there. As they moved closer, it grew louder. Daniel recognized the song. An oldie, one Dad had always liked. He relaxed a little. Funny how a familiar song could instantly have that effect. As he sang along in his head, it made him miss his father even more.

Heath was right. There was quite a crowd. It looked like over half the attendees of the morning meeting had come out for dinner.

Round bulb string lights stretched out in a 'V' shape from the awning of Pearl's Café to a couple of oak trees planted on either side of the little building. White tablecloths covered an extra-long *Last Supper* kind of table, and a couple dozen people huddled around it. Several candles of varied shapes and sizes ran down the center of the table, casting the diners in a warm, magical glow.

The inviting atmosphere calmed Daniel, and the overpoweringly tempting aroma of enchiladas reawakened his appetite.

The four of them found empty seats at the far end of the table. Daniel claimed a spot between Lena and a bald man who had spoken up at the meeting in the assembly hall. Heath sat across from them, next to a middle-aged plus-sized woman Daniel didn't recognize. He watched Heath acknowledge her with a polite nod, which she returned with a smile.

Daniel shifted around in his seat, trying to get comfortable. His body was still so freaking sore. He accidentally rammed his elbow into Lena's arm. "Sorry."

Her blue eyes sparkled as they met his, the reflections of candle-light dancing in her pupils. "It's alright."

He gaped at her. He'd been with her all day, but here now, in this setting, warmed by the golden glow of the candles and the string lights, she looked different.

Just before leaving the cabin, she'd pulled her white-blonde hair up into a messy French braid crown. She didn't wear her hair like this often, which was a shame. It made her look elegant, regal. Her sleeveless maroon blouse showed her bare shoulders, her collarbone, and a hint of cleavage.

God. She was beautiful.

Her brow furrowed slightly at him. "Are you okay?"

"Yeah, sorry." He realized he'd been staring a bit too intensely and shifted his gaze to the table, where baskets of nearly translucent tortilla chips sat encircled by small bowls of thick salsa and chunky, bright green guacamole.

From across the table, Heath reached into the basket and seized a chip. "You gotta try the guac," he said. "It's amazing." He scooped a generous heap of guacamole and devoured it with a crunch.

Daniel smiled and reached for a tortilla chip. Trusting Heath's recommendation, he sank it into the guacamole, shoveled a liberal amount, and ate. Crisp diced onions and succulently sweet tomato chunks filled the creamy goodness. He savored the bright, tangy cilantro and the tartness of freshly-squeezed lime. It was perfect. Absolutely perfect.

"Well?" Heath asked, brows raised.

"Damn."

"Right?" Heath grinned and reached for another.

Lena followed suit. Her eyes widened with her first bite. "Oh my god."

Heath chuckled, his too-pretty eyes watching her. "Told you."

Not exactly thrilled with the subtle micro-expressions being exchanged between Heath and Lena, Daniel went in for another chip. Someone's arm reached from behind with a plate at that exact moment.

"Whoop, careful! Right behind you!" a cheery female voice warned.

Daniel froze.

The slender brown arm set the plate on the table in front of the bald man next to him.

"Thanks, Zarah," the man said.

"No problem!"

Daniel nearly drooled when he got a look at the bald man's plate. The biggest enchilada he had ever seen sprawled across the dish, smothered in brown-red sauce, sprinkled with flecks of white cheese, and spilling roasted summer vegetables. Daniel's stomach ached with longing.

"You must be Daniel," the female voice behind him said.

He turned to find a shapely young woman with warm sepia skin and a big, luxuriant cloud of black hair. Her abundant, tightly-coiled spirals fell just past her shoulders. Daniel's breath snagged in his throat as he met her eyes. They were deep-set and heavy-lidded with striking, bright jade irises. He couldn't look away. She flashed him a toothy smile. She was pleasant and upbeat, but Daniel detected something like sympathy, perhaps pity, in her mesmerizing gaze.

"I'm Zarah. Zarah Crider. Welcome to the Compound. And, uh, welcome to Pearl's." She held up a hand, gesturing over-dramatically at Pearl's Café like one of the women on *The Price Is Right*. "Can I get you something to drink? I recommend the lemonade. It's my personal favorite."

Crider. Her features so closely mirrored those of Marion Crider, this had to be her daughter. "Um, thank you, it's nice to meet you. And sure, I'll try the lemonade. Please."

"An excellent choice, sir." She gave him a somewhat goofy grin before her brilliant green eyes drifted toward Lena. "What about your friend here? Lena, is it?"

"Yes, I'm Lena. Hello. I'll have the lemonade as well, please."

"Sure thing. Same for you Heath? Miss Geri?"

Heath nodded. Aunt Geri asked for water instead.

"Okay. Be right back, guys." She smiled at Daniel and gave him a gentle pat on the shoulder.

Daniel felt himself blushing after she'd gone, his shoulder still warm from her touch. Was she flirting with him? Probably not. He'd never been too smooth around pretty girls. He cast a sideways glance at Lena to judge her reaction to Zarah. She was munching on guacamole-covered chips, seemingly oblivious.

"You holdin' up okay, son?" the man next to him suddenly asked.

Daniel looked at him. Middle-aged with earth-brown skin, the man regarded him with kind, chestnut-colored eyes that bulged forward slightly. His shiny bald head gleamed in the candlelight.

"Yes, sir. Thank you."

"I know all this has gotta seem crazy to you," the man went on. He unwrapped a fork and knife from a folded napkin and begin cutting into his enchilada. Wisps of steam escaped, carrying delectable smells. "And it's awfully strange havin' everyone here know who you are, especially when you don't know a soul."

Daniel wasn't sure what to say.

"I know, 'cause I've been in your shoes. I came here four years ago, also not knowing a soul, except for Eddie and Marion. And your aunt." He paused to take a bite of his dinner. "They saved my life. Brought me to this place so I could stay safe."

Daniel waited quietly for him to continue.

"My name's Vern," he said. "I lost my entire family to a demon."

"Oh. I'm... I'm so sorry."

Vern stared down at his plate in quiet contemplation. After a few heavy moments, he said simply, "I'm glad you're here, Daniel." He lifted his eyes and looked at him once more. He gave him a small, reassuring smile. "I sure hope we find your dad, safe and sound. Maybe we'll hear somethin' soon."

As Daniel searched for the right words to say, he became aware of Zarah's presence again. She stood behind Aunt Geri, a tray of beverages in hand. His ears perked up as he heard his aunt ask Zarah:

"Have you heard anything from your parents?"

Daniel knew she was talking about the team that had gone to Crofton. He listened anxiously to hear her response.

"No, I've been here all day, helping Miss Pearl. I'm hoping Mr. Garrison will know something when he gets here."

Heath grimaced slightly at the mention of his father, Daniel observed.

"And I bet he'll be here any minute now," Zarah said. She set a glass of lemonade in front of Daniel. "Sit tight, okay? I'm gonna go grab y'all some plates."

No one spoke again.

The air suddenly felt tense.

Daniel's right leg bounced nervously. He distracted himself with chips and guacamole.

Zarah Crider reappeared, impressively balancing four heaping, steaming plates of deliciousness. Daniel licked his lips as he eyed the dish she set in front of him. The moment she walked away, he grabbed up his fork and dove in.

A fiesta of divinely blended flavors exploded on his tongue and melted there. Maybe he was just famished, but this was the best thing he had ever eaten.

Ever.

The next several minutes were a blissful blur as he attacked the enchilada, savoring every bite. He had forgotten his troubles until Walter Garrison showed up.

"Walter," Aunt Geri called him over. She swallowed the bite of enchilada she had been chewing and wiped her mouth with a napkin. "Have you heard anything?"

Mr. Garrison did not look well. Despite the warm light all around them, the man's face was pale. "Yes," he said solemnly.

The color drained from Aunt Geri's face as well, almost instantly. "What is it? What's wrong?"

Everyone at the extra-long table seemed to have frozen in place. The sounds of scraping forks, crunching tortilla chips, and friendly conversation shifted into agonizing silence.

Mr. Garrison gulped. "When the team reached Crofton, they had nothing to go on."

"What do you mean?" Aunt Geri asked.

"I mean, any evidence remaining is gone. Pete's trailer burned to the ground."

FOURTEEN

J UST LIKE THAT, DANIEL was homeless.

His shelter, his childhood home, four walls full of history, gone. Forever. Everything he owned besides the things he had stuffed into his duffel bag and brought to the Compound, was gone forever. Nothing but a pile of ashes.

It was strange the possessions he mourned first. His middle-school baseball jersey. His collection of novels and history books. The acoustic Ibanez guitar Dad gave him the Christmas of 2004.

The photographs of his mother.

It hit him like a roundhouse kick to the gut. The rest of his things were just that. *Things.* Stuff. Junk with a bit of sentimental value. But not the pictures of Helen Wester. Those pictures were the only living remnant of the woman who had given him life, the woman he had never been allowed to know. Those pictures were all he had of her.

Now they were dust.

Daniel stared down at his forgotten enchilada and felt his stomach quiver with nausea. Odd how the best meal of his life now seemed so unappealing.

Not only had he lost every material possession he and his father had ever owned, he had also been robbed of any chance at finding him. There were no clues for the team to find. No leads for them to follow. Any evidence had burned up in the flames.

"The demon knew we would go to Pete's place and look around," Walter Garrison said. "It went back to make sure there was nothing for us to find."

Out of the corner of his eye, Daniel watched his aunt hang her head in defeat.

"I'm just glad Daniel got out of there before that happened," Mr. Garrison said. "Things could have been much worse."

Daniel winced at the prospect of burning alive in the trailer. Would that have happened if the thunder hadn't managed to wake him? If he'd snoozed on 'til noon as he did sometimes as an unemployed twenty-one-year-old who often stayed up too late watching *Doctor Who* or playing video games, would he have gone up in flames as he slept? His stomach twisted as he realized how narrowly he had escaped.

"You're right," Aunt Geri sounded far away. "You're right about that."

Mr. Garrison took a step forward and looked at Daniel. His dark eyes brimmed with sadness. "I'm sorry, son. I wish I had good news to give you for a change."

Silence ruled the table. No one made a sound.

Daniel felt like he might be sick.

"Well, what now?" Lena demanded. She'd half-shouted, sounding uncharacteristically fierce. "What are they going to do now?"

Mr. Garrison breathed deeply. "They're examining what they can of the ruins. From what Eddie said, there's not much to see."

Daniel looked at Lena. Her jaw trembled as a tear forced itself out and slipped down her cheek. She brushed it away angrily with the back of her hand.

Mr. Garrison eyed the two of them sympathetically. "I'm sorry."

That was not what he was supposed to say. Not at all.

This was when he should have revealed some pivotal key they had been missing this whole time. He was supposed to give them hope, not crush whatever tiny bit of it they had left.

"Well, then, what do we do?" Aunt Geri asked. "We have to do something."

"I agree with you on that," said Mr. Garrison. "But right now, the only thing we can do is-"

Aunt Geri threw her napkin onto the table. "Walter, if you say the only damn thing we can do is *wait*, I swear to you, I will-" She stopped. Sweaty and red-faced, she lowered her eyes and took a deep breath. "Look, I just- I can't keep waiting. *We* can't keep waiting. This is my brother. Daniel's dad. If we keep sitting here, if we keep waiting around, we'll never find him."

"Then what do you think we should do? I'm open to suggestions." Mr. Garrison swept his eyes across the long table full of listeners. "Anybody? Do any of you have any ideas?"

Nobody said a word.

"See?" Mr. Garrison said. "There is nothing we can do." He swallowed. "Nothing."

The place went miserably silent.

Daniel's heart began to race. He had an idea, one that had been brewing in the back of his mind for a couple of hours now. His tongue felt dry as he spoke up, "There is one thing we could try."

"And what's that, son?" Mr. Garrison asked in a demeaning tone, as though he were indulging a toddler.

"We could summon a demon," Daniel said shakily. The words surprised him, even as they came from his own lips. "Evocation. I just read about it in one of Dad's books. We could trap a demon, torture it, force it to give us information about where Dad is."

"No," Mr. Garrison boomed. "Absolutely not. That is way, way too dangerous."

"Not if we go in prepared," someone said.

Daniel glanced up in search of the speaker. Zarah. The big-haired waitress planted her hands on her hips. Her arresting jade eyes stared shrewdly at Mr. Garrison.

"We could get a big group together, all of us armed," Zarah said. "Do a binding ritual to make sure the thing doesn't go anywhere."

Mr. Garrison shook his head. "The demon is too powerful-"

In what Daniel thought was an impressively bold move, Zarah interrupted him. "We wouldn't summon *the* demon. Just one of the bench-warmers. Think about it. All of us against one bottom-ranking brown-noser."

"Would that work?" Lena spoke up. She turned to Aunt Geri. "Is it possible to torture a demon?"

"Well, yeah, I guess it's possible," she replied. "But crazy."

"Yes, it's crazy. And highly risky," Mr. Garrison said. "Summoning one of those filthy things is asking for trouble. You open that doorway, you invite all sorts of evil in. I won't allow it."

"What if it was Heath that was missing out there?" Zarah tossed at him. "Your own son, gone without a trace, taken by a demon." She stared Mr. Garrison down without blinking even once. "Wouldn't you try anything to get him back?"

Everyone watched the graying leader now. The tension soared as they waited for his response.

"It's too dangerous," he said at last. "If we were to open this place up to demons..." He bit his lip. "We can't."

"No, not here," Aunt Geri said. "We wouldn't do it here inside the gates."

Mr. Garrison was taking longer and longer to respond. He was considering it. Daniel could tell. Slowly, the leader nodded. "The women and children could stay here while some of us men take care of it."

Daniel heard Lena angrily mutter something under her breath at that.

Aunt Geri huffed, her face flushing again. "Are you kidding, Walter? Get out of here with that misogynistic bullshit. You know damn well any woman inside these gates can run circles around your ass."

Wary grins appeared on most of the faces around the table, some more discreet than others. Heath was practically beaming.

Defeated, Walter shoved his hands in his pockets and cleared his throat. "Then who would go?"

"I would, of course," Aunt Geri said, still hot. "I'm sure others would volunteer."

"I'll go," the man next to Daniel- Vern- spoke up.

"Me too," said someone from across the table. A young white guy with shaggy brown hair and high cheekbones. He didn't look that much older than Daniel.

"Would you, Justin?" Mr. Garrison asked derisively. "How do you think Claudia and your boy will feel about that? You going outside the walls and conjuring up an evil spirit."

The young woman next to 'Justin' sat up straight. She was olive-skinned with catlike features and frizzy black hair prematurely streaked with silver. Her eyes darkened and narrowed at Mr. Garrison. "I would understand," she said sharply. This was Claudia, apparently, and she would for damn sure speak for herself. She stared resolutely at Walter Garrison and slung her brightly-tattooed arm around a small boy sitting next to her. He couldn't have been more than three. "And I'd come along too if I weren't needed here."

That quieted Mr. Garrison for a bit.

"I'll go too," Daniel heard himself volunteer.

Mr. Garrison let out a condescending chuckle. "This is all still a story to you, son. You have no idea what these things are capable of. You getting out of that gas station alive was pure luck, and that luck is bound to run out."

Daniel stiffened. "I don't care. I'll do whatever I need to do to find my dad." He glanced at his aunt, who surprisingly did not argue with him. Neither did Lena. She wore her fear clearly across her face, but he knew she understood.

"Hell, you know I'm in," Heath said.

The elder Mr. Garrison rolled his eyes. "Heath-"

"No, Dad, we're not having this argument twice in one day, and we're definitely not gonna do it in front of all these people. You know I'm a good fighter. I'm going."

Walter was silent.

"What's the point of this place if we're not gonna do anything when something happens to someone we care about? Did you start this place just so you could hide? Is that all this is to you? Just an escape, a way to forget about what's really out there? To pretend evil doesn't exist?"

Heath had the crowd's attention. Everyone around the table watched him, listening.

"We're not cowards here. Every single one of us inside this gate, we're here because we've faced these things at one point or another and made it out alive. We survived." Heath gestured toward Vern. "Four years ago, Eddie and Marion tracked demonic omens in Missouri. They didn't sit around on their asses. They drove up there and did everything they could to help. They saved Vern's life and brought him back here."

Vern nodded and stared down at the tablecloth as everyone's eyes found him. He looked as though he might tear up. Not wanting to stare intrusively, Daniel refocused on Heath.

"Two years ago. Wisconsin. Same story. A team went up there and came back with Beth and Logan."

Eyes drifted down the table to a thin middle-aged woman with a pale, heart-shaped face and a teenage boy who looked like a carbon copy of her.

"Everybody here has a story like this," Heath said. "We're all survivors. We're fighters."

The area outside the café grew quiet. Nothing but the late summer sound of crickets buzzing around them. Heath shifted in his seat and stared at his father, boring holes into the man.

"Pete was your best friend, Dad. Did you forget that? This monster came back for him, just like you'd always thought it might. And you don't wanna do anything but wait?" Heath shook his head. "No way. It's time to stop waiting around here, hiding. It's time to do something. It's time to fight."

Heath's speech seemed to move everyone sitting around the table. Even his father. Three additional people volunteered to leave the safety of the Compound's walls and conjure a demon. Others offered to help with guard duty, to increase security within the community in the absence of the summoning team.

However, the time and date of this expedition could not be agreed upon.

"We have to at least wait until the others get back from Crofton," Mr. Garrison insisted. He had taken a seat at the end of the table next to Aunt Geri. He placed his elbows on the tabletop now and leaned forward. "We sent out some of our best folks. If we send out more of them now, we put everyone at risk."

"He's right," Pearl said.

Pearl Olivares, the plump, silver-haired cook and manager of the little café had also joined the table somewhere in the middle of Heath's pep talk. She sat across from Daniel and Lena, still wearing her masa harina-dusted apron and smelling loudly of enchiladas. Her skin, the warm color of terracotta, looked exceptionally orange in the candlelight. Sweat glistened on her brow.

"What if something happened to both teams?" Pearl asked. "Then what would we do?"

"That's my point exactly," Mr. Garrison said. "As I said before, the demon *wants* us to do this. It wanted us to send people to Crofton, and now it wants us to do this. Think about it. These things would love to get more of us outside the gates, to pick off our best fighters, to weaken our defenses."

Everyone paused to consider this for a moment, then Zarah spoke up. "I think all of us would be more comfortable with waiting until my parents and the others get back to do this, but do we really have that option? Pete's already been missing for two full days. We can't keep wasting time."

Daniel nodded in agreement and noticed a few others around the table doing the same.

Mr. Garrison sat upright and crossed his arms over his chest. "Twelve hours," he said. "I call Eddie now, they can be back here within that time frame. That'll give us all plenty of time to prepare for this... ritual so we can make sure we do it right." He wrinkled his nose as he said the word *ritual*. Clearly, he still abhorred the idea. "Can we all agree to that?"

The members of the group looked at each other.

"I think that sounds pretty reasonable," Aunt Geri said for everyone.

Mr. Garrison dipped his bearded chin. "Alright, then. Geri, I want you in charge of finding a location for the ritual. Heath, you make sure everyone is fully armed."

"Yes, sir."

"Justin," Mr. Garrison eyed the shaggy-haired young man across from Daniel. "Make sure guard duty is doubled. I'm gonna get in touch with Eddie, then I'm checking my resources to find the safest way to do this." He frowned. "I suppose the rest of you can start digging six-foot holes and building coffins."

And with that snide remark, Walter Garrison turned, rose to his feet, and walked away.

"Wow," Lena murmured. "He's really optimistic about this, isn't he?"

"Listen, no matter what he says, this is our best shot," Heath assured the nervous crowd. "Our only shot at this point. Yeah, it's dangerous, but if we're smart and careful and we go in with a plan, we'll be just fine."

Daniel wondered how much Heath believed his statement. He didn't seem to be bluffing, but even normal people, people who lived outside of a secret gated neighborhood shut off from demons and the modern world, generally believed conjuring evil spirits was a no-no. How had A. R. Maxwell worded it? *Evoking spirits is morally wrong, associated with wickedness, and highly frowned upon.* He was still shocked at himself for suggesting this.

"Well," Aunt Geri sighed. "I guess we've got work to do."

"Any ideas about where we're gonna do this?" Zarah asked.

Daniel was wondering the same thing. On the drive in, he and Lena hadn't seen anything but trees for a very long time. It had been dark, of course, but he doubted there was anything but forest for at least twenty miles.

"There's the old foundry out on fifty-nine," Vern suggested.

"Yeah," a bespectacled man in flannel said. He was one of the others who had volunteered to go. "Nobody's bothered that place in years."

Pearl bit her lip. "It's a little far out, though, isn't it?"

"Isn't that the point?" the man in flannel said. "We don't wanna bring the thing right up to the front gate."

"Well, no, but I don't like the idea of you all being so far away from the rest of us," Pearl said. "What if something happened and you needed backup? Or, Heaven forbid, medical help?"

Lena released a loud sigh. "That's it," she said. "I'm going, too."

"What?" Heath asked in disbelief.

"I'm a nurse," Lena announced, looking around the table, making eye contact with each of the individuals gathered there. "A registered nurse."

"But, sweetie," Pearl said, "you're so young."

"Yeah. Didn't you, like, just graduate?" Heath asked.

"That means my knowledge is fresh." Lena pushed back her shoulders and kept her head high. "I already have over one and a half years of clinical experience in all areas of nursing, from orthopedics to pediatrics to surgery. I've done IVs, catheters, trachs, wound care. Plus, I'm BLS certified."

Daniel swallowed. "Aunt Geri, didn't you say there's a nurse practitioner here?" he asked. "Couldn't she go along instead?"

Lena shot him a look. "Daniel! No, I want to go!"

"Normally, I'd be with Daniel on this one," Aunt Geri said, "but Maeve is... well... getting along in the years." Daniel got the feeling his aunt was putting it nicely. "She's a fantastic caregiver and she knows her stuff, but I don't know if she'd be up to something like this."

Daniel glanced over at Heath and found him studying Lena, an odd look on his face. Something between amusement and, possibly, admiration.

"Geri has a point," Heath said. "But if you do go, Lena, you don't have any contact with the demon. You don't talk to it. You don't look at it. You are only there in case of a medical emergency."

Lena nodded. "Of course."

"So, we're going to the foundry, then?" Vern asked.

"I don't know," Aunt Geri exhaled. "Even with Lena along for medical aid, I think I'm with Pearl. The foundry is just a little too far. I was thinking about the barn at the old Jenkins' place."

Pearl responded with an enthusiastic nod. "Yes. I was just thinking about that barn too."

"It's an old barn at an abandoned home place a few miles down the road," Aunt Geri explained to Daniel and Lena. "The main house burned decades ago, but the barn's still standing. Some pretty dark stuff went down there a long time ago, which means there's residual negative energy that'll definitely help draw in the demon."

"Pretty dark stuff?" Daniel inquired.

"Back in the fifties, I think, the man of the house, Earl Jenkins, killed his wife and children with an axe, then set fire to the farmhouse, taking himself out in the process."

Holy shit. Daniel didn't like the sound of the old Jenkins' place at all, and he was growing increasingly concerned about what his aunt had meant by the phrase *residual negative energy.*

"I think the barn would be perfect," Vern said.

"Then it's settled," Heath stated. "Now we need to start rounding up supplies. Lena, you can get medical supplies from Miss Maeve at the clinic."

"I already brought a medical kit with me, just in case."

This news didn't surprise Daniel.

"Well, you need extras in case this thing goes south," Heath told her. "Come on. I'll walk you to the clinic."

"Thanks," Lena said, looking suddenly rosy as she stood from her seat.

"I'll go too," Daniel said, rising to his feet. He realized he wasn't thrilled about Lena strolling through the Compound alone with Heath Garrison.

"Actually, Daniel, I need help gathering up some other things," Aunt Geri told him, oblivious to Daniel's personal feelings at the moment. And for good reason. There were far more important issues at hand than his- was it... jealousy? "We need flashlights, batteries, candles, salt. A shit-ton of salt."

"Okay," he said, staring off after Heath and Lena as they strolled down the gravel pathway into the night.

"We'll go to Mr. Smith's place and get as much as we can," Aunt Geri said, standing up.

Mr. Smith's? He assumed she meant the beige building with *Smith's Store* painted across its large storefront window.

Daniel noticed that everyone else seemed to be abandoning their plates and hurrying off in different directions to prepare for the big ritual. Zarah began blowing out the candles on the table. Pearl pulled off her apron and helped her, quickly.

They had twelve hours.

Twelve hours before they set out to summon a demon.

FIFTEEN

T HE TEAM MADE RECORD time traveling from Crofton, Tennessee, to the Compound. When they returned in the wee hours of Wednesday morning, the community lay in darkness beneath dim stars and a pale half-moon.

Running high on strong coffee and Tuesday's batch of Pearl's famous lemon cookies, the residents of the Compound assembled in front of the Garrison farmhouse well before sunrise. In the shadows, the two-story, hundred-year-old, whitewashed homestead looked a bit spooky to Daniel. It was difficult to imagine Walter and Heath living here. It reminded him of the house from *Psycho*. Maybe it was just his nerves; he was quite on edge at the moment.

A caravan of parked vehicles lined the gravel road next to the aged structure, ready to go to the abandoned barn for the ritual. Aunt Geri placed a sack full of medical supplies into the rear hatch of her Jeep Cherokee. Daniel, Lena, and Heath would be riding with her to lead the convoy.

The second vehicle, a green Dodge Durango, would contain four other men who had volunteered to go: Vern Phelps, the kind, shiny-headed man who had sat beside Daniel at dinner, Justin, the young dad with the shaggy grunge haircut, a grumpy-looking man who wore bifocals and a flannel shirt despite it being mid-July (Daniel thought someone had called him Alan), and a stocky, fifty-something man with a ruddy, bulbous face and receding hairline. He had a long blonde ponytail flowing down his back and wore deerskin moccasins on his feet.

Eddie and Marion Crider, apparent androids who required no sleep, would follow behind everyone in a Ford pick-up truck with their daughter, Zarah, to make sure they got to the barn safely. Then the Crider family would keep watch outside while the others conducted the ritual.

Walter Garrison refused to go. He had researched the proper summoning ritual for them, but he would have no part of it. Presently, he stood off to the side, arms across his chest, watching in silence as the team packed their vehicles. He didn't even offer to help with the loading.

Heath was right. His dad was an asshole.

"We're ready," Justin announced as he walked around the front of the Durango. He flicked his head to the side, absent-mindedly knocking his messy brown bangs out of his eyes.

Justin didn't look all that scared, but his voice had come out weakly. He approached the crowd slowly, his hands stuffed awkwardly in the pockets of his blue jeans. His wife, Claudia, stood at the edge of the group, holding her little boy's hand. Her olive complexion looked a sickly shade of yellow. Daniel remembered how boldly and confidently she had spoken up to Walter Garrison at dinner. Now she looked as though she might puke.

Justin squatted down and placed himself at eye level with his son. He pulled the boy's tiny hands into his own. "I've gotta go now, buddy. Mama's gonna stay with you. You're safe, okay?"

The wide-eyed boy just stared at him, clearly frightened by all the commotion happening around him at a time he should have been asleep in bed.

"You're safe." Justin pulled him in for a hug. The child fell into his arms and relaxed his head against Justin's chest. "I love you, Riley." He stroked the boy's hair, thin brown strands that were as disheveled as his own. "I love you so much."

After a moment, he straightened and stood before Claudia. He stared deeply into her eyes. Daniel heard him suck in a deep breath before he said, "If I don't come back-"

"Stop," Claudia interrupted.

"If I don't..."

"No, don't say that shit."

"We have to be-"

"Do what you have to do, then get the hell out of there." Claudia threw her arms around her husband's neck and pinned their bodies together.

Daniel knew he was staring when he shouldn't have been, but his eyes were stuck on the maze of colorful artwork that covered Claudia's arms. His gaze drifted across sunflowers and tulips, ravens perched on tree branches, a full moon partially obscured by misty clouds, a barn owl in flight. The owl was particularly gorgeous and intricately detailed. He wondered what personal significance the symbols held for her, if any. Some people just liked the designs. Daniel had no tattoos, but he knew if he ever got one, it would be something personal and meaningful.

He noticed Claudia's upper body shaking as she clung to her husband. "I can't lose anyone else." She buried her face in his shoulder. Daniel was pretty sure she was crying. He realized his intrusiveness and forced himself to look away.

Exchanges like this were happening all over the place. The other volunteers on the team mingled with the crowd, saying their good-byes. He saw solemn handshakes. Prolonged hugs. Tearful kisses.

For the first time, Daniel was truly terrified of what they were about to do. Why had *he* suggested this? Maybe Walter Garrison was right. Daniel didn't know enough about demons. He didn't know what they were walking into.

Aunt Geri slammed the Jeep's lift gate shut. Her bangs clung to her forehead, damp with sweat. The air was hot and sticky, even for nighttime. "I reckon we're good to go," she announced with an unmistakable tremor in her voice.

"Wait just a sec," Zarah said. She approached Lena and Daniel, gravel crunching beneath her Chuck Taylor high-tops. "I made something for you guys," she said. Across her lithe frame, she wore a colorful embroidered satchel. She reached inside it and removed two leather bands with wire-wrapped black gemstones attached to them.

Necklaces.

"It's black onyx," Zarah explained. "A protection stone. In mythology, it protects the wearer from evil."

Daniel swallowed hard. He still wore Dad's silver medallion around his neck, its onyx stone and strange engravings concealed beneath his T-shirt.

In mythology, Zarah had said.

She went to Lena first and fastened one of the necklaces around her neck. "Let's hope it's more than a myth."

"Thank you," Lena said, grasping the shiny black stone in her palm. It hung just past her collarbone.

"You're welcome."

Zarah moved to Daniel next, a necklace in hand for him. His pulse quickened. Should he decline? Say something about the amulet from Dad? It was probably best to shut up and take the damn necklace, but what if supplies were limited and someone else could use it?

He glanced at Zarah, at the identical necklace hanging around her neck. He focused on the black stone, trying to avoid looking directly into her jade eyes. But they were like magnets. They pulled Daniel's gaze to them despite his best efforts. "I'm, uh, I'm okay, actually," he stammered. "Thanks, though."

Her eyes narrowed, assessing him carefully. Her astute gaze made him uncomfortable.

"I mean, I, uh, I already have one. From my dad. I'm sure someone else can use this one."

Daniel didn't miss the brief flicker of curiosity in her eyes. She gave him a smile. "Of course."

Zarah moved toward Aunt Geri, carrying the necklace Daniel had refused. His aunt accepted it graciously. Daniel watched Zarah drape it around Aunt Geri's neck, her fingers trembling as she tied the strap into a tiny knot. She completed the task with a bit of a struggle then gave his aunt a pat on the shoulder.

"See you at the barn," Zarah said to the three of them. She turned and walked away, perhaps in search of someone else to gift a protective necklace.

Aunt Geri fiddled with her new onyx stone anxiously. She looked slightly green as she turned to Daniel and Lena. "Okay. You two ready?"

Daniel stole a glance at Lena. Amid all the emotionally charged goodbyes happening around them, he'd avoided looking at her. She seemed to be doing the same to him. Their eyes met now, only for the briefest second, but it was long enough to communicate mutual terror, fondness for one another, and agreement that it was time to do this.

"I guess so," Daniel said.

Lena nodded. "As ready as we can be."

Aunt Geri pulled a ring of keys from a pocket of her jeans. She cleared her throat and turned to the crowd. "Alright, everyone," she shouted. "Let's move out."

Her announcement tore the volunteers away from the crowd. Much to Daniel's surprise, he spotted the Garrisons by their front porch, embracing. He gawked at them, watching as Mr. Garrison squeezed Heath and released him. Neither of them seemed like the hugging type. If the *Garrisons* were sharing a touchy, heartfelt goodbye, Daniel knew he should be fucking terrified.

His chest felt tight and fluttery as he climbed into the backseat of Aunt Geri's Jeep with Lena. Heath took shotgun, and Aunt Geri slid behind the wheel. Once all four doors slammed shut, there was a quiet moment of hesitation before anything else happened.

An *Are we really doing this?* moment, in which everyone exchanged fearful glances.

Aunt Geri almost dropped her car keys as she searched for the ignition. The Jeep came to life. She shifted into 'drive' and guided the Jeep down the dark, gravel road. The Durango and the pick-up followed behind them.

At the front gate, two armed sentries stood outside the aluminum guard shack. A loud metal screech sounded as the gate parted for their exit. One of the guards motioned for Aunt Geri to proceed. Everyone held their breath as the Jeep passed through the gate and crossed to the outside.

Outside the gate.

Daniel had lived in the world outside the gate his entire life, but right now, the idea of returning to it scared the shit out of him. He couldn't fully comprehend the reason for that. He supposed the nervousness of the others had simply rubbed off on him. Lena's anxiety was certainly affecting him. She kept fidgeting and bouncing her knees and looking like she might hurl at any moment.

His stomach threatened to do the same.

It was all so incredible. Not even two full days ago, he had been a complete skeptic. The idea of evil spirits roaming the earth still sounded like fiction, but Mindy's clear, icy eyes in that gas station had forced him to uproot everything he formerly believed.

As frightened as he was, he also felt an invigorating seed of hope for the first time in a while. If the ritual worked and they conjured and trapped an actual demon, they could interrogate it and find out where his dad was.

It still sounded crazy.

But what if it actually worked?

Daniel wished someone would say something. They had been riding for over fifteen minutes now, and none of them had uttered a word. Not even Lena, who usually prattled on endlessly when she was nervous. He peered out the window, hoping to find something out there to distract him from his thoughts.

But the darkness was so thick, it looked like a black curtain covered the glass.

He tried taking deep breaths. Counting in his head. Trying to remember the lyrics to the old Bee Gees song that had unfortunately been stuck in his head since he'd heard it at Pearl's nearly twelve hours ago.

The Jeep slowed to a stop.

Though it was too dark for Daniel to see out his window, Aunt Geri could see something, for she turned right. Daniel craned his neck to peer out the windshield. He could see now that they were turning down a bumpy dirt road.

And up ahead, in the center of an overgrown field, stood a crumbling old barn.

SIXTEEN

Aunt Geri and the other drivers backed in toward the barn, pointing the noses of their vehicles at the road to save them a few seconds if they needed to make a speedy escape. Everyone climbed out at once, moving with a careful, unsettling silence, and assembled at the rear of their vehicles.

The first thing Daniel noticed was the shocking, vacuum-like absence of sound. The field around the barn was too quiet. The knee-high wild plant growth should have been teeming with life, with chirping and buzzing insects. It was July. Shouldn't there have been something out here in the tall grass making noises?

Daniel had been standing on the property for approximately ten seconds, and already, he could tell something was wrong. A peculiar heaviness filled his chest. The air itself felt oppressive and dismal.

Residual negative energy.

Had Aunt Geri meant... ghosts?

Were lingering spirits of the dead real, too? Was the Jenkins' farm haunted? Perhaps knowing the history of the place, the mass murder that had occurred here decades ago, clouded Daniel's judgment. He'd been primed to expect an encounter with the ghost of Earl Jenkins. He could all too easily picture a transparent, overall-clad farmer wandering the field, blood-stained axe in hand, searching for his next victim.

Daniel's pulse quickened. This was a bad place. He could feel it, and he wanted to leave.

He forced himself to breathe and ultimately dismissed his feelings as nothing but anxiety about what they were here to do.

Aunt Geri raised the Jeep's lift gate and began unloading, the sounds of her movements echoing strangely in the silent field. She passed the bag of medical supplies to Lena, handed Daniel and Heath each a small duffel, then slung a backpack over her shoulder.

"Wait a second," Aunt Geri whispered. "Daniel. Let me see the bag I just gave you."

Daniel returned the duffel. With trembling hands, Aunt Geri unzipped it and reached inside. She removed a few flashlights and passed them around.

"Sorry," she said, looking annoyed with herself. "Damn nerves. Let's go."

Aunt Geri's group met Vern's at the barn entrance. The spacious wooden structure loomed ominously before them in the darkness. It was hard to make out many details in the shadows, but Daniel could see enough to make him even more uneasy. Its steep gabled roof had caved in so much in some areas that Daniel thought entering the place was a bad idea, period, regardless of ghosts or demons.

"Are we sure about this?" the bifocals-and-flannel-wearing man asked. He was staring up at the dilapidated roof, most likely having the same thoughts as Daniel.

No one answered him.

Eddie, Marion, and Zarah came up behind them. Daniel was alarmed, initially, to see shotguns in their hands. "Well?" Eddie sneered. "Y'all gonna stand around out here all day like a buncha pansies?"

Zarah rolled her eyes. "Knock it off, Dad."

Heath gripped the ivory-handled knife he carried around his waist and removed it from its sheath. He stepped ahead of the others. "Stay behind me," he whispered to Daniel and Lena.

Aunt Geri tapped Daniel's elbow and, keeping her voice low, added, "And stay close."

The bifocals-and-flannel-wearing man- Alan, Daniel was pretty sure- nodded at them and moved behind Daniel, a large iron blade in hand. The thing had to be ridiculously heavy. "I'll cover you from behind," he told them. The half-moon overhead reflected in each lens of his bifocals. "Just stay alert."

Lena had a complete deer-in-the-headlights expression on her face. She was doing her best to be brave, but Daniel could tell she was near tears.

He moved closer to her and discreetly slipped his hand into hers. Her skin was cool and clammy, and he could feel her shaking against him. He intertwined their fingers and squeezed.

"It's okay," he breathed in her ear. "We're gonna be okay." It was a stupid thing to say, and he knew it. He said it as much for himself as he did for her, hoping he could convince his stomach to stop cramping with anxiety.

Lena's hand steadied slightly. But she didn't let go.

The group inched through the doorway of the barn. It gaped open like a slack jaw, the door detached and likely missing for decades. Inside, the place was black. Someone clicked on a flashlight, but it didn't make much difference. Though it hadn't been used for years, the interior smelled like livestock. The walls retained hints of manure, ammonia, and the faintly sweet scent of hay.

Daniel heard a rustling sound as something scurried through the overrun weeds. He felt queasy. Rats. Snakes. Ghosts. Anything could have been in a place like this.

Aunt Geri turned her flashlight on and shined it around. Lena shrieked as the beam illuminated the large, worm-like tail of a rodent disappearing beneath the exterior wall.

That gave Daniel the heebie-jeebies. He didn't want to proceed, but Heath moved along, setting the example for everyone else to do the same.

A few other flashlights clicked on, allowing them to get a better look at the place.

The construction appeared intact. Everything was covered in dirt, cobwebs, and the occasional hornet nest, but all the structural posts and support beams Daniel saw looked sturdy enough, and the rafters overhead seemed to be soundly in place.

Several of the beams bore teeth marks where something had been chewing violently. The hairs on the back of Daniel's neck stood up when he noticed this. He tried very hard not to think about their rodent companion.

His thoughts pivoted to the last time he'd stepped foot inside a barn, which was quite recently, actually. Last month, a high school classmate had been married in one. Ashley F. tied the knot with a douchey-looking guy she'd met at her church college and career class, and they'd celebrated their nuptials with the rustic aesthetic that seemed to be the trend nowadays. Two months prior, back in April, he had attended the rustic barn wedding of Jayla Hambley, one of Lena's nursing school buddies. Lena was one of Jayla's twelve bridesmaids; Daniel had been her plus-one. All members of the wedding party had been forced to wear matching cowboy boots with their otherwise formal attire.

Daniel cringed at the memory.

He tried to imagine this place decked out with string lights and flowers and a long buffet table of food catered by a local barbecue joint. He could not.

"All clear," Heath proclaimed. He faced the others and sheathed his knife. "We'll set up right here in the center of the building."

"Good deal," Eddie said. "We'll see y'all later." The Criders headed back the way they came, ready to stand guard. As they passed, Eddie added, "Hopefully."

"Eddie," Marion chided him, slapping him on the shoulder.

Zarah flashed her toothy smile at Daniel. "This was a good idea. It's gonna work."

Daniel wished he shared her confidence.

The Criders exited and assumed watch outside.

As Heath plopped the duffel bag he was carrying onto the floor, others did the same. Bags unzipped. They pulled out candles. Spray paint. Little bronze burners for incense. Using an image in a large, leather-bound book as a guide, Justin spray-painted a giant symbol- an elaborate pentacle, Daniel had learned from Dad's books- on the ground in the center of the barn. Aunt Geri removed a container of black salt from her bag, and she and Vern began sprinkling it in concentric rings around the edges of Justin's symbol. Alan got to work encircling the salt rings with a vast circle of candles. The other man with them, the stocky one with the long blonde ponytail, helped Heath place incense in each of the barn's four corners.

Keeping close to Aunt Geri and Vern, Daniel and Lena stood in the middle of it all, just watching the team work. It was a strange scene. Grown adults hurrying about, creating something that looked like a set for a low-budget horror movie.

"Daniel," Aunt Geri called from her spot by the spray-painted pentacle. "Can you grab another thing of salt and help us finish up here? We need to make sure this circle is thick all the way around, with no holes or weak spots."

Daniel dashed to Aunt Geri's bag, grabbed a container of salt, and came to her side. He watched her and copied her moves. He tried very hard not to think about the fact that he was pouring salt in a big circle on the ground. He felt ridiculous. He followed Aunt Geri's instructions to fill up the gaps until they had formed a dense ring about an inch and a half thick.

"Now," his aunt said, "we need to make several more of these. Smaller ones. One for everybody to stand in. Lena, hon, could you give us a hand, please?"

Lena was clenching the handles of her medical supply bag so tightly, her knuckles had gone white. "Um, sure. Yeah. Be right there."

She set down her bag and retrieved some salt. They made eight smaller rings, each about a yard in diameter, to surround the outer edges of the salt-encircled pentacle. Each person would have their own circle of protection to stand in throughout the ritual.

When they finished the job and stepped back to assess their work, Daniel still couldn't see how a circle of salt would protect anyone from anything. Except goiters, maybe. But in a few moments, that circle would be the only thing between him and a demon.

If, that is, something actually happened when they performed this ritual.

"Alright," Aunt Geri said shakily. She carried herself with confidence, but Daniel could see the distress and anxiety in her wide blue eyes. "Everyone, get into position."

Daniel picked a circle in the back of the barn. Lena chose the one to his left, placing herself between Daniel and Heath.

As everyone stepped into their own personal salt ring, the group enclosed the pentacle Justin had painted and faced each other. Aunt Geri walked to the center of the pentacle, three unlit taper candles in hand: one red, one purple, one white. She placed them standing upright in a triangular formation. She struck a match and set their wicks aflame.

Quickly, she moved into the only empty salt ring, the one directly across from Daniel. The two of them stared at each other now. The obvious fear in his aunt's blue eyes unnerved him. He broke their gaze and focused his vision instead on the candles in the middle of the pentacle.

Justin cleared his throat. He looked down at the leather-bound book he was still holding and opened his mouth to speak. However, no words came out. He stared down at the pages, clearly struggling with his conscience, obviously reluctant to speak the words aloud.

His messy bangs fell into his eyes. He brushed them away.

Aunt Geri spoke up, her tone gentle and motherly, "Justin, hon, it's alright if you want someone else to..." She trailed off.

"No, it's okay," Justin sighed. He cleared his throat again. After several seconds, he wet his lips, closed his eyes, and forced out the first sentence. "Within this circle, I call thee. Within this circle, I bind thee." A pause. Justin focused extra closely on the text as he read, *"Bazz-oh-lay-ehl."* He broke the true name of the demon they were summoning into syllables, ensuring correct pronunciation. "To my will, thou art bound. I call thee forth."

Daniel shivered. They were really doing this.

"I conjure thee, Bazolael, in what place of the world ye may be, that ye tarry no longer in the air, nor in the earth, nor any other place, but that ye appear here immediately before us, to do our will."

Daniel wondered where Mr. Garrison had found this ritual. The book Justin read from looked ancient, but like a lot of things he had come across in the last forty-eight hours, the words he spoke had a very made-up-shit-from-the-Internet sound to them.

Justin stepped out of his salt ring and handed the book to Aunt Geri.

For a second, Daniel thought Justin was going to bolt, to dart out the door and run like hell back home, but instead, the young man squatted by a bag on the floor and removed two items. A small silver bowl that shimmered in the candlelight and a Mason jar full of dark liquid.

His hands shook violently as he placed the silver bowl in the center of the giant pentacle, eliciting a surge of empathy inside Daniel. Justin's face paled as he opened the glass jar and upturned it. Viscous crimson liquid streamed into the bowl.

Blood.

Whose blood? Daniel felt nauseous. That jar was full. Where the fuck did they get so much blood?

"W-witness this sacrifice offered unto thee, oh, Bazolael," Justin said. "Draw from it thine strength." He cast the empty jar aside and hastily moved back into his protective salt circle.

The interior of the barn suddenly felt cooler. The candles flickered.

"Come before us and fulfill whatsoever we shall command thee."

Thunder rumbled faintly overhead.

Justin grew silent. He stared at the flickering candles with a look of sheer terror across his features.

An icy chill ran from Daniel's scalp to his toes.

Justin gulped, then continued shakily, "Bazolael, we welcome thee into our presence."

A second peal of thunder sounded above them, closer this time. The flames winked out.

Darkness filled the barn.

"Shitfuck," someone nearby said. Daniel didn't know who it was. It could've been his own voice. He felt numb and detached. His heart was in his throat, pumping so hard and so fast he could barely breathe.

Someone clicked on a flashlight.

A figure had appeared, standing at the center of the pentacle.

Daniel heard Lena gasp. Or he thought it was Lena. It might have been him. A couple more flashlights came on and illuminated the figure. A male body, slim yet broad-shouldered. He wore a sharp, well-fitted black suit. Shiny black wingtips. A red silk tie, slightly off-center. He straightened it confidently.

"Thank you for the warm welcome," the newcomer said. His voice came out velvety smooth, almost like a song. "I appreciate it. It's nice. But would you mind if we turned up the lights? I want to see your lovely faces."

No one replied.

He raised his right hand and snapped his fingers. The three candles at the center of the pentacle burst into flames, somehow burning twice as bright as they had before.

"Much better." Perfectly white, *blindingly* white teeth gleamed between a pair of rosy lips as he flashed them a charming smile. "I can see all of you now."

Daniel was shivering. The barn suddenly felt fifty degrees colder. Just like it had at Lena's apartment and the gas station, the medallion pendant he wore now turned icy, and the frigid metal stung his skin. His teeth chattered as he studied the man. Well, *not* a man. Though he looked like an ordinary man. No, ordinary wasn't the right word either. He didn't look ordinary at all. Not with those dazzling teeth. And his bronze skin had an unusual luster to it. A glow, one that could never, ever possibly be achieved with a tanning bed.

Daniel focused on the thing's eyes. Blue. Impossibly blue. The bright, pure blue of a clear October sky.

Those blue eyes swept across their faces. "First of all, I *love* the venue. The old Jenkins' murder farm? You can almost taste the lingering fear of Earl's victims, it's just... chef's kiss." He pinched his fingers and thumb together, kissed them, and dramatically flicked them away. He smiled even wider. "So. Who's in charge here, hmm? I know someone wished to speak to me."

Justin pushed his shoulders back and puffed up his chest. "That'd be me."

The extraordinary man- Bazolael, was it?- released a delightful laugh. "No, Justin Foster. You may have been the one to dial my number, but you're definitely not the one in charge. No. You're not the one who wanted to talk."

As much as Daniel wanted to look away, to prevent eye contact, he could not tear his gaze away from the man. He was stunning.

It happened. The impossibly blue eyes met Daniel's.

"Daniel Wester," he said. His brilliant smile grew wider. "Maybe you didn't want to see me, but I'd certainly love to chat with you." His voice dropped to a seductive whisper. "There is *sooo* much you don't know about."

Daniel swallowed. It hurt when he did it.

"Leave him alone," a voice cried out. A husky, familiar voice. Aunt Geri, Daniel thought, but he couldn't be sure. He couldn't look away from the man's eyes.

"Ah. Now *there's* the lady I came to see," Bazolael said, pivoting toward Aunt Geri. "Dearest Geraldine. The faithful guardian. Thank you for taking such good care of Daniel. Pete will be so pleased."

Aunt Geri stood up a little straighter. "Yes. Pete. Let's talk about Pete."

"Now, now. Let's not rush things, my dear. Here we are, together at last. You and me." Bazolael glanced around at the barn, at the rafters overhead. "It's not the most romantic of settings, but at least we've got the candlelight." He flashed her a seductive smile. "I must say, the glow becomes you, Geri. It softens you. Helps take your whole butch dyke look down a few notches."

"We're here to talk about Pete," Aunt Geri replied, unbothered by the demon's commentary.

"All in good time, sweetheart." Bazolael winked. "Now, forgive me if I'm being too forward here, but truly, we're all dying to know: are you or are you not a vagitarian?"

Aunt Geri's skin flushed, but she remained resolute. "Don't make me shoot you this early."

"Oh, Geraldine, you won't hurt me. You *need* me. Obviously, or you wouldn't have summoned me here."

"Don't be so sure." Aunt Geri's right arm reached behind her, digging beneath her baggy plaid shirt into the rear waistband of her jeans. Her hand reappeared with a pistol. She aimed it at the demon. "Iron bullets."

Bazolael's expression didn't change in the slightest. "Mm, yes, go ahead and shoot me with your little iron bullets. It'll sting. Then I'll be back in a jiff. Ooh, I can remanifest with lady bits. Would that suit you better? Doesn't matter either way to me, I've got an open mind."

Aunt Geri kept her weapon steady on him. "The only thing you got that's open is your damn mouth. Why don't you shut it?"

"My, my. The crusty old auntie wants to skip the talking and get busy. I underestimated you, dirty girl."

"I said shut the hell up."

"I thought you called me here to talk."

"About my brother."

"Oh, Pete? Who needs him? You've gone twenty-one years without him, Geri, you'll be just fine."

"Cut the bullshit and tell us where Pete is," Heath cut in, growling at the demon.

Bazolael turned toward the sound of his voice and smiled. "Well, hello, there, Heath. You're looking extraordinarily fit these days."

"Where. Is. Pete?"

"Jesus F. Christ. You people are so pushy." Bazolael shook his head, then heaved a sigh of defeat. "Last I heard, Pete was taking a little road trip with a buddy of mine."

"Where did they take him?" Heath demanded.

Bazolael lifted a padded shoulder in a half-shrug. "They don't tell me those sorts of things, I'm afraid."

"You're lying," Justin joined in. "You know more than you're letting on."

Daniel glanced at him. Justin's expression was different. His brow furrowed in anger as sweat dripped down the side of his face. "That's what you do. Lie," Justin declared, his voice loud and emboldened by rage. "All of your kind."

Slowly, Bazolael turned to Justin.

"Justin," he said coolly. "*All your kind?* Don't stereotype. It's not my fault one of my brothers lied to you about your girl."

Justin's face fell.

"Not everyone here knows your history, Justin." His startlingly blue eyes returned to Daniel and stared through him. "You know, Daniel, Justin here used to have a daughter. Madison. No, no. Sorry. It was something else dreadfully common. Madeline. Yes. Little Maddie was only two years old when her doctors diagnosed her with terminal cancer. That's when someone- a very troubled human who likes to think of himself as a devil worshipper- told

Justin he could save her if he summoned one of us and made a deal."

"Shut up!" Justin roared, spraying spittle through the air.

"Poor, desperate Justin. He bought it. Did a ritual a lot like this one, actually. One of my brothers appeared to him and struck a deal. He agreed to cure Maddie's cancer." He grinned. "He just didn't say how."

"Shut the fuck up!"

"You know, sometimes, the best cure is death. Justin never has been able to understand this. But Maddie gets it."

Justin lunged forward out of his salt ring, hurling himself at the demon. "I said shut up!"

Without warning, Bazolael twisted around and thrust his left arm in Justin's direction.

Justin dropped to the ground with a thud.

Lena screamed.

Daniel looked down at Justin's body, horrified. Justin lay face up on the ground. Motionless. Blood trickled from his ears and nostrils. Where his eyes had been a second ago, only bloody sockets remained.

Instinctively, Lena started to Justin's side, medical kit in hand.

"Lena!" Heath bellowed. "Don't move! Stay in your circle."

Lena froze. Backed up.

"Oh, yes. Sweet, kind-hearted Lena Dillon," the demon hissed. "You can stay right where you are, honey. You really shouldn't have tagged along. Your little CPR skills are useless here."

Daniel heard a click as Heath cocked a handgun and raised its barrel in the demon's direction. The gun surprised him. He didn't know Heath carried a firearm in addition to his knife. "Tell us where Pete is. Now."

"I already told you. I don't know."

"Yeah, that's what you told us, but we know you're lying."

"Oh, come now, don't be another Justin. You saw how he ended up." When no one responded, Bazolael grinned. "Yes, Justin got all riled up and stepped outside his magic circle. I bet nobody else here makes that mistake tonight."

"Please," Aunt Geri sighed. "Just tell us where Pete is. We know you know."

"Don't beg, Geraldine. It's so unflattering. Nobody likes a beggar."

"Okay, well, we wanted to do this quick and easy," Heath said, "but you're not exactly cooperating. So." He looked across the pentacle at the stocky man with the blonde ponytail. "On to Plan B."

He gave Heath a small nod. The sanguine man's ponytail swished as he reached behind him, whisking a hunting bow off of his back. Swiftly, he threaded an arrow into place. Pulled it back. Released it. The arrow whipped through the air and struck the demon's left shoulder.

Daniel heard a sizzling sound, a sound like meat being tossed onto a blazing charcoal grill. He looked at the demon and saw little wisps of smoke rising from his shoulder around the arrow wound.

Bazolael's blue eyes turned to ice. The same empty, soulless translucence he'd seen in Mindy's once-hazel eyes. It was no less horrifying to witness for a second time.

"What did you do to me?" he- no, *it*- screamed, writhing in pain.

Looking quite satisfied with himself, the heavyset archer announced, "Black onyx arrowhead. Dipped in lamb's blood."

The demon cursed him.

"Now you wanna tell us where Pete is?" Heath asked. He kept his gun on the creature.

"I don't know!"

"Go ahead, Gravitt," Heath called out.

The red-faced, stocky man with the ponytail was apparently named Gravitt. He loaded a second arrow into his bow. He pointed it at Bazolael but held it in place.

Benjamin Franklin.

Daniel suddenly saw the resemblance between Gravitt and the Founding Father. He looked straight out of a funky graphic novel, a zombie-fied retelling of colonial America. *Benjamin Franklin, Zombie Hunter.*

Daniel was losing it. His mind couldn't process what was happening in front of him, and it was grasping at straws.

"You want another one of these?" Gravitt shouted. "This time, I'm aiming for a lung."

"I'm telling you the truth! I don't know where Pete is! It's classified; only the higher-ups know!" Bazolael panted for air. "All I know is that they took him to get him away from Daniel."

Daniel's stomach turned a cartwheel.

"What?" Aunt Geri asked. "Why?"

"Pete has protected Daniel for twenty-one years. But now they need Pete out of the way so they can get to *him*."

Daniel felt sick. This couldn't be real. None of it. Surely this was just the climax of some horrible nightmare, and he was about to wake up.

His lips parted anyway, eager yet afraid to ask the question he desperately needed answered. "Did they kill him?" Everyone, including the demon, turned to stare at him. The spotlight was excruciating, but Daniel refused to let it deter him. "Is my dad dead?"

Bazolael, still panting, eyed him for a few seconds, his gaze unreadable. "I don't know. I think the plan was to keep him alive, but honestly, I don't know."

Daniel swallowed painfully. He mustered the courage to ask another question: "W-why are you after me?"

The demon had caught its breath by now. Its lips curved into a devious smile. "I'll never tell."

"Gravitt," Heath said, giving Gravitt the sign to fire.

Gravitt tugged back the arrow but held it there, giving the demon an opportunity to respond.

"Go ahead. Shoot me. It won't change a thing."

"Oh yeah?" Gravitt raised an eyebrow. "Let's find out."

A second arrow flew from his bow and smacked Bazolael square in the chest. It threw its head back, releasing an agonizing scream. More smoke rose from this new wound, and the smell of barbecuing meat filled the barn.

"*Why* are you after Daniel?" Heath repeated Daniel's question.

Slowly, the demon lowered its chin back to a normal, neutral position. Sweat streamed from its forehead, dribbling down its neck. "You don't get the concept of loyalty, do you, Heath?" it snarled. "Then again, you wouldn't. You do have a hard time following your father's orders. You always have. Shall I share your story with the class?"

Daniel noticed Heath's legs were trembling. He was scared and clearly nervous about what personal thing the demon was about to reveal. But more than that, he could tell Heath was struggling to stay where he was, inside the ring of salt, when everything inside him wanted to jump out and clobber the creature.

"Last chance," Heath's voice thundered, waving his gun. "Where the hell is Pete?"

"Really, Heath? Haven't we been through that enough? I've told you all I know. How about we talk about you now?"

"How about we not?" Heath pulled the trigger.

The iron bullet hit the demon in the center of the forehead. Its head reeled back from the impact, then at once, its entire body disintegrated into gray dust. The dust swirled around in the air for a second like a tornado then zapped into nothing.

The demon was gone, with no trace that it had ever been there.

"What the hell?" Alan roared. His bifocals steamed over as the barn turned humid in the demon's absence. "That was stupid, Heath. Really stupid. I know that damn thing was getting to you, but we didn't close the ritual and send him back where he came from. That means-"

"I know what it means," Heath barked at him. "I don't care."

Feeling a bit lost, Daniel asked, "What does it mean?"

"It means he'll be back," Alan explained, giving him a bit of attitude. "He'll remanifest and pop up right back here in a few hours or so."

"Yeah, right back here. In the middle of a pentacle and a salt circle that'll keep him trapped," Heath said. "So let him stay that way. He can rot in here for all I care."

"Heath," Vern spoke up. The beads of sweat that now covered his bald head sparkled in the candlelight. "You know we can't do that. Anyone could walk in here and find it and break the circle. Then he'd be free."

"Well, I'll come back and finish the ritual, then." Heath tucked his handgun into a holster Daniel hadn't noticed before. "But he wasn't gonna tell us anything else. I hope you all know that."

"Yeah," Aunt Geri heaved a sigh. "We know."

"He was just fucking with us, wasting time."

Aunt Geri nodded sadly.

The barn went silent as they realized it was over. Their one chance was over. And what had they gained? Everyone's eyes drifted toward Justin's body.

"He died for nothing," Alan said.

Vern shook his head. "Man, don't say that."

"No, listen. Claudia's a widow, and that little boy is fatherless. And we learned nothing helpful from this. *Nothing,*" Alan said. "We're no closer to finding Pete than we were before."

Aunt Geri's eyes met Daniel's for a second, then she blinked fast and looked away.

"I gotta tell you, I'm getting real damn tired of this shit," Alan went on. He yanked off his glasses and wiped his sweaty brow with the sleeve of his flannel shirt. "I'm starting to think there's no hope here."

"Alan, please." Aunt Geri swept her greasy bangs aside and cupped her forehead. "Don't."

"No, I mean it, Geri. What else can we do? This was it." Alan threw up a hand in exasperation. "This was it."

"There has to be something else," Lena spoke up, her voice broken, trembling. She cleared her throat before she talked again. "What if... what if we tried summoning a different demon, one that knows more-"

"You mean a stronger, higher-ranking one? With more abilities?" Heath laughed dryly. "It wouldn't tell us anything either, it'd just be better at killing us off."

"No, we for damn sure don't need to bring more of those things here," Alan said. "Look, the only thing we learned today is that they're after Daniel for some special reason. If the demon only took Pete to get to Daniel... they're after us next." He gulped. "As long as he's in our protection, we're all in danger."

Silence returned as the group considered this information.

"Then I should just leave," Daniel said. "I should just go before anyone else gets hurt."

Heath looked at him, incredulous. "Go? Go where and do what?"

"No, no, you're not going anywhere, Daniel," Aunt Geri said. "So don't even think about it."

Gravitt, the pony-tailed Benjamin-Franklin-lookalike and skilled archer who had only spoken about ten words throughout their entire trip, suddenly set down his bow and arrow and plopped down on the ground. "What about a medium?"

Heath raised a brow. "Sorry?"

"We could find a psychic," Gravitt suggested. "See if they could sense where Pete might be."

Sitting cross-legged on the ground, with his long blonde ponytail, fringed suede leather pants, and soft brown moccasins, Daniel realized Gravitt was probably the strangest person he had ever met. He had already earned that title based on appearance alone, but now, he sat criss-cross-applesauce in the dirt, talking about psychics.

Daniel studied the man's face carefully.

Gravitt's skin was cratered and splotchy, weathered and red, as though he'd spent decades outdoors and the last hour burning in the sunlight. His beady eyes, set beneath a pair of pale, wispy, barely-there eyebrows, met Daniel's. *Old* eyes, filled with history and pain and weariness.

"Could that work? A psychic?"

Gravitt shrugged. "Possibly."

"I don't know," Aunt Geri said, scratching her head. "It'd be really hard to find a legitimate psychic, and we can't keep following dead-end trails."

"Yeah, sorry, Gravitt, but I just don't believe in all that psychic mumbo-jumbo," Alan said. His voice sounded heated, threatening further argument.

Vern cut in by clearing his throat loudly. "Look, as much as we all need to discuss this, I think hanging around here for much longer is a bad idea."

The others agreed. Half of them had already abandoned their salt rings. If the demon were to come back now, they would really be in trouble. They began packing their equipment hastily, being careful not to disturb any of the salt lines.

"I'm gonna let the Criders know what happened," Gravitt said, his voice heavy and somber. He slung his bow and quiver full of arrows over his shoulder as he moved toward the exit. "We'll need to use the back of Eddie's truck for Justin."

Justin.

Daniel's stomach clenched painfully as he stared at Justin's lifeless body. How could this have happened? How could the demon have killed him like that, without even a touch? He remembered Aunt Geri telling him about the murders in the diner all those years ago. She had described the same method. But for Daniel to see it, to witness it himself.

It changed everything.

That was the same way Dad had seen his friends die. Had his mother died this way too? Daniel's eyes stung with tears as he zipped up the duffel bag and picked it up from the ground.

Justin had died trying to help him find his dad. That made Daniel responsible for his death.

How could he face Claudia and her son? How could he go back to the Compound now, knowing the danger he placed on everyone with his presence? It was wrong. People's lives were at stake.

He wished he could disappear right there in the barn like Bazo-lael.

SEVENTEEN

DANIEL LAY SUPINE ON the bed in Aunt Geri's spare room, staring up at the log ceiling. Trying to sleep was pointless. After the experience in the barn, he doubted he would ever be able to sleep again.

A couple of feet away from him, on a foldaway cot, Lena lay in the same position. His aunt had encouraged them to rest today after spending the night preparing for and carrying out the ritual, so here they were. They had been awake for well over twenty-four hours straight now, but the exhaustion didn't seem to matter. Daniel couldn't sleep. He could tell from the sound of Lena's breathing that she, too, was wide awake.

Neither of them had spoken since their return to Aunt Geri's cabin. She probably knew he was awake also, but she kept quiet, which was highly out of character for her. He guessed the traumatic events had brought her to a loss for words, just like they had him. Surely she felt the same dull ache inside her chest. The same bitter, oppressive feeling of hopelessness. A sinking feeling, someone grabbing you by the ankles and pulling you down into a pit of darkness where no light could ever exist.

Daniel felt himself drowning in that darkness. Demons were real. Justin was dead. Dad was gone. There was no way to find him. Their home had burned. Everything they owned was destroyed. *Demons. Were. Real.* He was their target. Why was *he* their target?

Lying there in the dark, Daniel felt like crying. He had only truly cried once in his life that he could remember. When he and Lena were eight, on the elementary school playground, he had been pushing her in a swing when she suddenly jumped out and unintentionally sent the seat flying into his forehead. Even then, he wasn't sure he had actually *cried*. He was fairly sure his eyes had merely watered from the injury.

No. He had never really cried.

But right now, he wanted to. The tears didn't come, but he wanted them to.

He sighed deeply and racked his brain for something productive he could do. If he wasn't going to sleep, he was wasting time lounging around throwing pity parties in his head. He could get up and read more from Dad's books. The mere thought of returning to the lengthy occult texts gave him a headache.

Besides, he'd gotten the idea to summon Bazolael from one of Dad's books, and that had led to Justin's death and not much else. Maybe he should leave those books alone.

He wondered if anyone had started digging a grave for Justin. He should go ask around and see if he could help. The man's death was his fault, after all, wasn't it?

But he just couldn't make himself get up and do it. His body ached with fatigue. It needed rest. He closed his eyes and tried to relax. But when he did, images of Justin's dead body on the ground, the demon's too-white grin, its horrible translucent eyes, Justin's empty eye sockets, played one after another on the back of his eyelids.

Nope.

He could not relax. No matter how much or how hard he tried, there would be no sleep for him.

Even with his eyes open, the images flickered before him like scenes in a movie. Dad's broken coffee mug on the kitchen floor. The horror on Lena's face when Justin hit the ground. The enigmatic little smile on the evil creature's face when he had said to Daniel, *There's soooo much you don't know about.*

What had that damn thing meant? What did he not know about? Would this secret information put an end to all this, once and for all? He needed answers if he was going to find his father and protect himself. But how could he obtain this information?

He didn't want to cry anymore. He wanted to scream. To hit something.

Yet he lay silent and still, too weary to move at all.

The box.

Daniel's stomach twisted as the image of Dad's forgotten antique wooden box drifted into his thoughts.

All of a sudden, he had enough energy to move. He rolled onto his side and pushed himself up from the bed. His knees popped loudly as he did so, making him feel much older than he was.

He moved across the floor and stooped down in the corner where his luggage sat. The box had been forsaken here, beneath his extra clothes. Daniel had left it hidden, still wrapped in the bath towel from home. *Home.* This random towel suddenly had value as the last remnant from a place now gone.

The cot squeaked behind him as Lena shifted her body around.

Daniel glanced over his shoulder at her and felt his heart skip as he did. She lay on her right side, her eyes fixed on him. She had been crying. That was obvious. Thin, clear mucus dripped from her reddened nose. The whites of her gray-blue eyes had turned pink. Her lids puffed out around them, swollen and damp.

His heart ached for her. It truly did. He hated the fact that Lena was struggling to cope with this impossible, hopeless situation he had pulled her into.

Before he could think of something to say, she sat up on the cot, sniffled, and crossed her legs. "What are you doing?" she asked him, quickly dabbing her moist eyes with the back of her hand.

"I was thinking, maybe we should go through the rest of the things in Dad's box. With everything that's happened since we got here, I kind of forgot about it. Maybe there's something else in there that can help us."

Lena perked up a bit at this. "Oh, yeah, good idea." She sniffled again and wiped her nose.

She needed a tissue. Daniel knew she carried a pack of Kleenex in her purse, but she didn't move to get them. She was too exhausted to get up, no doubt. Carefully, he placed Dad's box on the bed, then he glanced at Lena's bags. Her purse sat on the floor next to her suitcase, unzipped. He could see the clear plastic corner of the

Kleenex pocket pack from here. He reached in, grabbed it, and handed it to her.

"Oh." She managed a small smile. "Thank you."

Lena withdrew a tissue and blew her nose as Daniel sat on the bed with the box. As he pulled the edges of the towel away, he felt a ridiculous sentimental attachment to it. The towel. It wasn't even one of their nicer towels. Just a plain brown one with a frayed seam and a couple of spots where the weaving had worn thin. But it felt like home. Smelled like home. It was a piece of the place he could never experience again. He inhaled it, wishing he were back there now, tweaking his LinkedIn profile, scrolling Indeed, and worrying about student loan repayment.

Lena rose and joined him.

Sitting on the bed next to her, Daniel felt a bit of *déjà vu* as he opened the box. Had it only been two days ago that they had done this for the first time? It felt like weeks.

The letter from Dad remained on top. Then the stack of un-opened cards from Aunt Geri, which he purposed to go through later. Next were the obituaries he had already read. He glanced at them again. Infant Jedediah *Crider- son of Eddie and Marion Crider*. It hit him now. And the other obituary was for ten-month-old Abigail *Garrison*.

> *Abigail is survived by her father, Walter, and her brother, Heath. She is predeceased by her mother, Lavinia.*

It made sense now, why Dad had held onto these newspaper clippings.

"Aunt Geri said the demon from the diner came back for the survivors and attacked their families," Daniel told Lena, passing the obits to her so she could have a closer look. "I bet that's what happened to these babies."

She shook her head sadly. "Heath lost a sister. And Zarah a brother." Her fingers shook as she held the clipping. "Eddie, Marion, Walter... shit. They've been through it."

The obituaries were as far as Daniel had gotten the last time, but the box held much more. Lena set the newspaper clippings aside on the quilt, and Daniel began digging deeper into the box.

An old journal. He had glimpsed it before, but he hadn't touched it yet. That seemed like a good place to start. He plucked it from the container and brushed his fingertips across its faded leather cover. The yellowed pages within emitted a musty odor that Daniel liked. Old book smell. A library smell.

The handwritten inscription on the first page took his breath away.

Property of Helen Louise Brown Wester

His mother's full name in flowing cursive letters. *Wester* appeared to have been added at a later time than her first three names. The ink and penmanship of the surname were slightly different.

With shaking hands, Daniel thumbed through the pages. His heart soared as he found page after page crammed full of the same elegant handwriting.

"Daniel," Lena breathed.

He looked at her and found fresh tears in her eyes.

Neither could speak. He gazed back down at this discovery, eager yet terrified to dive into its contents. This was his mother's diary. Her thoughts. Her dreams. Her day-to-day life recorded with a pen.

This was Daniel's opportunity to meet his mother.

He turned to the first page. The date at the top made his head spin.

February 4, 1986.

He stopped to do the math. He was pretty sure she would have been eighteen. Actually, she would have turned eighteen that very day. The fourth of February was her birthday.

Daniel knew nothing about her life at that time. Where she lived. Whether or not she knew Dad yet. Dad was a couple of years older than her and probably already in college by then, while he guessed his mom was probably a senior in high school.

As much as it pained him, he set his mother's diary aside. All he wanted to do now was get comfy and spend the rest of the day poring over the diary's contents, but they needed to look through the rest of the stuff in the box.

Lena tucked a stray piece of her collapsed up-do behind her ear. "What's that?"

She pointed at a corner of black fabric poking out from beneath more newspaper clippings. Daniel raised the papers to find out.

A shroud of black velvet protected some unknown object. He lifted the bundle from the box and unwrapped it carefully to find a tarnished metal cross. Not a crucifix; the x and y axes were of equal lengths, like a plus sign. The ends of the four metal rods curved into small hooks shaped a bit like ship anchors. These hooks all bowed inward and were painted black. In the center of the X, twine had been wound around and around, over and under, weaving a small web across the length of the metal rods. Six beads, each a different color- black, white, red, purple, blue, and yellow, had been strung throughout the web. The whole thing reminded Daniel of a Native American dreamcatcher sans feathers. It emitted the same strange, almost tangible energy of the medallion pendant. It contained history. And power.

"What in the world is that thing?" Lena wondered aloud.

"I have no idea," Daniel said, turning it over in his hands. "Maybe Aunt Geri will know." He re-wrapped it and added it to the pile beside the box.

They browsed through the remaining newspaper clippings. Several articles about various mysterious phenomena. A woman in Nashville claimed she had been visited by a horned devil. A couple from Sacramento reported that their child was a demon. Several campers at a Christian youth retreat in North Carolina died under inexplicable circumstances. A meteorologist in Phoenix had noticed a weird connection between thunderstorm activity and homicides. More stories like that. And more obituaries.

Daniel grew discouraged when he realized they were close to the bottom of the box. Maybe it had only been wishful thinking, but when he'd remembered the box's existence, he had felt strongly that something inside of it would tell them what to do next. But the remaining items, while interesting enough, offered no dramatic breakthroughs. They found a ragged woven bracelet, the kind teen girls made for their best friends, with a few black stones- onyx, he assumed- braided into the dingy, once-white cord. A homemade protective bracelet that his young mother had worn, no doubt.

Was she wearing it when the demon killed her?

One end of the bracelet had caught itself in the wire of a little spiral-bound photo album. Daniel disentangled it and opened the album with nervous excitement. He was hoping for some never-before-seen family photos, but the tiny book did not deliver.

It held pictures of scenery. Country landscapes. Verdant fields, a classic red barn, a pathway through a grove of maple trees that looked awfully familiar. He realized why when he flipped to the next photograph.

The old Garrison farmhouse, looking a bit younger and neater with a fresh coat of white paint and a few pots of orange marigolds across the porch.

"That's here," Lena said. "The Compound, before they built it up."

She was right. The pathway through the maple trees was the same path they had taken yesterday. One of the empty open fields now contained the assembly hall, the armory, the clinic, and Pearl's Café.

The last photograph in the album held an additional surprise. A very pregnant Helen Wester stood in a little clearing beneath a couple of gorgeous, centuries-old oaks. She smiled contentedly, hands folded and resting atop her swollen abdomen. Her auburn hair blazed in the sunlight like fire, contrasting vividly against all the lush greenery behind her.

"Wow." Lena smiled. "She was so beautiful."

Daniel simply nodded. Wanting a closer look, he slipped the photograph out of its plastic protective covering and held it between his fingers. He stared at her belly in amazement. This was how she had looked when she was carrying him. So pleased. So hopeful.

He turned it over.

Helen, our lot, June 1990.

Our lot. The space between those oak trees was an ideal spot for a house. This was the chosen location within the Compound where Pete and Helen were going to build a home.

The date on the photo threw him off. He re-read it carefully.

June 1990.

Here was his mother in the last stages of pregnancy in the summer of 1990.

Daniel had been born two years later, in January 1992.

A wave of nausea swept over him. What did this mean? Did he have an older sibling running around somewhere? Or did Dad, for some reason, lie to Daniel about his actual birth date?

The demon's words hissed through his mind again: *There is sooo much you don't know about.*

Aunt Geri would know about this.

Daniel slapped the picture onto the top of the growing pile of mysteries to ask his aunt about. They were going to have a nice little chat ASAP.

One more thing remained in the box. Another manila envelope like the one that had contained Dad's letter and driving directions to the Compound, except this one looked much older. Daniel's guts churned wildly, threatening a necessary sprint to the bathroom, as he lifted the faded envelope from the now-empty box and undid the gold clasp.

Papers. Several loose papers.

He hoped, wished, prayed one of them would be another letter from his dad. A second set of step-by-step directions on what they should do next.

But as he slid the contents out of the envelope, he found something quite different.

A state of Oklahoma certificate of live birth. *Aaron Isaiah Wester*. Born July 18, 1990. 3:04 AM. Male. Single birth. Mother- Helen Brown Wester, age twenty-two. Father- Peter James Wester, age twenty-six.

Attached was a copy of an infant's footprints. A shot record. A hospital crib photograph of a tiny baby boy swaddled in a yellow blanket. Messy tufts of dark brown hair stuck up all over the red-faced infant's scalp. A little sign hanging in the bassinet above the baby's head read:

It's a Boy!
Aaron
7 pounds, 14 ounces
19 inches.

Daniel didn't even look at the other papers in the envelope. He shoved these first few back inside and closed it. He sat there, staring into space for a second, letting these things sink in.

He had never seen a crib picture of himself in a hospital, but he knew this baby, Aaron, wasn't him. Dad had always told him he was a big baby, a nine-pounder, with a head full of thick black curls. The photos he had seen of his infant self fit that description.

No, this baby was his brother.

Daniel tucked all of the items back into the box and closed the lid. As he stood up from the bed, he grabbed the wooden box and started across the floor. His knees felt like jelly as he moved.

"Where are you going?" Lena asked, scooting toward the edge of the mattress after him.

"I've got a few questions for my aunt," he spat back. Daniel burst through the door of the spare bedroom and wandered across the cabin to Aunt Geri's room. The door stood open, lights out. But as Daniel poked his head in, ready to wake the woman up for a chat, he saw that the bed was empty.

And still made.

With a huff, Daniel went on to the living area.

He found a strange woman hunched over the pile of Dad's books at the dining table. He knew it was Aunt Geri, but she looked so dramatically different, it startled him. She'd changed into a loose v-neck tee and stretchy pajama pants that showed a curvy figure normally disguised by her layers of bulky clothing. A mass of coarse, salt-and-pepper curls fell about her face, freshly washed, freed from her usual bun. She wore a pair of reading glasses Daniel hadn't seen before and looked exceptionally exhausted.

Seeing his aunt like this felt intrusive. It was too intimate, like he should look away. He was just about to shift his gaze when Aunt Geri glanced up at him.

"We need to talk," Daniel blurted out before he could stop himself.

Aunt Geri merely nodded. "Okay." She pulled off her glasses, rubbed her forehead, and leaned back into her chair, folding her arms across her chest.

Daniel placed his father's box on the tabletop, inviting Aunt Geri to say something about it. He slid out a chair next to her and sank into it.

"I didn't know you brought that," she said, her droopy eyes widening with astonishment.

"What else do you know that you're not telling me?" Daniel didn't feel like wasting time being polite anymore. He didn't have the energy for it. He glanced over his shoulder behind them to see if Lena had followed him. She had not. Glad of that, he reached inside the box and yanked out the envelope that contained Aaron Isaiah Wester's birth certificate. He extended it toward his aunt.

Reluctantly, she took it.

"I found this picture of my mom taken in 1990. She was pregnant," Daniel said. He held up the photograph to make his point. "But I was born two years later."

Aunt Geri kept her eyes on the manila envelope as she reached inside and pulled out the papers.

"Then I found that stuff."

He heard his aunt release a shaky sigh as she clutched the photograph of the newborn. She looked at it for a long time before she responded. "This was your brother," she said at last. "Aaron. He died when he was only six days old."

Daniel gulped. It took too long to string together his two-word response. "What happened?"

"You remember when I told you that the demon came back and killed more people, more of our loved ones, after the diner?"

"Yeah."

Aunt Geri still hadn't looked up from the picture, and she didn't now. "The son of a bitch started with the children. Eddie and Marion, they had a sweet little eight-month-old boy. Jedediah. The demon killed him while he slept in his crib." She paused. "Heath had a baby sister. He was only three when the demon killed her." She went on, her voice watery and unsteady. "Right after your mom had Aaron, that thing came back for him. And it tore us apart. All of us. It damn near broke us, Daniel. All those innocent little lives taken for no reason other than to wear us down."

"So... why?" Daniel heard himself ask. "I still don't understand why the demon kept attacking. Why did it single out all of you?"

"I don't know." Aunt Geri looked at him now, tears pooling in her tired, bloodshot eyes. "None of us know. But it's still doing it."

Daniel drew in a sharp breath and stared at his aunt. "The demon said they took Dad so they could get to me," he exhaled. "What do you think that means? Why would they be after me?"

"I really don't know."

"And if they're after me, why hasn't anything happened before now? Dad left this place two decades ago."

Aunt Geri was quiet for a long time. An uncomfortably long time. Daniel could see the wheels turning behind the woman's blue eyes, and she had that look on her face, the same look she got right before she dropped a bombshell on Daniel. A look of indecisiveness as she debated about whether or not she should share something she knew.

Daniel groaned. "What is it?"

"Well, I have a theory." Aunt Geri blinked, snapping out of her little internal deliberation. "And trust me, sweetheart, it's just that, just a theory."

"Okay."

"After the demon came back and killed your brother, Heath was the only child we had left. The rest of the diner survivors had already lost their children, or like me, they didn't have kids. Some-time after Aaron was killed- it was in early ninety-one, I think- the demon came back for Heath. But by that time, we had started setting up here. Walter had learned enough to protect Heath. The demon couldn't get within twenty feet of him.

"That experience gave us hope. It showed us that, maybe, we could have some kind of a normal life. That we could be safe again. We built this cabin, and the three of us moved in. Your parents and me. We set up a life here. We grew our own food. It was a simple way of living; we didn't even have running water yet. But things were better. A little while later, Helen was pregnant again."

Daniel shifted around in his seat to get more comfortable. It seemed like it might take a while for Aunt Geri to explain her theory.

"You were born in January of ninety-two, of course. And actually, you were born here, in this cabin." She smiled briefly; it faded as she continued her story. "After everything we had been through, Pete and Helen especially, we worried about your safety. We took every precaution we knew to take. But when you were about six months old, you got sick. And there was nothing we could do here to help you."

Daniel's ears perked up. Dad had never told him about any childhood illnesses before. "What do you mean, sick?"

"Pneumonia. We didn't have Maeve yet, and we didn't have any way to treat you ourselves. You kept getting worse, so we had to take you to a hospital. Which meant leaving the safety we had created here." She swallowed. "They admitted you during the night. Pete and Helen stayed with you in the room constantly. I hung around outside and kept watch with Eddie and Marion."

All of a sudden, Aunt Geri's face lost its color.

Daniel braced himself for the rest of her story.

"I don't know what happened in that hospital room that night." Aunt Geri stopped. She wet her lips with her tongue. "But the demon found its way in there, and your mom got killed. While you were unharmed."

Daniel felt his pulse picking up a bit. Just what was Aunt Geri suggesting?

"Pete wouldn't talk about it, which I understood. His wife had just been murdered, and by the same thing that killed their first-born. I tried to get answers out of him, but he wouldn't budge. I hated to keep pushing him. I just- I don't know. I always felt like... it always seemed like there was more to it than we knew about. Like Pete knew something that we didn't."

Aunt Geri paused. Her shoulders stiffened as she sat back in her chair.

"You got better. You were discharged from the hospital, and we came back here. Then barely a week later, I found Pete packing his things. That's when he told me he was leaving, that he was sick of living in fear and didn't want you growing up afraid. It didn't make a lick of sense, 'cause we all knew the dangers of being unprotected outside the Compound. I mean, Helen had just lost her life because of that." She frowned. "What I'm saying is, Pete wouldn't have risked your life by moving away like he did unless there was more to it, unless he somehow knew you would always be safe."

"So... what are you saying?"

"I think he made a deal with the demon that night," she said it quickly. "It's just a theory, but there's plenty of lore about people making deals with demons. And the fact that you've lived twenty-one years in complete safety, without even knowing about the existence of demons…" She raised a brow. "I think that tells us something."

Daniel thought about it for a moment. "What the demon said about Dad being taken so that they could get to me, about Dad 'protecting me for twenty-one years'."

"Yep. I realized it today just as the demon said it. It's been twenty-one years since that night," Aunt Geri said. "Sunday night, the night your dad was taken, marked exactly twenty-one years since the night your mom died."

Daniel's heart kicked in his chest. There was no way that could be a coincidence.

No way.

"So, you think my dad made some kind of twenty-one-year protection deal to save me?" Daniel didn't like the way the words sounded coming out of his mouth. Even after everything he had seen and heard and read the last few days, the sentence still sounded preposterous.

"Basically, yes." She hesitated. "Well, either him or your mom."

Daniel's breath caught in his throat. "You think that's why she died?"

"Possibly. There are certain rituals I've read about where you can sacrifice yourself for something like that."

She was talking about a Faustian bargain. He remembered reading *Doctor Faustus* in English lit. He recalled how Bazolael had taunted Justin in the barn by describing the deal he had attempted to make to save his dying daughter. Could Daniel's mother have done that for him? Sold her soul to a demon? Traded her life for his? Was her death what kept him alive today?

"I just don't know, Daniel. I could be way off here. It's just something I've thought about."

Yes. Surely, Aunt Geri was way off. Daniel wasn't Harry Potter, walking around with a lightning bolt scar on his forehead marking where the demon had tried to kill him and failed because of his mother's sacrificial love.

Aunt Geri had to be wrong, because if she wasn't, that meant he was only alive because his mother had willingly died for him. He didn't know how to cope with that.

Actually, the more he thought about it, the more he realized Aunt Geri *was* wrong. Her theory didn't explain why Daniel's safety had always been somehow intertwined with Dad's presence. That was why the demon had abducted Dad in the first place. To get to Daniel.

But as he pondered this, a troubling thought he had continually suppressed rose to the surface of his mind. It had been roaming through his thoughts for the past few hours, and now he had to release it. "If the demon only wanted to get Dad out of the way so it could get to me, do you think there's any hope that he's still alive?"

The look on Aunt Geri's face told Daniel that she, too, was stuck on this thought.

"When I asked the demon," she reminded him, "it told us that it thought they were planning on keeping him alive."

"Yeah, but it could have just said that to shut us up."

"It could have."

"I mean, if all this is true, why *wouldn't* they just kill him?" Daniel asked numbly.

Her jaw tightened. "Maybe they're... holding him for some reason."

"Like what?"

"Maybe they're keeping him alive because they know that means we'll keep looking for him. As long as we think he's alive out there somewhere, we have a reason to leave the safety of the Compound and go looking for him."

"That doesn't mean he's actually alive, though."

"No. It doesn't."

They sat in silence for what felt like half an hour.

"We've gotta find him, Aunt Geri."

She bit her lip. Her right arm reached over toward him. She wrapped her callused fingers around his left wrist and gave him a comforting squeeze. "I know." Her voice cracked as she said it. "I know."

"What the man with the bow and arrow said, Gravitt, I think. About a psychic. Do you think we should try it?"

"Maybe. We are running out of options. But honestly, if I thought that would work, we would have tried it before summoning a damn demon."

Just then, Daniel remembered the other artifact he and Lena had found in the box, the weird metal dream catcher-looking thing.

"There's something else." He raised the lid and dug around inside the box until he found it. "Do you know what this is?"

Aunt Geri's eyebrows shot up. She took it and examined it closely, tracing the web of string with her fingertips. "What in the hell, Pete?" she muttered to herself, turning the thing over in her hands. She sniffed it, which Daniel found a bit odd. "I don't know what this is, but there's a good chance it's something else powerful that could come in useful right now. You mind if I hang onto it, see if I can find out anything about it?"

"Go ahead. I'd like to know what it is."

"Yeah. It might come in handy." She yawned. "Good lord, what time is it?"

Daniel checked his wrist out of habit, but he wasn't wearing his watch. He had left it at home.

One more thing lost in the fire.

He did, however, have his cell phone in his pocket. He didn't have cell reception at the Compound, but he still kept it on him at all times. He pulled it out to check the time. "Crap. It's nearly ten."

"Damn." She yawned a second time. "It's gonna be a rough day today, hon. You wanna grab something to eat at Pearl's?"

"No." He felt an annoying, gnawing hunger in his belly, but he didn't want to see anyone. He couldn't face the people of the Compound just yet. Not after what had happened to Justin.

Aunt Geri nodded. He could tell she understood his objection without any further explanation. "I'll bring you back a plate."

"Okay. That'd be good. Thank you."

"Is Lena awake?"

"Yeah."

Aunt Geri rose from the table. "Alright. I'll bring you both a plate. You two try to rest a bit while I'm gone. Please."

"Thanks." Daniel stood and stretched. His body ached even worse now. His throbbing knees felt like they would buckle at any second. As he started toward the spare bedroom, toward Lena, he caught a glimpse of Aunt Geri holding the metal dream catcher cross. Something in her posture seemed affectionate; she was almost cradling the cross.

The look on the woman's face sent a shiver up Daniel's sore spine.

He saw the truth, subtly displayed across his aunt's features.

Geri Wester knew exactly what the thing was.

And she was happy to have it.

EIGHTEEN

"**S**HE *LIED* TO YOU?"

Lena and Daniel stood together in the spare bedroom, speaking in hushed voices as they discussed the exchange that had just taken place between Daniel and his aunt. Aunt Geri said she was going to get them breakfast, but they hadn't heard her leave yet.

Lena was undoing her hair. The elegant French braid crown she had worn to the enchilada dinner at Pearl's last night (which now felt like a week ago) was slowly falling apart on its own. She ran her fingers through her pale strands and shook them out, unweaving the last of the braid. "How do you know she lied?" she whispered. "What did she say?"

"She said she didn't know what that cross thing was. But I could tell that she did."

"What do you mean you could *tell*?"

"I don't know, I just could."

"But why would she lie about it?"

"Why would she not?" Daniel huffed. "Every time I talk to the woman, she drops some huge, life-changing revelation on me.

She's been leaving out major details since the first time we spoke. And that's kinda the same thing as lying."

Lena stopped fiddling with her hair and looked directly at him. "Well, no, actually, it's not the same thing. She's been gradually telling you the truth. As you're ready. Do you think you could have handled *all* this on day one? If she had told you everything at once?"

Daniel frowned. "No."

"See what I mean?"

"Yeah, but still, she's lying now."

CLUNK.

The sound of a closing door. Aunt Geri's bedroom door. They stopped talking and listened as footsteps moved throughout the cabin.

CLUNK.

The front door closed. Aunt Geri had finally left for Pearl's. What had she been doing all this time? Aunt Geri was a no-frills kind of lady; getting dressed certainly wouldn't have taken this long. Had she been hiding the mysterious webbed artifact somewhere in the cabin?

"Your dad said we can trust her," Lena said. "And I think she's already proven that herself. I'm sure whatever reason she has for not telling you what that thing is, it's a good one."

That was the end of their chat. He didn't have anything else to say to her. She was supposed to be on his side. Why was she defending Aunt Geri?

He plopped down on the bed and folded his arms across his chest.

"I think I'm gonna take a quick shower," Lena told him. "I wanna freshen up before the meeting."

He said nothing. He watched her from behind, staring somewhat absently at her plump rear end as she bent down and dug through her suitcase on the floor to find a fresh change of clothes. She gathered a handful of items and left for the bathroom.

Daniel didn't want to think about the meeting. The daily assembly hall gathering had been pushed back from eight o'clock to noon to give everyone a few extra hours to recover from the failed ritual. Daniel's stomach ached, dreading it. What was the point of it, anyway? Walter Garrison would step up to the podium and give them all an 'I Told You So' speech, then everyone present would argue for an hour, blaming each other for Justin's pointless death. They'd whine about how the ritual had been a dangerous fool's errand, that it hadn't provided any new information about Dad's location. The mood would be gloomy and hopeless, and no one would have anything helpful to offer.

It would be a waste of time. Everything felt like a waste of time. His talks with Aunt Geri, the hours spent poring over Dad's books, their leisurely meals at Pearl's. The only thing that sounded like a good investment of time was sleeping. All of the stress was getting to him, and he hadn't rested properly. He was losing patience and turning into a real grouch.

He eased back and stretched out across the bed, sinking into the mattress. His heavy eyelids throbbed. The corners of his eyes watered from exhaustion. He allowed them to close as his head found the pillow. The relief was instant.

He wasn't sure how long he'd been lying like this when he heard a knock at the front door.

Daniel sat up too quickly, making his head spin. He hurried across the cabin to the entrance in the main living area. Suddenly nervous, he pulled open the door.

Heath Garrison stood before him, smelling like bacon. He held two black plastic food containers with clear lids in his hands.

"Hey," Heath said, his voice and expression neutral. "Brought you and Lena something to eat."

"Oh. Uh, thanks."

"Your aunt was going to, I guess, but she got caught up talking to Marion about something important. Asked me to do it instead."

Daniel wondered if the *something important* had to do with that damn metal cross. "Do you know what it was about?"

"Nope."

"Well, thanks. For the food." He took the containers. They were quite warm and smelled wonderful. He thought he got a whiff of fried potatoes.

"No problem."

Daniel expected Heath to turn and leave then, but he didn't. He lingered, hands in the front pockets of his jeans, looking like he wanted to say something. His hazel eyes met Daniel's, his irises more of a warm amber in the morning sunlight. They displayed a level of exhaustion that mirrored Daniel's. There was something else there, some intense emotion he couldn't quite make out. Sympathy, maybe. Probably.

Heath's lips parted to speak, then closed.

Normally, the moment would have been a little uncomfortable, but Daniel was too tired to care today. He was glad Heath was hanging around. He had an idea. Heath had grown up here, had spent his entire life in the Compound soaking up demon lore and mythology. There was a chance he might recognize the mysterious cross and know something about it. He decided to give it a shot.

"I, uh, I found something that belonged to my dad," Daniel told him. "I don't know what it is, but it looks important. I was hoping you might know."

"Why don't you just ask your aunt?"

"I did, but she won't tell me."

"Hmm. Okay. Let's see it, then."

"Well, she took it. But I can tell you what it looks like." Actually, when he thought about it, he couldn't. The strange object was quite difficult to describe. "Um, well, I can draw it. Come in."

Heath stepped inside the cabin and closed the door behind him. Daniel carried the food from Pearl's to the table and pushed Dad's books aside just enough to make room for the plates. Aunt Geri had abandoned an ink pen and a lined yellow legal pad covered in messy scribbles beside an open hardcover. Daniel grabbed the pen, ripped out a clean page from the pad, and tried his best to create a decent representation of the mysterious cross, which was a lot easier said than done.

"You're a shitty artist, Wester."

Daniel shrugged. "I never said I was a good one."

The bathroom door popped open and Lena emerged, barefoot and pink from the warmth of the shower. Her hair sat atop her head, twisted into a towel turban. She spotted Heath at once and froze. Though a fresh purple tank top and gray shorts covered her body, she looked as though she'd been caught naked.

Crimson pooled in her cheeks as she stared at their visitor. "Heath," she said in an atypical high-pitched tone that Daniel didn't like. "I didn't know you were here."

Heath reddened slightly and stared at the floor. "Sorry. I just came by to drop off breakfast for you guys."

"Oh," she said. "Thank you so much." She touched the towel on her head briefly. "Um, hang on, I'll be right back." She disappeared into the spare bedroom.

Heath watched her, looking slightly amused, then refocused on Daniel's rendering of the cross. "Help me out. What am I looking at here?"

"Okay, so, these intersecting lines are metal rods, both about six inches long," Daniel said, pointing out the parts of his drawing. "Those little dots in the middle are different colored beads. On twine."

Heath took the paper from Daniel to get a closer look. As he studied the sketch, Daniel tried to read his expression, but he honestly had no idea what Heath was thinking.

After a few seconds, Heath handed the piece of paper back to him. "Where did she put this thing?"

"I don't know. I have a guess, but I'm not sure."

Lena rejoined them now, looking more confident without the towel. She'd quickly piled her wet hair on top of her scalp in a messy bun. Rivulets of water dripped down the sides of her face. "It smells really good in here."

Daniel breathed in the comforting, familiar smell of her peach-scented soap or shampoo or whatever it was and privately agreed.

"Like bacon. Yum. Thanks again, Heath, that was really kind of you." Lena glanced at the paper in Daniel's hands, swiftly observing his drawing. Her eyes darted from the paper to Daniel to Heath. "Do you know what this is?" she asked Heath, sounding hopeful.

Heath fixed his gaze on Daniel. "I could be wrong, since I'm going solely off of his shit drawing," he said. "But yeah. I think I do."

Daniel's heart raced. "What do you think it is?"

"Have you ever heard of The Cross of Silvanus?"

Lena answered quickly. "No."

Daniel had to think about it for a moment. It sounded vaguely familiar, but he wasn't sure why. Perhaps it had been mentioned briefly in one of Dad's books.

"It's a mythological relic of a fifteenth-century European monk named Silvanus."

Silvanus. Monk from the fifteenth century. No, it wasn't ringing any bells.

"The story goes that the guy was plagued by demons. They visited him every night. Tortured him. He spent his entire life trying to find a way to fight back, and eventually, he fucked around with magic and came up with a device now known as The Cross of Silvanus." Heath paused to breathe. "According to legend, this thing can be used not only to protect the user from a demon, but to actually control a demon."

Daniel gulped. "Is that what you think that thing is? The real Cross of Silvanus?"

"Listen, I've seen drawings. A hell of a lot better drawings than yours, too, I should add. It's a metal cross. The rods are made of iron. There's six beads made from six different crystals with supernatural powers. Sounds freakishly like the same thing."

"Yeah, it does," Lena said. "This Cross of Silvanus, did it really work?"

"Supposedly. But then again, it was just a story. A myth, like King Arthur and Excalibur. Or Thor's hammer." Heath raised his eyebrows. "Of course, people *say* it was just a story. You never know."

"Aunt Geri must know the legend too," Daniel said. "That's why she acted so weird about it. And it must be true, or she must at least think it's true, because she seemed pretty happy to get it."

"Wouldn't you be?" Heath's eyes widened as he stared at him. "Think about it, man. If this thing works, we could tell every demon we ever come in contact with to go jump off a cliff, and they would fucking do it. They would *have* to do it."

"This could lead us straight to Dad."

"Exactly," Heath said. "Which is why we're about to try it."

"What?" Lena sounded horrified.

"Well, we have to find the damn thing first," said Heath.

Lena frowned at him. "You mean sneak around and pilfer it. If this thing really is so valuable, Geri wouldn't have just left it lying around, she would have put it away somewhere safe. Which means we'll have to look for it, and that means nosing around through her personal stuff."

"It'll be just like old times," Daniel scoffed.

That sent Lena's frown even deeper. "Not funny."

The trio grew quiet, each of them silently scanning the room. The modest little cabin couldn't have many hiding places. The old handmade cedar chest where Aunt Geri stored the scrapbook had been Daniel's first guess, but maybe that was too obvious. They should check it anyway. He reached behind the rocking chair and slid the trunk out from behind it.

With Heath and Lena watching over his shoulder, Daniel raised the lid. The leather scrapbook lay on top. He moved it aside so he could explore the rest of the items. He found several aging family photo albums and memory books that he wanted to thumb through but now wasn't the time. He uncovered a musty old quilt at the bottom. He almost ignored it, but it struck him that Aunt Geri might have wrapped the Cross of Silvanus in the blanket for protection. Carefully, he removed the quilt and unfolded it.

Nothing.

Just a quilt. Of course. Nothing was ever that easy.

"Any other ideas?" Heath asked, moving into the kitchen. He peeked inside a cabinet.

"I'll check her room," Daniel announced, heading that way.

Lena stayed behind with Heath, a turn of events that surprised and annoyed Daniel. Yet he said nothing and went on to his aunt's bedroom.

The second he crossed the threshold, Daniel realized Lena was right. The pit in his stomach screamed at him that, yes, he was trespassing. He felt like that nosy ten-year-old again, breaking the rules, tip-toeing around, rifling through Dad's stuff for fun and hoping he didn't get caught.

But this search *wasn't* for fun. He needed to locate and reclaim the item Aunt Geri had taken from him, the magical relic Dad had left in the box *for him*, the thing that might be the solution to all their problems.

Daniel told himself this over and over again to justify his actions and propel himself further into the room.

There were even fewer hiding spaces in the bedroom than he had anticipated. After his experience finding Dad's box in the trailer, Daniel's instinct was to check the closet. But the Wester siblings had taken a note from the Amish and not constructed one. Aunt Geri had only a hand-built wardrobe to house her belongings.

Daniel opened the wardrobe slowly, as though he feared something might leap out at him. He found about six or seven shirts and even fewer pairs of pants hanging from a wooden rod. Beneath this closet-like compartment, two shelves held stacks of folded T-shirts, socks, and underwear.

It seemed a little sick to dig through his aunt's undergarments. And really, who would stash a powerful, centuries-old relic in their tighty-whities? He checked anyway, as quickly as possible, and found nothing.

As a last-ditch effort, he slid the hanging clothing to the right. When he did, he found a miniature built-in cabinet just the right size for storing the object he was looking for. The tiny door let out a squeak as he pulled it open.

There it was, right on top. The Cross of Silvanus, neatly wrapped in the same velvety fabric Dad had used to protect it. Daniel grabbed it and closed the door.

Almost.

Something stopped him.

He caught a glimpse of another object in the cabinet. An envelope. Stamped and postmarked, addressed to Aunt Geri, and dated one week ago.

Dad had sent it.

NINETEEN

D ANIEL PLUCKED THE ENVELOPE from its hiding spot and turned it over. It had been opened carefully and neatly, with a letter opener from the looks of it. Inside, Daniel found a handwritten letter. He unfolded it and began reading his father's familiar blocky script:

Geri,

It's with shame that I'm picking up this pen to write you. I can hardly believe it's been twenty-one years since we last spoke. I was such a wreck then. I was so awful to you. So hateful. It's too little, too late, I know, but I'm sorry.

I want to tell you that I'll be sending Daniel to you soon. I'm leaving directions for him. The demon is coming back for me. The only thing that matters anymore is keeping Daniel safe. That's the only thing that has ever mattered. I know you'll know how to do that better than anyone.

I hope that you can forgive me for the last twenty-one years. I want you to know that I deeply regret not being a part of your life, and you not being a part of mine and Daniel's. I have so many regrets, Geri, but the way things turned out for us is the most painful one.

Take care of Daniel. Make sure he understands why it had to be like this, why I had to keep him from this. Make sure he knows how serious this is. I never wanted him to live in fear, I never wanted him to fight, but I know now that it's inevitable. That day is coming. So train him, teach him how to protect himself, the way I never did. I worry sometimes that I've been too protective of him, and that I've somehow crippled him. But he is strong, and I know that he'll do whatever he has to do for the people he loves.

I know how much you care about him. Please make sure he knows that. Above all, make sure Daniel knows how much he is loved.

Pete

Daniel's eyes grew watery as he read through his father's words again.
His final words.

That's how they sounded. Dad had written this letter as a man about to face his own death.

The sounds of Heath and Lena stirring in the other room snapped him back into the present. He folded the letter and slipped it back inside the envelope.

"I found it!" he called out, shoving the envelope back into the secret cabinet inside the wardrobe. He closed the unit, taking care to leave everything as he had found it, and hurried to where his friends were, grasping the velvet-covered cross tightly.

He met them in the living area. Daniel extended the object toward Heath, who unwrapped it gingerly.

"Holy shit," Heath exhaled. His eyes glazed over as he stared at it. "This is it. This is the real deal."

Lena's eyes bulged. "You're sure?"

"If Pete Wester had this, then yeah, I'm sure."

"If this thing can really control a demon," Daniel said to Lena, "we can make one tell us where he is."

Heath nodded with enthusiasm. "That demon, Bazolael, is gonna remanifest in the barn any minute. I say we sneak out with this right now and make it talk to us."

"Let's go," Daniel said, matching Heath's excitement.

Lena, however, looked skeptical. "Just hold on a second. That demon will only talk to us *if* this thing really does what the legend says it can do. And that could only happen *if* this is really, truly the actual Cross of Silvanus."

"You don't trust me?" Heath asked. His usual irritated look had returned.

"Well, no, it's not that, it's just..." she cut herself off. "It just seems like we won't know if this is gonna work until we're in there, with the demon."

Heath shrugged his shoulders. "Pretty much."

"But that's- that's crazy! Don't you see that? We can't go out there, alone, just the three of us. Daniel and I, we don't know how to use weapons-"

"We'll manage," Heath interrupted. "I'll cover you if I need to, but if you both stay inside a salt ring, you'll be fine."

"Did you somehow forget what happened to Justin?! We can't take this so lightly!"

"Lena," Daniel spoke up, his tone even and shockingly calm. "We don't have any other choice. This is the *only* lead we have. You can stay here if you want, but Heath and I are going back out there."

He shot a glance at Heath to make sure he wasn't going to argue. To his relief, Heath gave him a nod of approval.

Lena just stood there, trying to think of a comeback. In the end, she crossed her arms over her chest, inhaled deeply, and shook her head. "How do you even sneak out of a place like this?" she asked Heath. "There are guards everywhere."

"I'll drive," Heath offered. "They already know I've gotta go back to the barn and finish the ritual to get rid of the demon. You two can duck in the back seat."

Daniel turned to Lena. "Works for me," he said.

Lena kept standing there, hugging herself, tapping her toes involuntarily, anxiously, on the wooden floor as she pondered the situation. She released a defeated sigh. "I'll go get my med kit." She started toward the spare bedroom, then stopped and looked back at them. "But I'm telling you right now, if one of you gets hurt, it's your own fault, and I'm not helping you."

That was the biggest lie Daniel had heard all week.

"You won't have to," Heath said. He pointed at the Cross of Silvanus in Daniel's hands. "Not as long as we have that thing."

Lena's damp, messy bun wobbled as she turned on her heel and huffed all the way to the spare bedroom.

Heath's old Suburban had seen better days. The ragged interior of the vehicle smelled so strongly of coffee that Daniel wondered if Heath had dumped an entire pot of the stuff inside it recently. Or perhaps he had used coffee grounds to cover up an even worse odor. He had heard of people doing that, using coffee as an odor neutralizer. His childhood babysitter, Miss Priscilla, had done that once when a raccoon sneaked inside the trailer and used the living room carpet as a toilet.

Whatever the case was in Heath's Suburban, Daniel welcomed the distraction of trying to figure it out. He needed something benign to occupy his thoughts, for the closer they got to the front gate, the higher his anxiety soared.

As they reached the front entrance, Bear Solomon, one of the on-duty guards, flagged them down. Daniel recognized the burly man and remembered his odd name immediately. Bear was the one who'd driven him to Aunt Geri's cabin the night he and Lena had arrived.

Daniel crouched next to Lena in the back, out of sight.

Heath rolled down his window as Bear came to the side of the Suburban. "Morning," he said.

"Good morning," Bear replied. "Where you headed, Heath?"

"Back to the old Jenkins' place. I've gotta finish the ritual."

A long pause.

Then he heard Bear say, "I heard about what happened. I would have shot that damn thing, too." A beat. "I feel so awful for Claudia and her boy."

Heath remained silent and stoic.

"I'll be glad to go back out there with you if you need backup."

"No, uh, thanks, man, but that's alright. I'm the one who screwed up. I'm the one responsible for fixing this. I don't wanna put anyone else in danger."

Another long pause.

"Well, you just be careful."

Heath nodded. "Will do."

"See you 'round."

Daniel heard the sound of grating metal- the gate opening. Heath guided the behemoth of a vehicle successfully through the front gate and onto the road they had taken earlier to the abandoned barn. He waited until they were a good piece down the road to tell Lena and Daniel they could sit up.

"What time is it?" Daniel asked, scooting back into his seat. He felt jittery all over as he clutched the Cross of Silvanus, knowing what they were about to do with it.

Lena glanced at her watch. "Ten 'til noon."

Daniel's intestines slithered. The meeting would be starting soon. What would Aunt Geri say when she realized they had blown it off, when she inevitably figured out what they were doing? What would she do? He didn't know her well enough to know exactly how she would respond, but he guessed she would be furious. Not to mention terrified for his safety.

Lena mumbled something indiscernible to herself and grabbed her purse from the floorboard. She unzipped it and dug around until she found her cell phone.

"What is it?" Daniel asked.

"I'm checking for cell phone reception." She held up her phone. Nothing. Zero bars. "Dammit. I need to call the staffing office and let them know I'll be out again."

Shit.

Once again, Daniel felt like a selfish jerk. He had forgotten about her normal life. This was the beginning of their third day out of town. Another day absent from her job at the hospital. What kind of consequences would she have when she got back home? Would she still have a job? What explanation would she have to give anyone who asked where she had been?

He wondered if she had talked to her mother, if Carol Dillon had any idea that Lena was still gone. She hadn't said anything about it, but if she, like him, had no cell phone reception, they had not spoken.

Daniel pulled his phone from his pocket to check for service now that they were outside the Compound.

No service.

He wondered if anyone had tried to contact him. His dad had gone missing. His home had burned to the ground. Had anyone reached out?

Who would?

He had no supervisor or co-workers because he couldn't find a damn job. Dad and Lena were the only people he stayed in touch with regularly these days. The few buddies he'd had in high school were married now and focused on raising babies and racking up overtime at the mill. They didn't talk anymore. They couldn't relate to each other at all. The people he'd connected with at college had moved far away after graduation, scattering themselves across the United States, getting as far as possible from backwoods Tennessee.

Had anyone in Crofton even noticed his absence?

The likely answer depressed him.

Lena sighed and put her phone away. She looked paler than usual and a bit like she might vomit. She was stressed about her job, no doubt. Lena Dillon, a no-call-no-show. It was unimaginable.

Then again, wasn't everything these days?

As he watched her, he could feel her distress rising. He knew she was thinking about all she had left behind in Crofton. Mr. Darcy. Her mother. Not knowing their fate was tormenting her.

He wanted to say something to her, something comforting to ease her mind. He knew she needed it. But he couldn't find the right words. He couldn't find *any* words. They were going to an abandoned, possibly haunted, barn to face a demon. Nothing in Crofton would matter too much if they died today.

As they rode along, everyone remained silent.

The sky grew darker the farther they moved from the Compound. The clouds had gone from pale gray to deep lead. As they turned onto the bumpy dirt road that led to the barn, thunder growled around them. Lightning streaked the sky.

The demon was waiting for them.

Heath parked the Suburban facing the road, just as Aunt Geri had done earlier in preparation for a speedy getaway. With the motor off, the sound of raindrops pelting the metal exterior of the vehicle sounded like gunshots. The three of them stayed in their seats for a moment.

"If the demon is already in there," Lena said, staring out the window at the barn, "how will we be safe walking in? We'll be out in the open. We won't be able to get to the salt rings immediately."

"I don't think it'll hurt us on the way in," Heath answered. Daniel wasn't too thrilled about Heath's uncertainty here. "It should be happy to see us. I mean, if somebody doesn't go inside and break the salt line to set it free or finish the ritual to send it back, that thing is stuck in there forever."

That made sense. But there was usually a discrepancy between what made sense in theory and what actually happened.

Daniel's fingers clasped the medallion around his neck. The metal felt so icy, it stung his fingertips and sent a chill down his backbone. At least he had this amulet. This shield, as Aunt Geri had called it. It had protected him in the gas station. Hopefully it would do the same now if necessary.

He wished there were two more of them for Heath and Lena to wear. His eyes fell to Lena's collarbone, where the onyx necklace from Zarah rested. He wondered how well it worked against a demon's magic.

Hadn't Justin worn one when he died? Surely Zarah had given him one as well.

Heath turned around in his seat so he could face them. "I'll go in with my gun drawn, just in case. Lena, I want you to stay close to me." He looked at her to make his point, but his eyes darted away fast. "Daniel, with you carrying the Cross, you'll be fine."

If the ancient thing actually works, Daniel thought to himself. They were taking a lot for granted here.

"But Daniel, listen to me. This means you'll be the one with the power over the demon. You'll have to be careful about what questions you ask, what you tell it to do. Remember, the demon has to do whatever you say. Stop and think before you blurt something out."

Daniel squirmed in his seat. Why had he thought he could do this? He wasn't eloquent enough to be in charge of the conversation. He wasn't smart enough. Not knowledgeable enough. He'd only read a few of Dad's books over the last couple of days; that didn't make him an expert on demons. "Maybe you should do it," he said sheepishly, too embarrassed to look Heath in the eye.

"No." The word was definite. It forced Daniel to lift his gaze to Heath's face. He found Heath's wide hazel eyes staring intensely into his own. "Your dad left this Cross for you. He knew, somehow, that it would come to this. That you would end up here. And he knew you could handle it."

Daniel swallowed, fighting against the painful knot that had reappeared in his throat. Heath's confident words brought to memory a line he had just read in his father's letter to Aunt Geri:

He is strong, and I know that he'll do whatever he has to do for the people he loves.

Dad really believed in him.

So did Heath.

Or he was at least good at pretending he did. He knew the right words to say to kick his ass into gear.

Daniel looked down at the iron cross in his hands. The weird and slightly rank-smelling dream catcher-ish piece of medieval junk that was supposed to be the key to everything. He ran a finger across the smooth, cool beads that had been meticulously woven into the twine web.

"Heath's right," Lena commented softly.

Daniel glanced up at her.

"I don't even want to say it, because I am scared to death right now," she went on. "But yes. Your dad put that Cross in that box, and he left the key out for you to find it. He had to have known this would be the only way you could save him if anything ever happened." She hesitated, choosing her words carefully. "And I know your dad, Daniel. He wouldn't have left any of this up to you if he didn't think you could do it."

Despite the fear and anxiety that were unquestionably rising within her, Lena smiled at him. Color warmed her dimpled cheeks. Her gray-blue eyes sparkled. In that dreary landscape, against the backdrop of a lead sky and rivulets of rain trickling down the window behind her, Lena Dillon was a light. The warmth of her radiant presence soothed him, and he felt himself relax.

He smiled back.

TWENTY

T HE RAIN FELL AROUND the three of them in thick, white sheets. As they hurried through the downpour, headed for the barn, the muddy field squished beneath their shoes, making impolite noises.

Daniel did his best to shield the Cross of Silvanus from the elements. He hunched slightly and clutched it against his chest as he ran.

Heath was the first to reach the barn. Daniel and Lena came to a stop behind him. They stood there for a moment in the pouring rain, catching their breath. Procrastinating.

Daniel felt his neck for the umpteenth time. The shielding amulet still hung there. The Cross of Silvanus remained within his grasp.

"Okay," Heath said. He wielded a handgun. "Let's do this."

He dashed through the structure's opening. Lena and Daniel followed.

Inside, the barn's walls and roof contained countless holes for gray daylight- as well as rain- to stream through. Two dozen buckets could not have been enough to catch the leaking rainwater.

Daniel's heart skipped. For now, everything remained intact. But the dirt floor would be a muddy mess soon, and the salt circles and the pentacle Justin had spray-painted would be washed away.

It had never occurred to Daniel that maybe he shouldn't trust Heath. But now that he was here, in the middle of this increasingly risky setup, unbeknownst to his aunt, without any backup, with no protection but the amulet which *hopefully* worked more than once but he wouldn't know for sure until it was too late, Lena unarmed...

What if Heath had lied about the Cross of Silvanus? The guy might have made up the legend. The old relic could be useless. What if Heath was, for some reason, helping the demon? What if this was all a ruse to get Daniel unguarded and alone with the beings who wanted to kill him? Surely there were rewards for humans who did the bidding of demons.

Dad had told him to trust Aunt Geri. No one had said anything about trusting Heath. Perhaps he wasn't worthy of his trust.

He had only known the guy for two days. He seemed like their friend, but Dad had *seemed* like a normal, boring person. His entire life had been a lie. Daniel wasn't sure he could fully trust anyone ever again. How could he have blindly followed Heath here?

It was too late now.

The figure standing in the center of the pentacle spotted him.

Daniel was shocked to find that Bazolael's appearance was different. The smartly-dressed man with the perfect teeth and stunning blue eyes had been replaced by a taller, skinnier guy with shiny chestnut hair that swooped flawlessly across his forehead. The eyes beneath that perfect curtain of hair were glittering pools of deep, rich, chocolate brown that sparkled with energy.

"Well, look who's back," the handsome figure hissed. He glared at Heath. "You know, Heath, I really did *not* enjoy being shot in the head."

Heath didn't respond. He kept his gun aimed at the freshly regenerated demon and stepped into one of the empty salt rings. Lena and Daniel did the same.

"But I do like the makeover. What do you think?" Bazolael twirled to show off the new body, which now wore a more casual ensemble of stylish navy chukka boots, gray tweed trousers, and an untucked white Oxford button-down. "I'm quite fond of the new look myself. And I believe I've lost a few pounds. I feel lighter. Bouncier." He hopped lightly in place a couple of times to demonstrate. "Oh, yes. Springy. Good stuff."

The demon looked up. It raised a hand, grasped a lock of its perfect brown hair between its fingers, and tugged it down between its eyes, which crossed almost comically as the creature examined the new strands. "Hmm. Although the hair is nice, I was really hoping for blonde." It swept the stray lock back into place and set its sparkling brown eyes on Daniel. One of them winked as the demon produced an endearing friendly grin. "I know you have a thing for blondes, Daniel."

Daniel felt his ears growing hot. He kept his eyes on the demon, afraid he would catch Lena's gaze if he looked away.

"So," the creature said. Brimming with energy, he clapped his hands and skipped forward, still inside the pentacle. "Are we going to stand here and chat for a bit or are you going to complete your little ritual and send me along my merry way? Honestly, I don't have a preference, just as long as you don't shoot me again."

Daniel gulped. He knew what he had to do, but his palms were getting so sweaty, he feared the Cross of Silvanus would slip from his fingers if he moved an inch. He wiped his left hand on his jeans, then did the same with his right. With slightly drier fingers, he gripped the relic more tightly.

"How about we chat?" Daniel proposed shakily. Hoping with all his might that Heath had told them the truth, that this wasn't a trap, he held the Cross out so the demon could see what it was up against.

The brown eyes narrowed as the creature squinted at the object. "Is that...? *Noooo*. That can't be the Cross of dear old Silvanus. My old friend the monkety-monk."

"It is," Heath spoke up in a threatening tone.

"Where's that thing been? I haven't heard anything about it in ages. Where did you find it?"

"Hey," Heath snapped. "You're not the one asking the questions here." He turned to Daniel and cued him with a nod.

Instinctively, Daniel's eyes darted to Lena's face. Fear paralyzed her facial features for the moment, but she managed to give him an encouraging sort-of smile. Daniel drew in a deep breath and locked his attention on the demon's glittering brown eyes. He cleared his throat, mustered up his courage, and began. "Tell me where my dad is."

The demon's eyebrows shot up. "Well. Aren't we skipping to dessert first?"

Daniel clenched his jaw. He remembered Heath's advice. Think before speaking. Don't mindlessly blurt out anything. He spoke again, this time more forcefully. "*Tell me where my dad is.*"

"Tennessee," the thing spat. Its eyes transformed into twin chunks of ice as it did so, revealing its true nature. "He's still in Tennessee."

Daniel hesitated before continuing. If the Cross didn't work, this information was false. There was a very good chance the demon was playing along, screwing with him. He couldn't let himself get too excited over anything it told them.

"Where in Tennessee?" he asked.

"Weaver's Pass. Cabin eleven at the Pine Mountain Campground."

"Is the demon who took him there too?"

"No. Not anymore."

The mental image of his father bound and gagged and abandoned in a dark, empty cabin in the woods sickened Daniel to the point that he could barely breathe. He needed to ask another question, but he struggled to get the words out. "Is he still alive?"

"Yes."

Daniel's heart soared. He felt a fleeting, slightly hysterical urge to laugh, to cry tears of joy. But he focused on his task. On forming well-worded questions. "The demon who took him, where did it go?"

"Home."

Daniel paused to consider this for a moment. "Do you mean... Hell?"

Bazolael scoffed. "Hell is your pathetic, little, dying planet."

Daniel couldn't fully process that response. He hesitated once more, making an effort to choose his questions thoughtfully.

"What's the demon's name?" Heath cut in. "The one that has Pete, the one that's been killing us off since the diner massacre?"

"You heard him," Daniel said. "What is the true name of the demon who has been hunting and killing the people of the Compound all these years?"

Bazolael grimaced, not wanting to give up this powerful bit of information. "*Abalaroth.*"

Daniel gulped. When he spoke again, he did it slowly, repeating the name cautiously to make sure he didn't mess it up. "Will Abalaroth come after us when we go to the cabin for my dad?"

"Yes."

"Is there any way we can stop Abalaroth?"

"No." Bazolael grinned. "He'll kill you."

Daniel stopped and thought again. "Can *you* stop him?"

Bazolael twitched, obviously caught off guard by the question. It winced as though in pain as it uttered, "Yes."

Daniel felt his pulse quicken with excitement. If the Cross of Silvanus really worked, if this demon had to do what he commanded it to do, maybe, hopefully, he had found a solution.

He glanced at Heath and Lena. Both were watching him, wide-eyed, eagerly waiting for his next move. They were thinking the same thing, he could tell. He could see the hope on their faces.

Daniel looked back at the demon. He stared into Bazolael's unearthly translucent eyes as intensely as he could, willing it to obey him. "Go back home and tell Abalaroth you lied to us. Say you told us that my dad is in..." He stopped to think of a faraway place. "Montana." Random, but that was good. "Say you told us that to lead us astray and draw us out in the open."

A deep frown creased the demon's forehead. It hissed a curse at him. Daniel felt his confidence mounting. A light bulb had clicked on above his head, and the words came flowing from his lips. "Say you killed us."

The skinny arms of the demon's form convulsed uncontrollably. "Abalaroth will find out the truth," he spat. "And when he does, he'll kill us both."

"Do it anyway."

"Wait!" Lena cried out.

Startled, Daniel turned toward her. So did Heath. Lena remained in her circle of salt, but she had moved closer to its edge, closer to Daniel.

"What is it?" Daniel asked, worrying that he had majorly fucked up something.

"Before you send it away," she said, "ask why they're doing this. Why they're after you."

Daniel swallowed. He leveled his eyes with the demon's once again. He asked the question, not sure that he wanted the answer. "Why do you want me dead?"

"Dead?" Bazolael's glass-like eyes widened, looking genuinely surprised. "Oh, Daniel. Sweet boy. Nobody said we wanted you dead."

Daniel blinked. "What do you mean?"

"Look at your pitiful existence and think for a minute. You lack employment. Not a single prospect in sight. You have no plans for the future. No real aspirations. You're floating around through your life, as aimless as a kite bobbing about in the wind."

The accuracy of the demon's words stung.

"You don't have any friends back home. You never fit in there, did you? Not with those backward hicks and their Confederate flags. Teenage pregnancies and shotgun weddings. Their loud, pretend devotion to the hippie Jew, when we both know they serve no god but college football. No, you don't belong there with them, Daniel, and you never have. You've always been an outsider. And now, here you are, displaced. Homeless. You don't fit in at the Compound, either. You're a whole other kind of outsider there."

Daniel stared at the demon, too shaken to reply.

"Daniel, our little kite boy. Your line is tethered to Abalaroth. He's the one holding the spool." Bazolael grinned proudly, pleased with the metaphor. "We *like* aimless floaters, you see. There's so much potential there. You're like a blank canvas. We can do- and we have done- so much with aimlessly floating, robust, young, white males like yourself."

The demon wore an odd expression as it spoke. Something like admiration altered its features. The glassy ice eyes morphed back into normal human ones, soft brown ones that gravitated to the Cross within Daniel's grasp. "Take a look in the mirror, Danny. You can go places. Just think! You're a young mortal who has known the truth of our existence for a mere two days, and, already, you possess control over an entity such as myself. How flexible, how adaptable you are. Moldable. *Changeable*."

Daniel could scarcely breathe.

"Yes," Bazolael cooed. "With the right encouragement, the proper guidance, and tutelage, you, my dear, could do great things."

Daniel's heart hammered in his chest. He didn't like where this was going. He didn't think he wanted to hear anymore. He was tired of listening to and looking at this thing, at its mocking smiles and soul-piercing glances. He had obtained all the information they needed to find Dad. He should banish Bazolael now, get the creature out of their sight and proximity. Then they could get out of here. They needed to hurry to the campground in Weaver's Pass, Tennessee, to save Dad while they still could.

But something told him to wait.

A quiet voice in his mind reminded him that he held within his hands a rare power. He could compel this demon to spill any secret it knew. It could tell him the truth about his mother's death, if she or his father had indeed made a deal with Abalaroth. It could tell him why the group in the diner had been targeted in the first place back in nineteen eighty-eight. Why it had come back for the children.

This creature held so much knowledge. Perhaps it could even see the future. With Silvanus's Cross, Daniel could know anything, if he only had the guts to ask.

"*There* it is," the demon said, smiling with smug satisfaction. "The mind races, does it not? I can just see the little wheels turning inside your head. The possibilities of what could happen here are only now dawning upon you."

It was true. Daniel could know anything. He could *have* anything.

"Yes, yes, come on, there it is," Bazolael urged, waving his hands toward himself as if trying to magically extract the words from Daniel's lips. "Think about it. You have control here. I am now your servant, and I can get you anything you want. Anything." The thing snapped its fingers, did a little shimmy of its shoulders, and sang, "*You ain't never had a friend like me.*"

"Daniel."

A loud hum had grown in Daniel's ears, drowning out everything but Bazolael's voice. But a different voice had spoken his name.

"Daniel, don't listen to that thing."

Heath. It was Heath's voice calling out to him faintly. He sounded muffled, almost like he was shouting underwater.

"We both know that new college degree is nothing but an expensive piece of paper. It's been useless to you so far. I can make those student loans disappear. And if you really wanna work in a museum, I could make you chief curator of the Smithsonian. We're talking six figures, Daniel."

"This is a trap," he heard Heath say. "This is what they do. Stay focused. Send it back, now."

"I could make anyone fall in love with you," Bazolael promised. "Lydia Flynn, the hottest girl in your graduating class. I could reunite the two of you, if you like. Or we could go bigger. How about Scarlett Johansson? You've always admired her, haven't you? How would you like to escort her down the red carpet at her next premiere and bang her afterward?" The demon bobbed its head toward Lena and whispered, "Or even *her*."

"Stay focused, Daniel! This is…" Heath's voice faded into silence.

"Anyone can see you've been carrying a torch for Lena Dillon for quite some time. You haven't looked at her the same since your senior prom, when the two of you shared the last dance under a cascade of balloons. How romantic. You had a little epiphany during that Death Cab for Cutie song, didn't you? Bless it. You and I both know Lena is the *real* reason you went to Hamilton University. You went there because she did. And when you found out about her new nursing job at the county hospital, her new apartment in your shithole hometown… that's when you decided you'd keep staying with dear old Dad. It's sad, Daniel. Really sad. How about I give you a hand and pull you out of the friend zone?"

Daniel's heart pounded harder. His entire body seemed to have frozen, literally. His skin was like ice. He felt dizzy.

"Or- this one's a goodie-" the demon said, grinning maliciously, "I could bring back your mother. I know you can't wait to delve into that old journal of hers, just so you can have some sense of what she was like. But we could skip all that. I could bring her back to you, alive and in the flesh. How does that sound, hmm?"

Daniel's ears were roaring now. The room had started to spin around him.

"You have to focus!" Heath's garbled voice called out. "Send it out of here now!"

The Cross of Silvanus felt as heavy as a cement block in his trembling hands. He knew, deep within, that he needed to regain control and speak out against this horrible creature before he gave in to its temptations, but that formerly small voice inside of him was screaming at him now.

Do it, Daniel. Claim Lena for yourself. Resurrect your mother.

"Thaaaat's it," Bazolael encouraged him. "You're the one with the monk's Cross, Daniel Wester. You're the one calling the shots. The world is, as they say, your oyster. What do you want? Tell me, and it's yours."

Beads of cold sweat trickled down his forehead, slipping through his eyebrows, blurring his vision. His intestines crawled sickeningly within his abdomen. His chest tightened until it ached.

"Come on, Daniel. Just say the words. A fat paycheck. The girl you're pining for. The mother you never met. Just say the words. It's that easy."

"Daniel, don't!" Lena shouted.

Ignore her and do it, Daniel.

Say the words.

Just say the words.

No. He wanted to. Oh, how he wanted to. But he couldn't. He had to act before the temptation grew any stronger. He had to act now. Right now. He gasped for breath and nearly choked on phlegm as he swallowed. *"No."*

The ferocity of his own voice snapped him out of his stupor.

Resolutely, he steadied himself and glared into the demon's loathsome face. "Do what I already told you to do," Daniel ordered the demon. "Tell Abalaroth what I told you to say and get the hell out of here." He gulped. *"Now."*

The demon released an awful shriek as it crumbled to coal-like dust. It dissolved instantaneously into oblivion with a flash of white light and an ear-splitting *POP*.

It was gone.

A deafening silence fell upon the barn.

Daniel's knees felt like gelatin. Heat rushed through him from head to toe now in the demon's absence. His entire body quivered as he felt bile climbing his esophagus. He was going to vomit. He couldn't control it. He turned away from the others and pitched his torso forward, spewing the contents of his stomach on the ground.

He felt Lena at his side. Her hands were on his back. She was saying something, but he couldn't make it out.

Stomach empty, he remained bent at the hips, one hand gripping his thigh. Sweat poured from his brow. He needed to sit. To lie down.

But more than anything, he needed to get the Cross of Silvanus out of his hands and far away from him. He hurled it into the dirt.

"We need to go," Heath said. At some point, he had appeared on the other side of him. "Can you walk?"

He nodded and pushed himself upright.

Heath grabbed the Cross from the moist earth. "Come on," he said, leading the way. "We've gotta get moving."

Lena stayed with Daniel. "Lean on me if you need to," she told him as they started toward the door. Her eyes were wide with concern as she offered her arm to him.

Still quite unsteady, he latched onto her arm gratefully.

"Everything's gonna be okay now," she whispered to him as they lagged behind Heath. "You did it. You actually did it, Daniel."

TWENTY-ONE

DANIEL STRETCHED ACROSS THE loveseat in Aunt Geri's cabin. He propped himself up on a pillow as Lena handed him a glass of icy water. The rush of coolness felt incredible to his parched tongue and throat. He gulped it down too quickly and gave himself a headache.

Lena pressed a cool, damp washcloth across his forehead. "God, you're burning up," she told him. She pulled a plastic medicine bottle from her med kit on the floor, unscrewed the cap, and shook out two reddish-colored tablets. "Take two of these. It's just ibuprofen, but it'll help."

He took the pills from her and downed them with a sip of water.

"Just sit here and drink that for a moment," she instructed him. She slid the antique rocker closer to his side and sat in it. "Heath will be back with the others in a few minutes."

Daniel followed her directions. They sat without speaking for several minutes. As he guzzled water from the glass, he became aware of her eyes upon him. He glanced up at her. He couldn't tell what it was, but something in her gaze had changed.

She looked at him differently now.

"What?" he asked.

"I'm sorry, it's just..." Lena redirected her gaze to her lap and began inspecting her fingernails. "I was really worried about you back there." She stopped. Plucked a fallen blonde hair from her shorts. "I could see how that thing was affecting you. All the stuff it said." A nervous pause. "All the... things it offered you."

Things like her.

Daniel had to look away.

"I just- I saw you struggling, and I hated it. I wanted to do something, to help you so badly, but I couldn't do anything. I was just stuck there in my stupid little circle."

He didn't know what to say.

Lena shifted around in her seat. "I can't imagine what you were feeling." She crossed her legs. Folded her hands and placed them in her lap. "And for a moment, I really wasn't sure what you were going to do."

"Neither was I," he admitted.

"But you stayed strong." She smiled. "You didn't let it have control over you, and because of that, we're going to be able to get to your dad now."

Daniel looked at her doubtfully. "You really think so?"

"Yes, I do." She frowned. "You don't?"

"Well, things haven't exactly been going too great for us so far. The demon could have lied to us about where he is." He swallowed. "Or about him being alive."

"Daniel, no. You have to stay positive."

"Why the hell would I do that?"

"Daniel!" She scooted forward in her seat, staring at him, incredulous. "You just defeated a demon! You should be proud of yourself right now."

"It wasn't like *that*."

"Yes, it was!"

Daniel shook his head. "Whatever."

"Yeah, whatever. Act all modest about it, but I'm proud of you. And your dad, god, your dad is going to be so proud of you too."

"Lena, please. Don't."

"What?"

"Don't talk about him like that. Like he's okay. We don't know for sure. We're going off of a demon's word. We can't just assume that he's alive and fine."

"No, we can't. But like I said, we have to stay positive."

He shrugged. "I don't wanna get my hopes up."

"But you have to." She leaned forward and hugged her knees. "I know the past couple of days have changed the way we think about... pretty much everything. It's been one insane blow after another. Your dad. Your home."

He glanced away and focused on the water inside the glass he held. It sloshed around a bit. He was shaking. He tried to steady his hands.

"It's been a lot. *A lot.* And it's all depressing and scary as hell." She paused, looking as though she might cry. "But Daniel, you can't let all of the bad stuff get to you. You have to hope that there's good out there too. That good things still happen. I mean, think about this place. Heath said everybody here has a story. Some tragedy led every single person here. They all started over. They built this place, this incredible, beautiful community. And they're thriving."

He had a few words to say about Justin's newly widowed wife and fatherless child, but something told him to keep his mouth shut.

"Hope is what has kept these people going," Lena said. "And hope will keep you going." She smiled at him again. "I know that you haven't given up entirely, or you wouldn't have even tried using the Cross of Silvanus. You definitely wouldn't have been able to withstand the demon. You would have given in to its offers. Something kept you fighting."

He knew that part, at least, was true. He heaved a sigh. No matter how much he didn't want to get his hopes up, they already were. They always had been.

Daniel gulped down the last of the water and set the empty glass on the coffee table. He eased back into the pillow.

"Thank you," he said.

"For what?"

Too embarrassed to look at her, he fixed his eyes on the back cushion of the plaid loveseat. "For coming here with me. For not freaking out over any of this." He felt his cheeks and ears warming with color. "For just being here. Always."

Silence.

Daniel had expected some kind of a response. A *you're welcome* or something. Her silence puzzled him. Worried him. He turned his head to search her face for a clue as to what she was thinking.

She was definitely looking at him differently now.

Still leaning forward, elbows propped on her knees, her face seemed closer to his than it had before. Her thick, whitish-blonde braid draped gracefully over her shoulder, ed by golden afternoon sunlight that now streamed through the window behind her. Her silvery-blue eyes glittered as they gazed into his.

How lovely she was.

He felt their faces inching closer together. As gravity tugged him toward her, he realized he wanted to kiss her. And Lena didn't seem to be opposed to it.

Lena Dillon, the pig-tailed eight-year-old girl who had accidentally smacked him in the forehead with a playground swing. The ten-year-old who'd gone on searches with him to find Dad's mysterious wooden box, who'd giggled with him, making up silly theories about its contents. The thirteen-year-old with braces and that stupid Bumpit thing in her hair who liked to watch *American Idol* with him. The eighteen-year-old in the shimmering blue gown at senior prom, *A Starry Night;* he'd held her against him, swaying to their favorite songs, silver balloons floating magically down around them. And now, the young woman who had faced a demon alongside him.

She'd always been there.

His lifelong best friend.

Were they really doing this?

A mere two inches separated their lips when they heard the sound of boots stomping up the front porch steps. They pulled away from each other just as the front door flew open.

Aunt Geri lumbered inside, her face splotchy and red with hot fury. Smoke practically fumed from her nostrils. "What the fuck were you thinking?"

The tone of the woman's voice disturbed Daniel. He hadn't known his aunt could get so frighteningly loud.

"Sneaking out to face a demon alone like that," Aunt Geri bellowed. "You could have been killed! There's a damn good reason I didn't tell you about the Cross, why I hid it from you, Daniel! Did Heath tell you what happened to Silvanus?"

Heath wandered in behind him, looking guilty.

Aunt Geri didn't wait for an answer. "Yeah, that device gave him power over demons, power that he couldn't handle. Instead of using it to banish his demons, he conjured up more of them. He used them to bring him money and women and whatever the hell he wanted until finally, he was so indebted to them, so deeply under their control, he went mad and gave up his own soul. *And he was a goddamn monk.*"

Yeah, Heath had omitted that part. But it didn't make any difference to Daniel. Nothing would have changed. No matter how dangerous the Cross was, it had been their last hope. He would have done nothing differently.

"Uh, listen, Geri," Heath spoke up, his voice gravelly. He cleared his throat. "No disrespect, but we don't have time for this speech right now. Save it for the car ride."

Aunt Geri sighed so hard, her bangs blew out from her forehead. "Come on, then. Get up."

Daniel hurried to his feet. He couldn't bring himself to look at Lena right now, but he heard her moving around. His head swam as he stood. Apparently, the demon's effects- or the Cross's- had not yet worn off.

"We're leaving for Tennessee right now," Aunt Geri informed them. "Lena, do you have the medical supplies ready?"

"Yes, ma'am," she replied. Her voice came out as an unnaturally shrill squeak.

"Bring them. We have no idea what kind of shape Pete may be in when we get there."

From the corner of his eye, Daniel saw Lena snatch her hefty medical kit from the floor and sling it over her shoulder.

"Alright," Aunt Geri said. She glared at Daniel for an agonizing second, then looked away. "Let's get moving."

TWENTY-TWO

T HE THIRTEEN-AND-A-HALF-HOUR CAR RIDE to Weaver's Pass, Tennessee, was without a doubt the most uncomfortable experience of Daniel's life.

He spent the entire trip crammed in the backseat of his aunt's Jeep between Heath and Lena while Aunt Geri kept giving him intermittent lectures and dirty looks in the rear-view mirror. Alan, the bifocals-and-flannel-wearing man who had joined them for the summoning ritual, rode shotgun. He wore a different flannel button-down this time, a dull gray plaid, and a permanent sour expression on his face. He stayed silent the whole time, clearly out of place in the middle of Aunt Geri's chiding and the backseat trio's rebuttals.

Thanks to their relationship-altering almost-kiss in Aunt Geri's living room, Lena wouldn't look at Daniel. And he couldn't bear to look at her. Heath had noticed this and kept shooting mildly questioning looks at Daniel, which certainly didn't help things.

On top of all that, the ibuprofen Lena had given him was starting to wear off. His head throbbed dully, and he felt clammy all over.

All he wanted was to find Dad and go home.

Wherever *home* was now.

The Jeep whirred past the Pine Mountain Campground welcome sign Thursday morning as the sun appeared over the eastern horizon, streaking the sky with brilliant orange and pink hues. Gravitt, the Benjamin Franklin doppelgänger, followed closely behind in a Dodge minivan, accompanied by Eddie, Marion, and Zarah.

As Daniel peered out the window, he took the cloudless, sunny sky as a good sign. No thunder and lightning meant no demon. Hopefully this meant Bazolael had done what he'd been instructed to do, and they could find and collect Dad without interference.

Hopefully.

The winding mountain road narrowed, and Aunt Geri had to ease up on the gas. Daniel's ears popped as they climbed higher in altitude. They passed cabin one. Ten more to go.

The closer they got, the higher Daniel's heart rate rose.

Cabin six. Cabin seven.

He had never been to this corner of his home state, but the scenery was gorgeous. He had always loved the mountains. And having grown up in a secluded home encircled by forest, he felt a comforting familiarity, a special kinship, with the towering pines that surrounded them. He would have enjoyed the views if he hadn't been on the verge of puking again.

Cabin eight. Cabin nine.

Daniel's knees bounced involuntarily, knocking both Heath and Lena in the thighs over and over again. He tried to make it stop, but his frazzled nerves wouldn't cooperate.

Cabin ten.

He held his breath.

Cabin eleven.

The quaint little lodge, a boxy structure made of logs and a hunter-green metal roof, reminded him of Aunt Geri's house. It was the kind of place his father would have picked for a weekend getaway. He wondered, somewhat oddly, if Abalaroth had chosen this place for that very reason.

Aunt Geri guided the Jeep down the dirt driveway. She did a three-point turn to park the Jeep facing the way they'd come in, just as she had at the barn. Gravitt's van did the same beside them. Slowly, cautiously, everyone climbed out of the vehicles and gathered at the rear of them.

Daniel glanced up. Overhead, the sky remained crisp and clear, the first golden slivers of sunlight banishing the shadows of night and bathing the cabin in warmth. Birds chirped pleasantly as they flitted around in the pines that surrounded them.

It was all a bit surreal. A little too delightful, too charming.

"We need to move fast," Aunt Geri reminded them as they unloaded weapons and supplies from the back of the Jeep. "It looks safe enough here, but we don't know what we're walking into, and we don't know how much time we have before Abalaroth shows up."

Daniel grabbed a container of black salt. He watched Lena as she shouldered her medical kit, still avoiding his gaze. He couldn't read her expression as she stared at the cabin before them.

Aunt Geri had already insisted that she carry the Cross of Silvanus, and Daniel had happily agreed to that. He didn't want to touch the thing ever again. She had threaded a long leather cord through the center of the relic and tied it around her neck before they'd left. It remained there now, secure against her body, mostly concealed by her baggy green overshirt.

Daniel hoped they wouldn't need it, but he was glad his aunt was the one responsible for it this time.

Aunt Geri led the way toward the cabin's entrance. She kept her right hand on the Cross as she moved. The others followed closely behind her, moving swiftly but remaining cautious and hyper-alert to their surroundings.

From the outside, there were no signs that the place was inhabited. No movement. No lights in the windows. No sounds but the birdsong all around them and the accelerated thumping of Daniel's heartbeat roaring in his ears.

Aunt Geri was the first to reach the door. She gave Daniel a nod, his signal to lay the salt across the threshold. He opened the container with trembling fingers and crouched down, carefully pouring a thick line of black salt across the entrance. Behind him, he heard soft *KSSSSSSSH* sounds as Marion and Eddie spray-painted demon-warding sigils onto the log walls like neighborhood vandals.

Zarah, Heath, Alan, and Gravitt split into two even teams and hastened around the sides and back of the cabin, salt and spray paint in hand, hurriedly implementing the same protective measures on the rest of the structure. They rejoined the others at the front in under a minute.

Aunt Geri clutched the Cross of Silvanus as she sized up the entryway. Two small, square windows sat side by side at the top of the rustic wooden door, like a pair of glass eyes watching them. She peeked in, then twisted her head back to the others and nodded, not looking particularly alarmed. She reached for the doorknob. Turned it.

It was locked.

That was no surprise. Daniel stood with Lena in the middle of the group, watching Aunt Geri closely to see what she would do next. He was anxious to see if she would impress them all by kicking the door in. As Daniel had predicted, Aunt Geri's left leg flew up into a Chuck Norris-style kick. Her heavy steel-toed work boot pounded into the door, chipping the wood but not enough. She stepped back and gave it another try.

On the third attempt, the door blew inward with a bang. Aunt Geri's breath hitched as she reached inside her billowing shirt, into her waistband, and removed a pistol. She stepped across the threshold.

Eddie, Marion, and Alan were supposed to go inside next. Daniel and Lena were to stay back, where they would be covered from the rear by Zarah, Heath, and Gravitt.

But Daniel couldn't do it.

He couldn't stand around outside, waiting, wondering what the hell was going on within the walls.

He'd gone up against Bazolael in the barn and succeeded. He had the protection of the amulet. This was *his father* they were here to rescue. Maybe it was a little reckless, but there was no way in hell he was going to wait.

He bolted ahead, almost knocking Marion down as he pushed in front of her to get inside the cabin.

"Whoa-whoa, what the hell?!" a man's voice said behind him, Eddie probably.

Daniel's wobbly legs nearly gave way as he raced through the door.

Aunt Geri whipped her head around at him, her eyes wide with shock and maybe a little fury, as he joined her in the living area. She didn't make a sound, though. She stood silently, pistol at the ready, scanning the empty cabin.

Empty.

Daniel's breath snagged in his throat as his eyes swept across the place. Clean stone fireplace. Bare coffee table. Vacant brown couch.

He fought a rising panic as they moved together through the barren living space, around an empty wooden dining table for two. A small kitchen sat neat and tidy, untouched by visitors.

Had Bazolael lied?

Daniel's bones turned to water. Of course the *demon* had lied to them. This was a trap, a ruse to lure Daniel and Lena and all the others outside their protective iron gate. Here they were, out in the open where their defenses were lowered, where demons would surely pick them off one by one. They would be forced to watch as their friends' eyeballs exploded in their sockets.

But he heard no thunder. A quick glance out the front door confirmed a clear blue sky and unfiltered daylight.

"There," Aunt Geri mouthed, bobbing her head toward the open doorway of an adjacent room.

The bedroom.

Daniel's anxiety mounted with each step as he and his aunt approached the only place inside the cabin that remained unchecked.

What would they do if it, too, was empty?

What would they do if it wasn't?

Daniel saw him.

Sprawled across the bed on his stomach. Hands tied behind his back. A red bandana covered his mouth, knotted tautly at the base of his skull.

Dad was here. He was really here.

Daniel saw a finger twitch. He was alive.

People rushed in around him, all talking at once, spouting off instructions, but it all was a slow-motion blur to Daniel. His eyes locked on his father. Beneath heavy eyelids, Pete Wester gazed back at him. His blue eyes flickered with recognition. He blinked slowly before his eyes rolled back into his head.

He looked worse than Daniel had imagined. Patches of blood stained his pants and his T-shirt, the gray Hamilton University tee he had proudly purchased at the campus bookstore the day they'd registered Daniel for his freshman classes. Cuts and bruises marred his face, his neck, and his arms. Just about every area of exposed skin bore some product of abuse.

Aunt Geri flicked open a pocketknife and sliced through the bandana that gagged her brother while Heath worked on the hand restraints. Lena darted to the other side of the bed and set down her medical bag, working impossibly fast to dig out supplies. Daniel stood frozen at the foot of the bed, helplessly watching them work.

"He's severely dehydrated," Daniel heard Lena say. He detected no hint of fear in her voice. She had switched into full-on medical professional mode. "I need to start an IV."

"There's no time for that," Heath snapped at her. "The demon could show up any second. We need to get out of here, *now*."

Lena looked somewhat flustered as she blew out some air. "Okay. Then help me roll him onto his back."

Working together, Heath, Aunt Geri, and Lena log-rolled Dad into a supine position. His head bobbed groggily as they turned him, his eyes still closed. Daniel wondered if he had slipped into unconsciousness.

"Oh, god." Lena's features twisted in horror. "I think his legs are broken."

Daniel's eyes shifted immediately to his father's legs. His stomach turned. Each leg curved unnaturally to the left despite Dad's altered position.

"Fuck," Aunt Geri breathed. The color drained from her suntanned skin as she looked at Lena. "What's the best way to move him?"

Lena gave Dad a rapid head-to-toe scan. "We can use the bedspread as a stretcher. Roll up the sides so we'll have something to hold onto." She demonstrated by pulling up her side of the bedspread and rolling it up toward Dad like a burrito. "Geri, Heath, you get that side. Alan, will you help me lift this side?"

Alan, whose eyes had turned to saucers behind his bifocals, hurried to join Lena. Daniel watched numbly as Heath and Geri followed Lena's example and rolled their side of the bedspread toward Dad until they had a sturdy scroll-like formation to grasp hold of.

"Someone will need to stabilize his neck. Daniel?"

The sound of his name pulled Daniel from his stupor. He stepped forward, eager to lend a hand. "What do I do?"

"Put a hand on each side of his head to hold him steady as we move him. We just don't want his head moving around too much, in case he has some sort of spinal injury. Try to keep his neck, head, and spine in a straight line."

Daniel nodded and placed his hands on either side of Dad's head as directed. The skin on his temples felt unnaturally dry and cool beneath Daniel's touch.

"Okay, everyone," Lena said, gripping her portion of the rolled bedspread, "team lift on three. One, two, *three*."

The group raised Dad from the bed, cradling him in a sort of makeshift hammock. Daniel gripped the sides of his father's skull as they moved, hoping he was keeping him stable enough. They carried him through the cabin and outside.

Gravitt yanked open the back of his van for them. His blonde ponytail swished as he hurried around the side of the vehicle and folded the rear seats down flat, creating a roomy space for Dad to stretch out.

Very carefully, the team transferred Dad to the back of the van. Daniel moved into the rear cargo space beside him, still doing his best to keep his head steady.

Lena knelt in the back on the opposite side of Dad. "If we had some sheets or towels, we could roll those up and put them around his neck for the drive. That'll help keep his spine stabilized."

"On it," Heath said, breaking into a run and disappearing back inside the cabin.

"Lena, there's a blanket in the compartment to your right," Gravitt told her, indicating a large built-in storage console.

She opened it and removed a rust-colored blanket. A large protective sigil had been woven into the center of the fabric. Lena draped it across Dad gently.

Heath reappeared with a stack of bath towels he'd swiped from the cabin's bathroom.

"Perfect, thank you," she said, taking them from him. She rolled them into logs and created a crude cervical collar around Dad's head and neck. Satisfied with her work, she drew in a deep breath and eased back onto her heels.

"Everybody load up!" Aunt Geri hollered, climbing into the back of the van. "We gotta get going!" She handed her key ring to Alan. "You mind driving the Jeep for me? I'd like to stay with my brother."

Alan nodded. "Of course."

"You two are with me," Aunt Geri said, her wide eyes darting between Lena and Daniel.

The group hastily redistributed themselves into the two vehicles and left the empty, vandalized cabin behind them just as the sun slipped behind a cloud.

Daniel and Aunt Geri sat hunched very close together at Dad's right side. Lena remained across from them, kneeling at Dad's left side. Heath rode up front, with Gravitt at the wheel. As the van zoomed down the road, Heath glanced over his shoulder to check on the situation in the back every thirty seconds or so.

Lena had confirmed Daniel's suspicions. His father was unconscious. But she assured him that his vitals were decent and that his present state was probably a good thing due to the intense pain from his shattered legs.

She reached into her med kit and withdrew a line of clear plastic tubing, a bag of translucent fluid, and a handful of other medical supplies. She tugged on a pair of nitrile gloves. "I don't have an IV pole, obviously," Lena said, removing the stopper from the bottom of the fluid bag. She inserted the white pointy end of the tubing into its port and twisted it firmly into place. "We'll just have to take turns holding it up, I guess."

Daniel glanced around the back of the van. "Could you hang it up there?" He pointed at the built-in plastic coat hook above the window behind her.

"Ooh, good idea," Lena told him, meeting his eyes appreciatively for a quick second. She slipped the bag onto the hook. It held there perfectly. She squeezed the clear cylindrical chamber that hung beneath the bag and liquid poured into it.

Daniel stared at her as she worked with the tubing, rolling the little wheel on the blue clamp, allowing the fluid to fill the length of the tubing. *Priming the line*, he remembered.

It was about a year and a half ago, before Lena had her own apartment, and they were both full-time commuter college students living with their parents to save money. Daniel sat at the fancy mahogany table in Carol Dillon's formal dining room, his arm outstretched on the wooden surface and growing sore from the too-tight tourniquet Lena had wrapped around it. A slightly younger, slimmer version of Lena leaned over him, poking and squishing his veins.

He was always her patient. She needed someone to practice her skills on outside the classroom, to help her get things right before her highly stressful, downright terrifying skill check-offs at school. Daniel was happy to volunteer.

He had good veins, she said. She didn't actually pierce his skin, though; she practiced that part on a Navel orange. The IV tubing was next, and Lena had to practice spiking the bag and *priming the line*. She had all the real equipment to practice with at home, which Daniel thought was cool. She followed her instructor's directions, step by step, clumsily attaching the tubing to the real bag of fluid. When she undid the clamp on the tubing, saline solution gushed down the line and squirted everywhere, all over both of them, sending them into a fit of laughter until they realized it was also all over Carol Dillon's oriental rug.

Daniel smiled at the memory as he came back to the present, back to Dad's motionless, battered body lying on the floor of Gravitt's van. He watched Lena as she worked, admiring the ease and confidence she possessed now as she quickly performed the tasks she had fumbled back then. She seemed oblivious to his stare as she tied a rubber tourniquet around Dad's forearm and swept an alcohol pad across the back of his hand. The strong astringent smell turned Daniel's stomach. He felt even queasier as he watched Lena find a vein and expertly guide the needle into it. When he saw his father's dark blood shoot into the needle's clear chamber, he was glad he was sitting down. He glanced away as she connected a syringe of clear fluid and pushed the barrel.

"All finished," Lena said a couple of minutes later.

"Thank you," Aunt Geri told her in a watery voice.

Daniel looked at his aunt and saw that she, too, had been watching Lena work on her brother this whole time.

"Yeah, that was awesome," Daniel said to Lena, his heart racing as he spoke. "Really. You did great."

She blushed as she met his eyes. "Thanks."

They held each other's gaze for a moment. Daniel felt heat rising within him as he looked at her, studying her features. Her tired silver-blue eyes looked a bit exhilarated from the action of rescuing Dad. There was something else there too, behind the fatigue and excitement. Something new, something he hadn't seen until earlier in Aunt Geri's cabin. It felt... sultry. Alluring. His eyes involuntarily dropped to her lips. Rosy and wide, slightly parted. They'd come so close to his mere hours ago.

For the second time, Aunt Geri interrupted their moment. "What about his legs? What can we do?"

Lena inhaled sharply and tore her eyes away from Daniel. She cleared her throat. "We've gotta get him to a hospital."

"Dammit to hell," Aunt Geri said. "We can't do that. It's too dangerous."

"But I think he'll need surgery."

"Abalaroth could come back for him at any time. We have to get back to the Compound."

Lena dropped her professional persona. "Geri, listen to me," her voice was gentle but firm. "If Pete doesn't get the right medical help, he may never walk again." She paused. Her eyes glistened with tears. "And that's the *best* outcome. Other complications are likely to happen first."

"What kind of complications?" Daniel wanted to know.

"Well, um, depending on the type of fracture he has... infection, fat embolism, pulmonary embolism." She gulped. "This could be very serious."

"Could Maeve do a surgery like that?" Heath asked from the front seat.

"From what I've seen of the clinic, absolutely not," Lena replied. A tear slipped down her cheek. She wiped it away forcefully. "And he'd need x-rays first anyway so we can see what we're dealing with."

The inside of the van fell silent.

Daniel watched his father as they rode along. He looked so horrible, he could have been easily mistaken for dead.

"I hate it, but we can't take the risk of going to a hospital right now," Aunt Geri said.

Another tear slid down Lena's face, and she looked deeply annoyed by it as she brushed it away. "Any one of these complications could kill him!"

"Pete wouldn't want us to do it," Aunt Geri insisted. "If I know anything about my brother, I know he would never let us put anyone else in danger just for him to get treatment. Not after all he's done to protect Daniel."

Daniel recalled the letter he'd found in his aunt's wardrobe. His words had been so final. He hadn't expected to come out of this alive.

"If anything happened to Daniel, it would nullify everything he's sacrificed to keep him safe," Aunt Geri went on. "I'm telling you, if Pete survived but someone else didn't, he wouldn't be able to live with himself."

After everything he had learned about his father these past couple of days, Daniel felt that to be true. But it didn't make the decision to forgo proper healthcare any easier.

They weren't living in the Dark Ages. This wasn't Colonial New England. They weren't roughing it out on the prairie in the eighteen-hundreds. Nor were they living in some kind of post-apocalyptic *Walking Dead* version of modern America. Dad had perfectly valid health insurance, and there were countless clinics and hospitals between here and the Compound.

But broken legs could be the death of him because the people at the Compound didn't possess the medical capabilities he required.

It seemed so incredibly stupid and backward and outright cruel to bypass all of the available options and leave him to the limited resources inside the gates. And Daniel knew that, as a nurse, Lena felt even stronger than he did about that.

But Aunt Geri had decided for them.

They continued to the Compound without further discussion.

TWENTY-THREE

Maeve Lewis was much more spry than Aunt Geri had made her sound.

While the nurse practitioner did have a slight humpback and a braided bun of snowy white hair atop her head, everything else about her radiated youth and wellness. Beneath a crisp white lab coat, she wore a teal knee-length dress that swooshed when she walked and showed off her stunningly toned calves. Instead of granny loafers, she wore a pair of stylish wedge sandals. Turquoise beads dangled on silver pendulums from her ear lobes.

Though he felt a bit creepy for thinking so, Maeve Lewis was the most attractive older woman Daniel had ever seen.

She fastened a blood pressure cuff around Dad's left arm and slipped the earpieces of her stethoscope into her ears. Daniel watched her closely as she placed the stethoscope diaphragm into the fold of his father's arm and began pumping up the cuff.

The medical clinic at the Compound was more impressive than Daniel had expected. Maeve had four beds, actual working hospital beds that they had mysteriously acquired from somewhere, each separated by the same standard blue curtains he'd seen in emergency rooms.

She had all the miscellaneous basic equipment too. Thermome-ters. Otoscopes. Oxygen tanks. Several open storage cabinets held clear canisters of cotton balls and cotton applicators and all sorts of other things Daniel didn't know the names of. A whole lot of intimidatingly pointy things he didn't want to know the names of.

Overall, Maeve's clinic had the same cold, sterile atmosphere as any normal medical facility, and Daniel found that incredibly reassuring.

"One-twelve over seventy," Maeve announced to the group as the blood pressure cuff deflated.

Daniel sat in a rocking chair next to his father's bed. Lena propped an elbow on the back of his chair while Aunt Geri stood on the opposite side of the bed, hands planted on her hips, drum-ming her fingers anxiously against her shirt tails. Maeve had pulled over a couple of extra chairs for them, but everyone was tired of sitting after the long car ride. Daniel, however, still felt weak and sickly from the Cross of Silvanus and had gladly taken the rocker.

Maeve removed the stethoscope earpieces from her ears. "That's a good sign. All of his vitals remain stable. None of the fractures broke the skin and his temp is normal, so he doesn't appear to have an infection at this point. I've started IV antibiotics to cover our bases though. I'll continue to monitor him regularly, of course, but as of right now, I feel confident that he's in the clear."

Maeve looked at Lena and smiled warmly.

"You did everything perfectly, dear," Maeve told her. "It's a good thing you started the IV therapy when you did. Being left without food and water for the past couple of days combined with the blood loss from all these wounds had him severely dehydrated."

Daniel glanced up at Lena and smiled. Even in the madness, he recalled her using that exact terminology. She couldn't help but return a proud smile.

"I gave him something for pain as well," Maeve said. "I'm afraid the pain will be quite intense when he wakes up."

"When do you expect that to be?" Aunt Geri asked.

"There's no way to be sure, but he'll probably be out for a while. And that's perfectly fine. After all he's been through, he certainly needs some rest."

Aunt Geri nodded. "Thanks, Maeve, for everything. And thank you again, Lena."

Maeve gave her a sweet smile. "You're welcome. I'll check back in on him shortly." Her smile turned a tad mischievous. "For now, I need to go check on young Caden's hand. He cut it mending a chicken coop, and I'm afraid he might need a few stitches."

Apparently, the privacy rules of HIPAA were irrelevant here in the Compound.

Aunt Geri winced. "Go right ahead."

In the older woman's absence, Lena replaced her by going into caregiver mode again. "Do either of you need anything?" she asked. "Maybe something to eat?"

They hadn't eaten all day. Daniel's stomach growled audibly at the mere mention of food.

Lena grinned. "I'll take that as a yes."

"Why don't you stay here with Pete, just in case," Aunt Geri said. "I'll be happy to walk over to Pearl's and get a plate for each of us."

"Okay, thanks."

Aunt Geri smiled, shoved her hands into the pockets of her baggy jeans, and shuffled toward the door. "I'll be right back."

As she left, Lena settled into the straight-backed metal chair next to Daniel's rocker. Neither of them spoke. They just sat together, each of them staring at Dad's unmoving body.

When they had initially arrived, Lena had helped Maeve clean him up. They had removed his soiled clothing and gotten him into a blue hospital gown. Together, they had cleansed and bandaged his many wounds, only one of which needed stitches.

Thanks to their efforts, Dad looked more like himself now.

Daniel relaxed in the rocker and began to move the chair slowly back and forth. A euphoric rush of peace had swept over him the moment he had been reunited with his father. Even though Dad's future was uncertain, and Daniel couldn't speak with him yet, he felt a new calmness just being in the same room with him.

As he and Lena waited silently for Aunt Geri to return with dinner, Daniel began mentally preparing himself for the first conversation he and his father would have. They had so much to talk about. The diner massacre. His mom's death. How he had protected him for the last twenty-one years in Crofton.

Where would he even begin?

And Daniel had his own updates to give him. He wondered if Dad knew about the fire at their trailer. The demon had probably bragged about burning it down just to taunt him, but it was possible he didn't know yet. They had to discuss the future. Where they would live. He had a feeling they would be forced to remain at the Compound for a while, at least until he had recovered. But what would they do then? Or what would Daniel do if Dad didn't recover?

He glanced down at his father's legs sadly. It would be a long time before they knew the extent of his injuries. What if he never walked again?

He suddenly felt Lena's hand on top of his. The spark of her skin on his pulled him from his thoughts. He looked up at her and found her smiling brightly.

"What did I tell you?" Her smile widened, showcasing her dimples. "You did it. You got him back to us."

Daniel couldn't say anything to that. He stared sheepishly at the blue and green tiled floor.

Lena squeezed his hand. "I'm so proud of you, Daniel."

"I'm proud of you too. You kicked ass." He grinned and shifted his hand around, moving his fingers to intertwine with hers. "It was really cool to see your nursing skills in action."

A hint of pink flushed her cheeks. "I'm just glad I could help."

Daniel wondered where their future lay now. With Dad back, alive and on the mend, Lena could freely return to Crofton, couldn't she? She would have to address the life she had abandoned at some point. She had left behind a job, an apartment, a cat, and her mom. She had to go back, at least temporarily to take care of things. So, when would she leave?

And another pressing issue: were they going to address the moment they had shared at Aunt Geri's, when their lips had come so close to meeting? Were they pretending that didn't happen?

"So, uh," Daniel started. He stopped just as fast. He let go of her hand and scratched his ear. "Um, now that Dad's back, are you gonna head back home?"

His question seemed to catch her off guard. Her face paled as she breathed, "What?"

He couldn't make himself repeat the question. He knew she had heard him the first time.

"I-I can't just leave," she said, eyes wide with disbelief. "Not after everything." She hesitated. "Is that what you're asking me to do?"

"No," Daniel said quickly. "*No*. That's not what I meant at all. I just thought that, you know, with work and your apartment... and Mr. Darcy... you'd have to be getting back soon."

Lena looked down at her lap. Picked at her nails. "I don't know." Her tone had changed. She sounded flat. "It all seems pretty pointless now, doesn't it?"

"Pointless?"

"Well, I mean, knowing what we know now. That demons are real, that they're a threat." She blinked. "How can I just go back to that everyday stuff? You know? It's like... the world's different now. I feel different, too. I don't know. I just don't see how things can go back to the way they used to be."

Neither did he. Everything had completely changed for him. He didn't even have a home anymore and his dad might be paralyzed.

Not to mention the demons were stalking him. His previous existence was over and done with.

"Are you saying you want to stay?" Daniel asked. "Here, at the Compound?"

She sighed loudly. Shrugged her shoulders. "I know this probably sounds ridiculous to you, but I like it here. It's beautiful. And it's simple." She smiled. "It's a real community, and there are... some great people living here." She blushed slightly as she said it.

Daniel felt a twinge of jealousy as Heath's face appeared in his mind. Surely he was who she was talking about.

He found her hypocritical. Only a few hours ago, she had been judging the place for its backward medical practices. Now she wanted to move here?

"I don't know," she said again. "I just... I can see why all these people came here. I think it'd be nice to have a fresh start."

"What about your mom?" Daniel asked.

She released a heavy sigh. "What about her?"

"What the hell would you tell her?"

"I don't know. Ugh, I don't know." She rubbed her temples, clearly frustrated. "I don't know what I would do. I can't leave her on the outside, not knowing how to protect herself if anything ever happened. But at the same time... can you see her living here?"

No, Daniel could not. He couldn't help but chuckle aloud when he tried to picture hoity-toity Carol Dillon leaving behind her big, comfortable house and her Ann Taylor shopping sprees, roaming around the Compound, black onyx on her collarbone and a sheathed iron machete slung over her shoulder.

Lena giggled heartily, evidently envisioning something similar. "We're awful."

Daniel just smiled.

She sighed again, wearily this time. "I guess I have to go back," she decided. "She's my mother. I'm all she's got. I have to make sure she's safe, and I think maybe I've learned enough here the past couple of days to do that."

He nodded. He had expected this response from her, but he still felt something deflate inside him. He was stuck here. And not so deep down, he had hoped she would choose to be stuck with him.

"Yeah. I should probably head back by Monday, at least. I don't know how many days they'll let me miss work before they fire me, especially with me still being a new hire."

She had made her decision, then. She didn't seem too happy about it, but she had realized what she needed to do.

Daniel didn't bring it up again.

TWENTY-FOUR

THURSDAY NIGHT CAME AND went.

Daniel stayed at his father's bedside, only getting up to use the restroom or pace the floor when his rear-end went numb and he remembered Lena's warnings about how sitting for too long could cause deep vein thrombosis. Maeve had insisted he lie down on one of the other hospital beds and try to get some sleep. He did manage to doze for about seven hours, and for that, he was grateful. He woke up feeling recharged and slightly less anxious.

Friday morning, Lena brought him breakfast and his mother's old journal. This was the perfect opportunity for him to read it, she told him. He agreed. He dove into it the moment she left him alone.

He spent the next several hours engrossed in the day-to-day adventures of his eighteen-year-old mother. She had begun the diary on the evening of her eighteenth birthday (it had been a gift from her Aunt Nora). From that point on, she described, quite thoroughly and oftentimes a bit over-dramatically, the various occurrences she encountered each day. He found a lot of typical teenage angst. A few slightly embarrassing descriptions of boys she liked who didn't notice her existence.

The way she continually referred to some guy in economics class named Tony made Daniel uncomfortable.

By her nineteenth birthday, she was a freshman at the University of Tulsa, majoring in history, like Aunt Geri had said.

In September of 1987, she mentioned "Peter" for the first time. She described him as the friend of a friend she was introduced to at a football game. She and Peter it off quickly and bonded over their shared disdain for a particular mathematics professor, Dr. Calsmith. By the end of the entry, she was rambling about Peter and his *"incredibly gorgeous, piercing blue eyes that seemed to stare into one's soul."*

Daniel laughed to himself. As cheesy as his mother's words were, there were a few times when he had felt the man peering into his own soul. Like that time eleven years ago when he had found Daniel sitting in his bedroom closet with the secret wooden box. He would never forget *that* piercing stare.

In October, his mother dropped the formalities and began calling him Pete.

November consisted of one dreamy date after another.

They shared their first kiss on Christmas Eve while sitting on the wooden swing on her parents' front porch. A surprisingly bold move for his shy father, Daniel thought. Young Helen said it was *"nothing short of magical in the glow of the twinkling Christmas lights."*

She met Pete's sister, Geri, who she described as *"a little odd but nice, though she didn't say much,"* the next day at the Wester family

Christmas gathering, where everyone made her feel welcome and she could easily see herself becoming a part of that family.

The way his mother wrote about Dad warmed Daniel's heart. She had truly been in love with him. Their romance was straight out of a Nicholas Sparks novel. Until the following April.

Daniel felt his anxiety rising as he watched the dates of the journal entries drawing closer to April 4, 1988.

He paused on April 3:

> *Tomorrow, Pete and I are going with Geri to grab some dinner and see a movie. I'm not sure what's playing, but I'll be happy just to have a break from studying. Biology is killing me! Ted and Jenny may go too if Ted can get off work. I hope he can; I haven't seen them in ages.*

That was it. Her last entry before the demon's massacre at the diner in Tulsa. She had no idea how her life was about to change.

Daniel's stomach fluttered as he turned the page. The date skipped to April 8.

> *I don't know what to say today. I don't know what to think. What to feel. Everything is over. Everything has been turned completely upside down.*

> *On Wednesday, the five of us did go out for dinner and a movie. Ted got to leave work early. What a*

horrible twist of fate! He should have been at the body shop. If his boss had made him stay, this wouldn't have happened. He would still be alive.

His funeral was this afternoon. One of six funerals because of what happened in the diner. The entire city has been affected by this tragedy. But for those of us who were trapped inside and forced to witness it- we are broken. We will never recover.

Daniel closed his eyes and tried to imagine how she had felt as she penned that entry. What it had been like to see her friend, Ted, killed in front of her by an inexplicable force. After witnessing Justin's death, Daniel possessed a greater understanding of what their shock, horror, and confusion must have been like.

As he read the entries that followed, her tone changed. The mood darkened. Even her penmanship evolved. Her long, delicate strokes grew short and careless as she scribbled her jumbled thoughts in a hurry.

Sometimes, anger and bitterness seethed from her sentences. Other days, she poured out her sadness in the melancholiest strings of words. A few droplets of dried liquid dotted several pages, making the ink run, blurring the words. Daniel wondered if they were tears.

July 5, 1988.

Will the funerals ever end? I'm so tired of going to fucking funerals. This one today was by far the worst. Eddie Crider, the busboy from the diner, was one of us who made it out alive. On Tuesday, his wife, Marion, found their eight-month-old son, Jedediah, dead in his crib. His eyes had burst in their sockets; blood flowed from his ears and nose. The doctors can't explain such a horrific tragedy.

As I stood next to that tiny casket today, I lost it. I don't have to wonder what happened to this poor baby. That man, that horrible THING, came back for this precious, innocent baby. I wept openly. I felt this powerful, bitter rage growing inside of me, so strong I could barely contain it. I wanted to scream. I wanted to find that damn monster and make him suffer the way he's made all these innocent people suffer.

I'm not the only one who feels this way. As we left the cemetery, a man approached us. Anders Melrose, a theology professor at the university. Pete took one of his classes last semester, actually. Pete said he was pretty strange, kind of eccentric, but seemed like an okay guy. He wants to meet with us. He says he knows things and can help.

Dr. Melrose.

Daniel remembered Aunt Geri saying something about him. He had been an instrumental figure in their lives after the diner massacre. He noticed his mother's entries growing more positive and more hopeful the more she mentioned the professor.

July 20, 1988.

Pete, Geri, and I went to speak with Dr. Melrose again. Eddie and Marion Crider were there. Walter Garrison came this time, too, and brought his two kids with him; two sweet babies now without a mother. Walter's wife, Lavinia, was one of the victims in the diner. I helped keep an eye on the children while Dr. Melrose taught us more about demonic entities.

As impossible and insane as it sounds, this demon theory is the only thing that makes sense. I think I knew that the moment that "man" walked into the diner. There was something so strange, so unique about his presence that seemed unearthly, even before I saw his eyes transform into those horrible, clear, chunks of glass.

I still see those eyes every time I close my own.

Dr. Melrose says that never really stops, but we can take comfort in knowing we can fight back. He's showing us ways to protect ourselves. I have to admit, some of his ideas and methods are a little out there, but I'm trusting him. What else can I really do at this point?

That sounded familiar.

He read her accounts of the next few months, captivated by her descriptions of their lessons with the professor. They met in the demon-proofed cellar of his gorgeous, authentically restored Victorian abode that lay a few miles outside of Tulsa. He gave them books, taught them a handy new way to use salt, and showed them which protection symbols were nothing but made-up hogwash and which ones actually worked.

But apparently, not everyone took Dr. Melrose's theories seriously.

September 9, 1988.

The demon hit us again. Hard. It came back for Walter's children.

It crept into the bedroom that his son and daughter shared and went for his youngest, Abigail. She was only ten months old. Her brother, Heath, who is still practically a baby himself at three, managed to run to his father before the demon got to him.

Poor little Heath hasn't stopped crying since it happened. He keeps saying over and over that he messed up, that he did wrong, because his dad always tells him to watch out for his baby sister. During the attack, Heath hid under the covers and ran to his father. Even at three, he feels guilty for his baby sister's death. No kid should grow up with that in their head and on their heart.

But that's what this demon is doing to us. Dr. Melrose says it's trying to break us. To not only harm us physically, but to get inside our heads and weaken our spirits.

If anyone is on the verge of breaking, it's Walter. The demon killed his wife in the diner, and now it's come back and taken his little girl. I don't know how he's coping. I'm not sure he is. And I worry about Heath. What if the demon comes back for him again?

We're going to have to take protecting ourselves more seriously, and I hate it. I hate wondering who's next.

Daniel closed the journal for a moment, holding his place with his thumb. He leaned forward in his seat and inhaled deeply as he let his mother's story sink in.

His heart ached for these people. It literally ached. His parents and his aunt. Eddie and Marion. Walter and Heath. The guilt Heath felt over his baby sister's death had never left him. Daniel knew it. The demon in the barn had known it too. *You do have a hard time following your father's orders.* It had taunted Heath, spoken those words just to dredge up all those old feelings, only to upset him.

Daniel dog-eared the page and set the book aside. He didn't feel like reading on at the moment.

He eased back into the chair and moved around to get more comfortable. He looked at his father, who continued to lie stationary in the hospital bed next to him. His eyes had fluttered open a couple of times during the night, but he had drifted back off to sleep immediately. It was a good sign, though, that he had regained consciousness and was now only sleeping. Maeve said he would be sitting up and talking very soon.

As he sat there, Daniel just stared at him, wondering how he had done it. How Pete Wester lived the life he had lived. It seemed impossible that this man, this gentle, kind-hearted man who liked to get up early and watch the sunrise, who instigated *Andy Griffith* marathons on rainy Sunday afternoons, who cracked corny dad jokes at the dinner table, had seen such darkness.

In twenty-one years, not once had that darkness slipped through.

How had he hidden it? How had he fought it?

Admiration for his father rushed over him like a warm summer shower. Dad had never wanted Daniel to live in fear. He did all he could to keep him from facing the same terrors he had faced. He had been so brave, so strong, for Daniel.

Feeling his eyes growing a bit misty, Daniel reached over and closed his fingers around his father's hand.

TWENTY-FIVE

As long as Pearl stayed in charge of the cooking, Daniel thought he would enjoy life at the Compound.

Heath brought two of her lunch plates from the café to the clinic a little before noon. One for Daniel, the other for himself. When Daniel had first removed the lid, he had been disheartened to find a large pile of salad. A very pretty, colorful salad, but still. Salad. Rabbit food, Dad always called it. Was Heath eating this too, or was this the guy's passive way of calling Daniel a sissy?

Trying to be discreet, he checked out Heath's plate. It was the same as his. A few different types of vivid leafy greens, cherry tomatoes, diced cucumbers, thinly sliced radishes, white cheese crumbles, and some kind of shredded meat that looked tasty. That was just on the surface. No telling what else Pearl had tossed in there.

"That's lamb barbacoa," Heath said, staring at him, probably sensing his reluctance. "It's freaking delicious."

"Lamb, you said?"

Heath nodded. "They had to slaughter one for the summoning ritual. We'll be eating lamb for a while, which is fine by me."

Daniel remembered the large jar of blood Justin had emptied into a silver sacrificial bowl at the barn. Poor lamb.

"Go ahead, try it."

Daniel had never eaten lamb. It wasn't commonly consumed in rural Tennessee. But he was hungry, and Heath hadn't steered him wrong yet. Daniel shifted the meat and vegetables around with his fork. He took a cautious bite.

The meat was impossibly tender, warm and smoky, with a pleasant but sharp tang of citrus. And the boring raw vegetables? They didn't taste like this on the Outside. The vegetables grown here at the Compound were so fresh, so juicy, and so richly flavorful. Each one had its own vibrant taste, and when tossed together, they were heavenly. And the tangy dressing Pearl had drizzled over the mixture was amazing by itself.

Much to Daniel's astonishment, he almost liked Pearl's salad as much as her enchiladas.

Heath stayed with him at Dad's bedside while they ate. Neither of them had much to say, but that was okay. Daniel appreciated the company, and he was too busy scarfing down the most incredible salad of his life to worry about the awkward silence.

But after a while, Heath spoke up. "They're burying Justin this afternoon."

"Where?"

"We have a, uh, a small cemetery at the edge of the property." He scooped up a large bite of salad. Before he popped it into his mouth, he added, "Mr. Smith's gonna say a few words."

"The guy that runs the store?"

Heath nodded. "Yeah. He's an ordained minister."

"Oh."

They went back to their lunch.

Daniel knew he should go to Justin's funeral. The poor guy had died trying to help Daniel find his father. At the same time, he feared leaving Dad's side. He needed to be there in case he woke up.

He knew everyone was aware of that. Surely no one would blame him. He decided to change the subject. "Have you seen Lena lately?"

Heath's left eyebrow twitched. "Um, yeah," he said, keeping his eyes on his salad. "I've been teaching her to shoot, actually. Showing her some self-defense tricks. Thought it'd be good if she knows some basic stuff before she leaves." A heavy pause. "I think she's at Geri's now. Packing."

Daniel felt his heart sink. Perhaps it was selfish, but he had hoped she would change her mind about going home. He could tell from Heath's countenance that he had been hoping for the same thing.

Daniel had mixed feelings about that. And he felt unreasonably annoyed by the fact that Heath and Lena were apparently spending so much time together without him.

"Do you think that's a good idea?" Daniel asked. "For her to leave?"

"Hell no," Heath replied hotly. "If the demon is after *you*, there's a damn good chance it may hurt Lena to screw with you."

After the things he had been reading in his mother's diary, Daniel knew Heath was right. "Did you tell her that?"

"Yeah, but I think that made it worse."

"Why?"

"Now she's really worried about her mom being on the outside alone." He slapped his fork down onto his plate, sending a tiny piece of cucumber airborne. "I don't get it. Why can't she just bring her mom here?"

"You haven't met Lena's mom."

Heath rolled his eyes. "Look, I don't care what kinda life the lady has right now. I don't care if she's a hermit with fifteen cats. If she doesn't have any skills or any experience, it doesn't matter. We can train her. You wouldn't believe what some of the strongest people here used to be like. Eddie used to be a restaurant busboy. Marion was a waitress. Vern sold insurance. And Alan, when he moved in, he was like a hundred pounds overweight with bad type 2 diabetes. Look at him now."

Daniel's brows raised in surprise.

"Anybody can change." Heath stabbed a cherry tomato with his fork and devoured it.

"Yes, but I'm not sure Mrs. Dillon would be willing to change," Daniel told him. "She's... old-fashioned. Super conservative. Image, looks. Shopping. That's all she cares about. She's a snob. The most judgmental, critical person I've ever met. And I'm telling you, she's *very* set in her ways. I don't think she'd buy into all this."

"Okay, well, let's all wait around 'til a demon is up her ass. Maybe then she'll buy it."

Daniel kept quiet after that. He stared at his salad, grinding a radish slice with his teeth.

Heath exhaled loudly. "Sorry. I guess it's not easy uprooting yourself when you've had a decent, normal life out there."

Heath wouldn't know, Daniel realized. He couldn't understand "normal" life. This separate life within the gates had been the only life he had ever known.

The guy drew in another deep breath and calmed down. "I'm sorry, man. I'll try to talk to Lena again."

Daniel forced a smile. "Thanks."

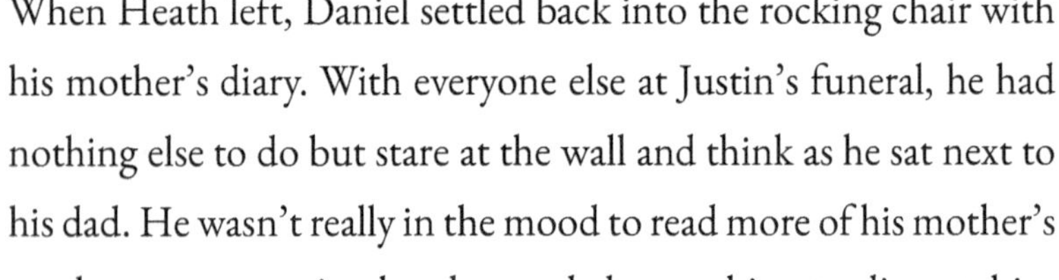

When Heath left, Daniel settled back into the rocking chair with his mother's diary. With everyone else at Justin's funeral, he had nothing else to do but stare at the wall and think as he sat next to his dad. He wasn't really in the mood to read more of his mother's unpleasant memories, but he needed something to distract him from thoughts of Lena leaving.

He picked up where he left off. Autumn of 1988, right after the death of Heath's baby sister, Abigail.

They buried her. Walter Garrison struggled with depression. The survivors kept training with Dr. Melrose.

In November, Helen's mom, Daniel's grandmother, was diagnosed with terminal cancer.

Pete graduated college at the beginning of December.

On Christmas Eve, exactly one year after their *"nothing short of magical"* first kiss, Pete asked Helen to marry him. They had a short engagement; they wanted to have the wedding before her mother passed away. They tied the knot on Valentine's Day of 1989 in her parents' front yard, on the porch, and had their first kiss as Mr. and Mrs. in the same spot where they had shared their very first kiss.

Helen's diary entries became much less frequent after that. She wrote briefly about their first home, a one-bedroom rental in Vinita, Oklahoma. She wrote when her mother died in March. But apparently, nothing else worth writing about happened until December of 1989, right before their first anniversary, when Helen learned she was pregnant.

Daniel was pleased to see that her writings became hopeful again. Her pretty, careful penmanship returned. She made lists of names she liked and doodled her favorites in the margins. Nearly all of the names were biblical, he noticed. He saw his own name coming in at third place for boys, with Aaron topping the list. For girls, she couldn't decide between Leah and Hannah.

Then in May 1990, she wrote for the first time about the land Walter Garrison owned that would someday become the Compound.

May 18, 1990.

Walter isn't just dreaming out loud anymore. He's officially opened up all those acres of farmland he inherited to the rest of us. His idea of building our own armed, demon-proof community is on the verge of becoming reality.

I think it's wonderful. I have some kind of a pioneer spirit inside me that really wants to do this. It sounds like the perfect opportunity to start over, to build a home, to raise this baby growing inside me in safety around people who love us and are going to look out for us.

A couple of the others aren't too sure about it just yet. But we all know we're stronger together, so why don't we just do it?

Daniel turned the page, curious to find out what happened next. But the rest was gone.

Except for a few blank sheets at the very end, every page from that point on had been ripped out of the diary. Only wavy shreds remained at the journal's core, tantalizing anyone who read it with the unsolvable mystery of what the pages had contained, why they had been removed, and who had been the one to remove them.

Daniel flipped carefully through the final blank pages, just to make sure each one of them was, in fact, blank.

They were.

Helen's short entry about Walter's land was the last piece of history that the diary held.

Irritated and disappointed, Daniel clapped the book shut. He felt cheated. Just when he was getting to a pivotal point of his mother's story, the part that could have filled in so many gaps, it ended.

It might not have been so upsetting if his mother had just stopped writing. If the remainder of the diary had been left blank. But the remnants of the pages that had once been there proved she had written more, and their absence left nothing but more unanswered questions.

TWENTY-SIX

Two hours later, Daniel was still theorizing about the diary's missing pages. He hadn't come close to formulating any kind of solid hypothesis. Nothing he thought of felt right. He still knew too little. He was so lost in his thoughts, he didn't hear Aunt Geri come in until she made her presence known by clearing her throat.

His body jerked in surprise, startled by the sound. He glanced up and found his aunt standing at the foot of Dad's bed. She was all dressed up, at least for Aunt Geri. She had traded her usual baggy layers of plaid work shirts and jeans for loose-fitting black slacks, scuffed-up black loafers, and a crisp black button-down with a starchy-looking pointed collar, two sizes too big. She'd pushed the sleeves of the shirt up to her elbows. Her cheeks were flushed and damp, and her thick, silver-streaked dark bangs clumped together, soaked with sweat.

"Didn't mean to frighten you," she told him. "You looked like you were someplace else."

"I guess I was," he replied.

Aunt Geri held two stainless steel tumblers with attached lids and straws in her hands. "I brought you some coffee," she said, extending one of the tumblers toward him. He took it. "I'm no damn barista, but it's iced. It's hotter than blue blazes out there."

"Thank you."

"Sure thing." Aunt Geri exhaled loudly as she sank into the empty chair next to Daniel. She took a sip from her tumbler and stared at Dad. "How's he been? Any changes?"

Daniel shook his head. "Just sleeping."

She nodded.

They sat in silence for a while.

Daniel tasted his iced coffee. It wasn't too bad. But yeah, Aunt Geri was definitely no barista.

"Well, I just came from the funeral," she told him. "It was... rough." She kept her eyes fixed ahead of her, on the hospital bed. "Claudia and little Riley..." She sighed. She leaned forward, propping her elbows on her knees, letting her shoulders drop. "It's been a long time since we buried one of our own, but I'm just so damn tired of going to fucking funerals."

Daniel was pretty sure he'd read the same line from his mother's diary. He stared at her slumped shoulders in sympathy. Her friend Ted from the diner. Lavinia and Abigail Garrison. Jedediah Crider. Her infant nephew, Aaron. Her sister-in-law, Daniel's mother. Probably countless others. Aunt Geri had certainly attended her fair share of funerals.

She took a drink from her tumbler. Daniel suddenly wondered if her cup contained something stronger than coffee. Like whiskey. "But," Aunt Geri breathed, "as awful as it sounds, we're lucky to have buried only *one* person today."

"That's true, I guess."

After a few moments passed, Aunt Geri straightened and sat upright in her seat. She wiped her sweaty bangs off of her forehead and turned to Daniel, locking eyes with him for the first time. "I need to apologize to you. I'm sorry I wasn't truthful about the Cross of Silvanus. I knew exactly what that damn thing was the second I laid eyes on it, and I knew if I told you that, you'd go out and do exactly what you did. So, I lied. Right to your face." She frowned. "I'm so sorry for that."

"It's okay."

"No, it's not. I was scared as hell, I wasn't thinking straight, but that's no excuse. I broke your trust."

Her uncannily familiar blue eyes bored into him, glistening with dampness as she spoke. Her sincerity unwound the knot in his stomach that had been there since he'd seen her inexplicably cradling the Cross. Since she'd stormed into the cabin later and shouted at him for his foolish actions.

"And I underestimated you." She blinked hard, forcing away the wetness. "Heath told me how you fought the demon's temptations. All the things it offered you. How you didn't give in. I couldn't believe it. You heard what I said about Silvanus; he couldn't withstand the demons at all." She paused. "You're strong, Daniel."

He could see the adoration, the wonder, building in his aunt's gaze. It was too much. He looked away.

"I am so proud of you. Your dad, he's gonna be so proud, too."

"Thank you, Aunt Geri," Daniel replied timidly, staring at the floor tiles. "That means a lot to me."

The room felt uncomfortably warm now. He took a drink from the tumbler and let the frosty, bitter beverage wash over his dry tongue.

Neither of them spoke again for a while. They sat in companionable silence, watching the rise and fall of Dad's chest as he slept.

"Did you- were you and my mom close?" Daniel heard himself ask. The question probably seemed left-field to Aunt Geri, but Daniel's thoughts kept going back to the missing pages of his mother's diary.

Aunt Geri crossed her legs. "We were."

"I found her diary. In the box from Dad."

Her eyes widened, but she didn't say anything.

"I've been reading through it." He reached over to the bedside table where the leather journal lay. He picked it up. "My whole life, Dad has never talked about her much at all. It's been... really great to read her writing."

"I-I can imagine."

"The thing is, the last few pages are missing. Somebody tore them out." He opened the book and showed her the ripped edges that remained after his mother's final entry. "It feels important."

Her brow furrowed in response to this. "What the hell?"

"Do you know anything about this? Could *she* have done it?"

"Well, I mean, yeah. It was her personal diary. But I'm with you, it does feel important."

"What can you tell me about her? What was she like?"

Aunt Geri drew in a deep breath. She got a far-away look in her eyes as she sat there, taking her time before she responded.

"Your mother was the kindest person I've ever known," she finally told him, a small smile forming on her lips. "She always accepted me, right from the start, even though she could tell I was... different." Aunt Geri glanced away as she said it.

Different. The word was loaded.

Daniel didn't want to make assumptions, but he thought he understood the inference. Her guarded body language and avoidance of eye contact told him she was uncomfortable discussing this, so he kept his questions to himself and sat quietly, giving her time to speak again when she was ready.

"It was the eighties," Aunt Geri went on, still looking away. "A lot of people, well, they weren't so kind. But Helen was always my friend."

His heart swelled at the sentiment. Of all the things Aunt Geri could have said about his mother, she chose to speak of her kindness. That choice contained so much information, so much profound truth. How you treated others, how you made them feel, that's all that mattered in the end.

"She was a wonderful mother," Aunt Geri continued. "She went to college, you know, she got her education. She was smart as a whip and could've done anything she wanted. And what she wanted, more than anything, was to be a mother. She loved you so damn much, Daniel. You were everything to her. Especially after the loss of your brother."

He felt a lump growing in his throat. It would have been easier, he thought, if Aunt Geri had nothing nice to say about her, if the diary had revealed a cruel, selfish, manipulative young woman, someone slightly more deserving of her fate. The reality was too unfair. Abalaroth had put Daniel's kind, admirable, loving mother through so much heartache, then taken her life, tearing her from the child she'd wanted so badly, the child who needed her.

He'd longed for her as far back as he could remember. The loss had hit him for the first time in kindergarten, when he realized he was the only one in his class without a mommy. He didn't understand it. He'd needed her then. He ached with grief now.

Daniel became aware of his pounding pulse. His ears roared as he began to realize just how much he loathed Abalaroth for killing his mother.

"I know Aaron was born in July 1990," Daniel forced out. His dead brother's name felt strange and foreign on his lips. "The last entry in the diary was in May, just two months before that. She talked about Mr. Garrison wanting the survivors to move to the farmland he'd inherited. She sounded upbeat and excited. And that's it. Whatever happened after that is missing."

"Hmm. Well, I remember that summer," Aunt Geri said. "Just weeks before Aaron was born, we visited the Garrison farm and chose where we wanted to build. We picked out the spot for the cabin. We made plans. But we didn't have the time or the resources to get this place up and running as fast as we needed to. We were still working regular jobs then, just to pay rent and eat. And Helen was nine months pregnant, she couldn't do too much. It was a rocky start. Then, of course, Aaron came." She paused. "And Abalaroth found him."

Daniel nodded.

Aunt Geri was quiet for a moment, lost in thought. "I don't know, hon. Helen... well, she struggled after that. Understandably, of course. It was a dark time." A beat. "Maybe she wrote about it all to help her process things, and maybe what she wrote was *too* dark. Maybe she felt ashamed and ripped it out so nobody would ever find it."

This was a logical conclusion. He decided this was probably the case.

The silence returned.

Aunt Geri left.

Alone at Dad's bedside once again, Daniel's thoughts obsessively returned to his mother's diary. Aunt Geri's idea of a distraught, grieving Helen destroying her own dark, cathartic writing made sense, but Daniel couldn't shake the feeling that there had been more to it than that.

His mother had lived for two more years after writing that hopeful entry about Walter's farmland. *Two years.* What had happened from 1990 to 1992? There wasn't enough space in the back of the diary to contain regular entries for two whole years. And there were still a handful of blank pages at the end. At what point in that time frame had she stopped writing?

Eventually, he went back and reread her earlier entries to look for clues. A few things stood out to him, but it felt like he was reaching too hard and taking things out of context.

He flipped through and found April 1988. He read everything she wrote about the diner over and over again until her words didn't even look like words anymore. Maybe Aunt Geri's conclusion was the right one after all.

"Daniel."

At the sound of his name, he glanced up from the diary.

No one was there.

Maeve was on the other side of the clinic with her back to him, jotting down notes in a patient file. She had not spoken to him.

Daniel's heart kicked in his chest.

Dad.

He looked over at the bed. At his father. His blue eyes were open and staring at him.

TWENTY-SEVEN

"**D**AD!" DANIEL LEANED FORWARD excitedly. "How-how are you feeling?"

Slowly, Dad's lips curved into a little smile. His voice came out raspier than usual as he gave his one-word response: "Hungry."

Daniel laughed. "I bet you are."

Dad's smile widened as he reached for his son's hand. Daniel took it gently, cautiously, afraid he would somehow hurt him. He scooted to the edge of his seat to get closer to his father.

"Are you hurting a lot?"

"Not too bad." Probably a lie. But he did have morphine pumping through him, so maybe it wasn't.

It might have been too soon, but Daniel had to ask him, "Do you remember what happened?"

He blinked slowly. "Yes. I remember."

"Well, um, you're safe now."

Dad's eyes widened with panic as they darted around, taking in the IV lines, the hospital bed, the blue privacy curtains.

"It's okay. We're at the Compound."

Daniel watched his father's panic dwindling, questions forming. "Th-this place? The Compound?"

He nodded. "I promise. They've gotten pretty fancy since you left."

Dad peered around in astonishment at their hospital-like surroundings then returned his attention to his son. "You did it, then." He smiled. Gave Daniel's hand a weak squeeze. "Good boy."

Looking at his father now, fully awake, Daniel thought he had aged a lot in a week. His hair seemed grayer, his forehead more wrinkled, his eyes more tired. But his smile was the same.

Daniel smiled back. Before either of them could speak again, he heard the clacking of high heels against the clinic floor. Maeve slid the curtain aside and hurried to Dad.

"Look who decided to wake up," Maeve said, smiling brightly. "How are you feeling?"

"Very hungry," Dad repeated.

Daniel grinned. "He's already back to normal."

Maeve let out a pleasant laugh.

"This is Miss Maeve, Dad. She's been taking great care of you."

"Thank you, Maeve."

"Of course! Oh, this is wonderful!" she exclaimed. Her eyes sparkled as they darted from Dad's face to the water pitcher on his bedside table. "Here. Let's try drinking some water." She poured some into a glass and popped a straw in for him. "I'm going to raise your head up a bit." She pressed a button on the bed and slowly elevated Dad's upper body about forty-five degrees.

"Are you alright?" Maeve asked.

Dad grimaced slightly but nodded.

Daniel watched anxiously to see what happened next. Though no one had talked about it, they all knew Dad might be paralyzed. Now was the moment of truth.

Maeve held onto the glass. She didn't make herself obvious, but she was waiting to see if he could reach out to take it from her. Both she and Daniel held their breath as they watched him.

Sluggishly, Dad lifted his left arm and grasped the glass.

Daniel sighed with relief. Dad's arm muscles were weak, but he could at least move them.

Maeve couldn't hide her happiness from her voice. "Daniel, dear, would you help your father with the water? I'm going to listen to him swallow."

Without hesitation, he hopped up from his seat and assisted Dad in raising the straw to his lips. Maeve slipped the earpieces of her stethoscope into her ears and placed the diaphragm on Dad's throat.

He gulped down the water fervently. He didn't cough or gurgle or anything, so Daniel guessed that was a good sign.

Maeve nodded as she removed the stethoscope. "Perfect. I think you're safe to try to eat something. I'm going to let Geri and the others know that you're awake. And I'm sure Pearl will be delighted to whip you up something special."

"Pearl?" Dad's eyes brightened as he said her name. "Pearl Olivares?"

"Mm-hmm."

"Oh boy. Does she still make those enchiladas?"

"Indeed she does. But I was going to suggest some bone broth. Why don't we try that out first?"

"*First,*" Dad echoed the word with a mischievous grin. "Bone broth appetizer. Then enchiladas."

Maeve shook her head, smiling. "We'll see." She started to leave, then halted. She turned to him with her warmest smile yet. "Welcome back, Pete."

Dad tolerated the bone broth well enough that Maeve gave in to his demands. Pearl was more than happy to declare Friday night Enchilada Night 2.0. To Daniel, this batch was even tastier than the first. With his father awake and safe at his side, he could relax and enjoy the meal properly.

It seemed like half the Compound stopped by to visit Dad that evening. Maeve hadn't liked the idea at first, but when she saw how much the familiar faces perked him up, she stepped back and let him enjoy it. He had one joyful reunion after another. Any hard feelings anyone held against him for leaving all those years ago evaporated as they welcomed him back. Hearing the story of his rescue, seeing his smiles and his laughter, and just being around his positive presence were what the people needed that night after Justin's funeral.

And their affectionate embraces were exactly what Dad needed, too.

Especially one in particular.

When Geri Wester stepped into the clinic, everyone grew quiet. Daniel could tell his aunt was nervous as she approached his bed. She advanced slowly, wearing an uncertain expression across her features.

With the two Wester siblings now in the same room, side by side, Daniel realized for the first time just how much they truly favored. They had matching noses, matching smiles with the same fine wrinkles at the corners. And they shared the exact same clear blue eyes, the ones Daniel had inherited.

Now at the bedside, Aunt Geri looked down at her brother with tears in her eyes.

Dad mirrored her look.

Without saying a word, they pulled one another into a tight embrace. They held each other for a long time, exchanging a few muffled words that no one else could make out.

When they let go, Aunt Geri stood upright and wiped her wet face with the back of her hand. "Damn you, Pete," she exhale-laughed. "It's so good to see you again."

"You too," Dad said in a broken voice. He dabbed at his own watery eyes. His gaze moved across the clinic, over the faces of the people gathered around him. "It's so wonderful to be back here. Thank you all for making me feel at home again. And for taking such good care of my son."

Daniel glanced around the room and caught several people staring at him. Heath was one of them. He acknowledged Daniel with a nod. Zarah Crider was another. She flashed him a warm smile.

"You all risked everything by what you did for me this week," Dad said. He strained his voice so they could all hear him. "I just want to tell you how grateful I am."

Daniel looked at Lena, who was sitting next to him. He saw a tear slip down her cheek. She'd always been a contagious crier. Not many people in the room *weren't* shedding a few happy tears right now. Lena felt his gaze upon her and glanced at him. She managed a shaky smile.

"Every single one of you," Dad went on. "Thank you."

One by one, the crowd filed by to say goodnight to Dad until only Geri, Lena, and Maeve remained in the clinic with Dad and Daniel. As soon as everyone else left, Maeve left them alone to get back to her work, whatever that was. Probably just an excuse to give them some privacy, which was appreciated.

A slightly awkward silence fell over them.

Aunt Geri shifted her weight around and shoved her hands in her pockets. "You know, Pete," she said, "you coulda just quietly showed up here any time. We would've taken you back. You didn't have to have such a dramatic return."

Dad let out a little chuckle. "It was rather dramatic, wasn't it?"

Aunt Geri grinned and settled into the chair at his bedside. "Well," she sighed. "It looks like you're stuck with us now. It's too risky to go back out there."

Daniel turned to Lena when she said that. She didn't look back at him.

"It is," Dad agreed. A wistful smile formed upon his lips. "Plus, I'm kind of homeless."

"No way. You always have a home here, with me," Aunt Geri told him. She cast a meaningful glance at Daniel, then Lena. "All of you."

Daniel's mouth suddenly felt dry. "Thank you," he heard himself say. And as he said it, he knew this was home now.

His family was here. His only blood relatives. New friends. Dozens of people waiting to get to know him better, people who would protect him and continue to teach him how to protect himself. What did he have outside of those gates anymore?

Unacknowledged job applications. A handful of job interviews from which he'd never received a callback. Former acquaintances and school friends who'd moved on with their lives.

There was nothing in Crofton for Daniel.

Except for, probably, a few demons who were lingering there in case he returned.

And Lena, if she really was going to leave.

Everyone's eyes now seemed to be upon her. Daniel could tell the attention made her uncomfortable, but he didn't look away. He studied her as she looked down, wringing her hands.

"Geri," she said quietly. "I, um, I am so thankful for everything that you've done for us while we've been here. You made us both feel at home from the start."

Aunt Geri gave her an affectionate smile.

"And you helped us when we didn't know what in the world to do." Lena sighed. "But I... I can't stay here."

Daniel felt his stomach turn as his hopes crashed once again.

"Lena, I know you're grown," Dad told her. "You're old enough and mature enough to decide what you want for yourself. But you've seen what's really out there now. It isn't safe."

"That's why I have to go. My mom is still out there. In Crofton. She doesn't have anybody else but me. I need to be there for her." She paused. "And I have a job. And an apartment." She stopped again, thinking. "Maybe when my lease ends, I'll reconsider..." She trailed off. When she spoke again, she sounded more focused and determined. "But for now, I know I have to go back home."

Daniel glanced up at his aunt, who was already staring at him. He blinked and looked away.

"My bags are packed," Lena said, her voice faltering. "I'll leave in the morning."

"Well, if you do go," Aunt Geri spoke up, emphasizing the word *if*, despite Lena's clear resolution, "promise us all that you'll be careful. I know Heath's been teaching you some self-defense stuff. Keep yourself armed. And wear the necklace Zarah gave you."

Daniel spotted the black onyx stone suspended against Lena's chest. Aunt Geri still wore hers as well. The two of them had remained unharmed, so perhaps the stones really did hold some protective power.

"I will," Lena promised. She glanced at Daniel, but he turned away. She wanted him to say something, to approve her decision or perhaps even protest her departure, but he had nothing to say to her. "Well, um, it's a long drive tomorrow. I better go get some sleep." She rose from her seat and went to Dad, leaned over, and pulled him into a hug. "Goodnight."

"Goodnight, sweetie," Dad told her, giving her a fatherly kiss on the forehead. She squeezed him tighter before she let go.

"You need to rest too," Lena told Dad firmly as she straightened. She looked at Aunt Geri. Then Daniel. "Goodnight." She gave him an unnatural, strained smile, then she was gone.

Both his father and his aunt stared holes in Daniel the second she disappeared.

"What?" Daniel spat out at them, embarrassed.

"Are you not gonna try to talk some damn sense into her?" Aunt Geri asked, incredulous.

"I already tried. She won't listen."

"Well, try again," Aunt Geri told him fiercely. "We can't let her go. She's in danger as soon as she steps outside these gates."

"Your aunt's right," Dad agreed.

Daniel hung his head. "I know."

The clinic went silent.

Aunt Geri sighed loudly. "Well. It's late. You've been through a lot today, Pete. I'm gonna head out too, let you get some rest. Can I get anything for either of you before I go?"

"No, but thanks," Dad said. A tired smile curved his lips. "For everything."

"Don't mention it. I'll check on you first thing in the morning." Aunt Geri patted him on the shoulder. Then, a little unexpectedly, she kissed him on the cheek. "I am so glad to have you back, Pete. This is where you belong."

She left.

They were alone.

Daniel looked at him. The man just sat there in the hospital bed, staring down at the white woven blanket spread across his lap. He was fiddling with the blanket's hem. Avoiding Daniel's eyes.

It suddenly felt awkward between them. A new, almost palpable tension filled the space they shared. Dad had made amends with everyone else, with all the people from his past who had lined up to see him. Now it was just the two of them, and there was a lot to say.

But neither of them wanted to say it.

Daniel's stomach fluttered nervously as he tried to decide how to start the conversation they needed to have. Where should he begin? What point in Dad's lifetime of secrets should he address first? The diner massacre? Mom's death? The way he had irresponsibly fled the safety of the Compound with a six-month-old infant in 1992? How that reckless decision had eventually led to the events of the past few days?

The air-conditioned medical clinic was chilly, but a jolt of anger heated Daniel's blood. When his father was missing, he had been rightfully worried about his condition, frightened for his safety. Now that he was here, right here in front of him, safe and sound, talking and smiling and making jokes with everyone, Daniel could acknowledge the anger that had been mounting within him for days. He'd been marinating in resentment for a while now, since he'd first opened the box and discovered his reality was a lie.

The man before him no longer felt like *Dad*. The guy in the hospital bed was a stranger.

This was Pete Wester, survivor of the Tulsa diner massacre, founding member of the Compound, retired demon hunter, collector of magical artifacts. The Pete Wester *he* knew- the humble, quiet man who worked at a lumber mill, went to church, made meatloaves and peach cobblers, raised his son on his own with little external support- that guy was dead. Or had never existed. *That* Pete Wester had always been a façade.

Daniel trembled as he bit back the anger.

How had Pete managed to continue his act day after day with no slip-ups for twenty-one years? How had he kept the truth buried for so long? He could never trust his father again.

He was hot now, ready to explode.

Unload on the guy, let him have it.

Or get up and leave.

Daniel wavered between these two options. His pulse throbbed in his ears as he moved his dry tongue and parted his lips to say something.

But Pete spoke first.

His voice was barely more than a whisper when he choked out, "I'm sorry, Daniel."

TWENTY-EIGHT

For what? A lifetime of lies and secrets? Putting his only child at risk for twenty-one years? Isolating him from his aunt? Making him feel responsible for Justin Foster's death when there was no one to blame but Dad?

His father looked up from the blanket that covered him, not bothering to wipe away the tears that flowed freely from his eyes. His chin quivered as he said, "I am so sorry."

Daniel felt his anger cooling as he studied his father's haunted eyes. The depths of sorrow and regret stared back at him.

Dad buried his face in his hands and wept.

Daniel watched the man's shoulders shake as he sobbed. He didn't know what to do. He'd never seen him, or anyone for that matter, in such a state. He racked his brain for something he could say to make it stop, but he already knew there was no such thing. As painful as his father's breakdown was to witness, Daniel didn't think it *should* be stopped. He had the feeling Dad needed this, that maybe he was unleashing twenty-one years of pent-up emotions.

Daniel leaned forward, propped his elbows on his knees, and sat next to his father in silence, waiting for it to end.

Eventually, it did.

Dad flopped his head into the pillow behind him and began wiping his face with his palms. He released a shaky sigh. "I can't imagine what this has been like for you, son."

Daniel struggled to swallow. It felt like a golf ball had lodged itself inside his throat.

"I-I just... I never wanted things to end up like this. I thought it'd be different. I'd hoped it would." He shook his head and sighed again. "I'm sorry I didn't tell you about all this sooner." He gestured at the clinic around them, but Daniel knew what he meant. "I'm sorry you had the burden of finding me on your shoulders. I never meant for that to happen. At all."

"Wh-what *did* happen? Back home, in the trailer?"

Dad was quiet for what felt like several minutes. "Sunday night... I stayed up all night. Praying and reading the Bible. I even fasted." He scoffed. "Lotta good that did me. I knew the demon was coming back, and I was begging God for help, searching for an answer in the scriptures. And then... there it was. The demon. Inside our home. He zapped me out of there, somehow. I don't know. I blacked out and woke up in a strange cabin."

"Why weren't you wearing the amulet? If you *knew* that thing was coming back, why didn't you put out salt? Or warding sigils?"

A proud smile upturned Dad's lips. "I see you've learned a lot."

Daniel found this response deeply irritating, particularly the smile. "You didn't answer me. What's your excuse for not protecting us?"

Dad's smile vanished, instantly replaced by pain. Daniel's words had struck a soft spot. "The amulet was always for you, Daniel," he said, "to protect you when the time came. And I put salt above your bedroom door and windows. I carved warding sigils into their frames while you were still in diapers."

"Why didn't you try to protect yourself?"

"Because… my time was up."

"What the hell does that mean?"

Dad glanced away and focused on the water pitcher atop the bedside table. "The demon gave me twenty-one years." His voice faltered. "Twenty-one years with you. Twenty-one years of guaranteed protection."

Daniel's stomach seemed to drop into his pelvis. "In exchange for…?"

"Me." Dad didn't look at him. "My soul."

Aunt Geri's Faustian bargain theory had been correct after all. "Why… why would you do something so stupid?" The question wasn't adequate, but it was the best Daniel could do.

"I did it for you, Daniel. I couldn't lose you." Dad looked at him now, fresh tears pooling in his eyes. Maeve was going to need to increase his intravenous fluids. "I don't know what all Geri's told you, but when you were a baby, you got sick, and we had to take you to the hospital."

Daniel's heart raced as he listened, eager to finally hear Dad's version of this story.

"It was the first time in months that we'd left this place, the Compound. We were terrified. You'd just been admitted and moved to a private room on the pediatric ward. Your mother and I were there with you, next to your little bassinet, when there was a knock on the door. We thought it was just another nurse coming to check on you. But it was that monster, all smug and proud of himself. He waltzed in and raised his arm up at you. Then your mother jumped in front of the bassinet to save you." A pause. "He killed her. Instantly."

The golf ball in Daniel's throat seemed to have expanded in size.

He expected his father to cry again now, but he spoke with a strange, cool detachment now as he told his story. A coping mechanism, probably. The only way he could relay the horrible details.

"I couldn't lose you, Daniel," he repeated. "I couldn't. I got that demon to talk to me, to listen. I begged him to spare you. We had lost so many people already. I'd just been blindsided. I'd lost Helen out of nowhere."

He paused for a few seconds, collecting his thoughts.

Daniel cut in, "*Aaron.*"

Mentioning his deceased brother's name didn't surprise Dad. He merely nodded. "I could not, as a parent, lose another child. I would rather die myself." He drew in a deep breath and went on. "So, the demon made an offer. He agreed to leave the two of us alone for twenty-one years. We could have a life together. You could grow up. He promised they wouldn't touch you, for over two decades. Then he'd be back."

Daniel stared at him. "For your soul."

"I was so desperate to save you, I barely hesitated. I took his offer. Twenty-one years sounded like a lifetime. It seemed so far away. I figured that was plenty of time to find a way out of the pact."

"But why did you leave the Compound? You *really* trusted the demon's word?"

"Your mom... she was... I loved her more than I-" He broke off, his eyes welling with tears again. "Maybe I went a little insane with grief, but I couldn't stay at the Compound. Everywhere I looked, I saw Helen. The fruit trees she planted. The cedar boxes she wanted for her first garden. That place was our dream. We'd built it together. And the cabin... that was *our* place, for our new, safe life together. I couldn't be there without her."

Daniel felt his own eyes growing misty. Conversations about his mother were so rare, it shocked him to see how deeply his dad still cared about her. He had always wondered why Dad didn't speak of her, but now he realized it was simply agony for the man.

"And I watched the way Walter was with Heath," Dad continued, dabbing at his eyes with the back of his hand. "Walter... his paranoia sort of... infected Heath. He was so depressed after losing his wife and his daughter, so angry and afraid. He put all that on his son. Heath never got to be a kid. I mean, at five, the poor boy carried around his own iron knife. I remember he used to go around drawing warding sigils on everything. He was just so scared all the time. Always on alert."

Daniel's chest ached at this. He liked Heath. It saddened him to imagine this terrified miniature version of his new friend.

"I didn't want that for you. And I knew, if we stayed at the Compound, that's how your childhood was gonna be."

From everything he had witnessed, Daniel agreed this would likely have been the case. He could kind of understand his father's motives now. But still. "In twenty-one years, you never mentioned *any* of this to me."

"How could I? I kept waiting for the right time to bring it up, but there was never a right time."

Daniel nearly laughed. They could have been discussing sex. That's what normal fathers struggled to find the *right* time to have conversations about. The birds and the bees. Or *just saying no* to drugs. Definitely not demons.

"When we first moved to Tennessee, I didn't completely trust the demon. I took every precaution I knew of. I got a secluded place, buried iron nails in each corner of the property. I put up warding. I got all the books I could find. I studied and researched more than I ever have before." He paused. "The years went by, and nothing happened. What I was doing was working, or the demon was true to its word. Or a little of both, maybe. Anyway, everything was good. We were living a normal life. I started focusing less on pure survival and more on ways to get out of the pact I made, to save my soul. Religion seemed the obvious place to start."

That did seem like a somewhat logical train of thought, Daniel had to admit.

"I thought maybe the Christians were right, that maybe Jesus could be my salvation. I really thought religion could be the solution. So I buried myself in it."

All those years of faithful church attendance, of private Bible study at home. It made sense.

"I thought that surely, if there was *this* much evil, there had to be a good side too. There had to be a balance to the world. Yin and yang and all that." Dad hung his head. "I was a fool." His voice cracked, threatening tears again. "I was a damn fool."

Daniel's shoulders sagged. He sat quietly, waiting for his father to go on. It seemed like hours before he did.

"It was all a waste of time. The only thing I found in religion was a bunch of self-righteous hypocrites who twisted the Bible to suit their own agendas. They were loud, but their God was always silent. I wanted to believe so badly, I tried so hard to believe... but... there is no good side." Dad's piercing blue eyes bored into him. "There's nothing but darkness, Daniel."

The words sent a shiver down Daniel's spine.

No good side.

Nothing but darkness.

If that was true, they had no hope.

Even as a young kid, Daniel had been too rational to put any stock into religion. He'd picked apart the gaping doctrinal holes in their pastor's sermons as he listened to them. He always had questions none of his Sunday School teachers or church leaders could answer. He had never placed any hope in the faith of his father.

Despite all this, he found the man's words deeply upsetting.

As silly as it probably was, he realized he'd been secretly hoping for a good side, too. He had since he'd first spoken with his aunt.

But some part of him had known all along that any existing good side wasn't very *good* if it continually allowed the murder of so many innocent people, even babies in their cribs, without any attempts at divine intervention.

"Are you sure about that?" The question surprised Daniel as it came from his own mouth. "No good side? I mean, your twenty-one years are up, and here you are. Alive and safe. You got away from the demon. Even if the *good side* is just... *us,* isn't that enough?"

A smile tugged at the corners of Pete's lips. "I think so."

Daniel felt his head bobbing up and down affirmatively. "You got away. The demon can't get in here, right? This is your way out of your pact. As long as you stay here, you're saved."

"I believe you're right, son. I hope you are, anyway. Though the demons won't be happy about that. I'm afraid we've really riled them up. We're all gonna have to be extra careful."

Daniel gnawed on his bottom lip. He had already been thinking about this.

"Which is why Lena absolutely cannot go back to Crofton tomorrow," Dad said.

Daniel sighed. "How can we stop her, Dad? She's worried about her mother."

"I know. And she probably should be. If the demons can't touch us in here, then going after people we care about on the outside to punish us, provoke us, get us to leave... that's bound to be their next move."

"What can we do? Do you think we could get Carol here?"

Dad's forehead puckered in response.

Daniel bit back laughter.

"I... I know how Carol is," Dad said delicately. "Bringing her here would be something else."

"I know. But what are our options?"

"I don't know. I think I'll need to sleep on it."

As that remark sank in, it occurred to Daniel that his father did look exceptionally sluggish and drained. Maybe all the visitors and this heavy conversation had been too much for him. He was recovering from a brush with death and could still have complications at any time. Daniel felt a stab of guilt for pressing him for answers. He should've waited until he had regained more strength.

"Of course. I'll let you get some rest."

He rose from the rocking chair, reclined the head of the hospital bed, then rearranged pillows and blankets until his father felt comfortable.

"Thank you." Dad gave him a weak pat on his forearm. "Goodnight, son."

"Goodnight, Dad."

His drooping eyelids closed. He was snoring in under a minute.

Daniel, however, wouldn't sleep. He didn't even consider trying. He sat in the rocker next to the bed and glided back and forth, back and forth, back and forth, thinking about Lena.

What if she *really* left? What if he couldn't stop her?

She would go back to her apartment, back to work. Even if the hospital decided to terminate her employment due to her absences, she was a registered nurse. She would find another job quickly.

The lack of cellular service at the Compound would cut off all communication between the two of them, for good. If Abalaroth or one of his minions didn't attack her immediately, she would move on with her life. No matter her fate, Daniel would have to move on without her.

He couldn't imagine being separated from her. They had always been together, since befriending one another in elementary school. Throughout every stage of life thus far, she was there, facing it with him, his closest companion. Maybe it was an unhealthy codependency, but he truly couldn't picture a future without her in it.

How could she leave?

Daniel felt sick. This couldn't be happening.

The more he thought about it, the more out of character this move seemed for her. Lena had always been faithful to him and his dad. They were her family as much as her terrible mother was. Hadn't she just blown off a week at her new job to go with him across state lines, in search of his missing father? She hadn't thought about herself at all during that time. She dropped everything to help him, to support him, without hesitation.

That's how she was. That was Lena Dillon.

Maybe he was being a selfish ass. Lena was capable of making her own decisions, and she deserved to live a normal life with a normal occupation in a normal town far away from him. She was the most intelligent, resilient, and determined person he knew. She would take the knowledge they had gained at the Compound and put it to use without missing a thing. She would find some protective black onyx jewelry for her mother. She would carve sigils in their door frames. She would take self-defense classes. Stock up on salt and iron weapons. She would train and practice with fierce resolve until she was a strong opponent to any demons that came calling.

He knew this was true. Maybe he should have left it at that.

But sometime around midnight, he decided there was more to this. Lena was too reasonable, too rational to leave now. She'd seen firsthand the dangers that existed outside the Compound. Something about this didn't feel right to him. He hadn't even seen much of her the last couple of days. What exactly had she been doing? They'd barely spoken.

Daniel jerked the rocking chair to a halt. He glanced at his father. He slept deeply, mouth open, snoring softly.

Careful not to make a sound, Daniel stood from his seat and left the clinic.

TWENTY-NINE

Aunt Geri's cabin was dark. As Daniel slipped inside the front door, navigating the furniture in the tiny, shadowy space, he banged his shin on the coffee table. He cursed as the shocking pain shot up his leg, radiating into his hip.

The wooden plank floor squeaked. He wasn't sure if he had made the sound or if someone else had entered the room.

Something poked the center of his back. Something cold and hard.

The barrel of a gun.

Terror coursed hot throughout him, dousing him instantly in a sickly sweat. The temperature of the medallion stayed neutral against his chest, letting him know this armed threat was not demonic in nature.

"Daniel?"

"Yes!" He sighed with relief. "Lena, it's me!"

The pressure of the gun against his back eased, and he whipped around to face her.

"Daniel, what the hell are you doing here?" she demanded. It was too dark to see her face, but she sounded furious. "I thought you were staying at the clinic! I almost shot you!"

He swallowed hard. "What're you doing with a gun?"

"Heath gave it to me. He's been teaching me to shoot."

Right. He flushed with irritation. He'd barely seen Lena because she was spending so much time with Heath.

"I have to be able to protect myself when I go back home."

"Well, you're safe in here now. Put it away. Please."

"Why the hell did you sneak in here? In the middle of the night, in the dark?"

"I-I wasn't sneaking. I'm sorry I scared you-"

"I almost shot you!"

"Shh, you'll wake up Aunt Geri," he whispered. "Look, I came here to talk to you."

"At midnight?"

"Something told me you'd be up. Come on. Let's go outside."

They moved quietly together across the living area, out the front door, and onto Aunt Geri's front porch. Daniel eased the door shut behind them. Lena descended the porch steps, the outline of a small revolver now visible in her hands. She sat down on the bottom step and placed the weapon on the ground before her.

The night air was crisp and cool and healing after the terrifying moment in the cabin. Daniel followed Lena down the steps and sank onto the bottom one next to her. He glanced at her, her features illumined by the whitish moonlight.

He was surprised to find mascara smeared around puffy, red eyes. Blackish streaks stained her cheeks. Her hair was a wild, luminescent, silvery mane framing her face. A few strands clung to her cheeks, damp and sticky from tears.

"Lena." His voice came out quiet, strange. "What's wro-"

Before he could even finish his question, her bottom lip began to quiver. Tears formed in her eyes.

"Lena," he repeated, now deeply concerned. He scooted a bit closer to her. "Hey. What is it?"

She shook her head as fresh tears spilled down her cheeks.

"Tell me what's wrong."

She released a shaky sigh. "I'm sorry, I'm just so... on edge. I can't calm down. I can't- I can't sleep, because whenever I do, I have these nightmares. About the demon. Abalaroth." Her voice dropped to a near-whisper as she said the name, as though she were trying to thwart eavesdroppers. "I should've told you. He-he's been coming to me in my dreams, telling me to... do things."

"What things?"

She covered her face with her hands. "I am so sorry, Daniel. I am so, so sorry."

His stomach churned uncomfortably as he asked, "For what?"

"He told me to destroy the final pages of your mom's journal. He didn't want you to know what was at the end."

His heart lurched. "*You* ripped out the pages?"

"He said he would kill my mom if I didn't. That he'd..." Her jaw shook violently as she paused. "'Slice open her belly and tie her guts into a pretty little bow for me, like... like they did to Mr. Darcy'." Her voice shattered into an uncontrollable, heart-wrenching sob.

Daniel's breath snagged sharply in his throat. The stars overhead suddenly seemed to be spinning. "You- you don't know that's true," he offered. "You know they lie."

She ignored his comment and managed to choke out, "I was so terrified, Daniel, I just tore out the pages and burned them in Geri's fireplace. I was such a fucking idiot. I didn't even look at what was on them. I'm so sorry."

"It's okay-"

"No, I should have read them first. Whatever your mother wrote was obviously something important that the demon doesn't want you to know about."

"We'll figure it out. Maybe Dad knows what those pages said."

"Maybe. But I *have* to go. I have to get away from you, Daniel, before I do anything else stupid and dangerous. Abalaroth is in my head, and I'm not myself. I mean, for Christ's sake, I almost shot you!"

"That's why I came here to talk to you. You can't leave, not now."

"Oh! So you *do* care that I'm leaving?" she spat out bitterly.

"*What?*"

She sniffled. "You haven't said one word to me about it, not since we got back with your dad. You've barely even talked to me."

"Uh, because I haven't seen you?"

"What are you talking about?"

"Lena, I haven't left Dad's side. I've been sitting there, in the clinic, waiting for him to wake up for the last day and a half. If you wanted to talk to me, you should've come by the clinic and told me that. But instead, you've been too busy keeping secrets and running around with Heath." He felt his skin burning. He shouldn't have said that last part.

Her eyes narrowed at him. "I've been by the clinic, Daniel. I was just there. I *just* told you my bags were packed, that I'm leaving in the morning, and you just fucking sat there. You didn't say anything. You wouldn't even look at me."

"You sounded like you'd made your mind up already. What could I say?"

"Something! I was hoping you'd follow me out the door, that you'd stop me and try to make me stay. But you act like you don't care at all."

He swallowed a lump of phlegm that was accumulating in his throat. Was that really how he came across? Apathetic? He forced himself to stare into her watery eyes. "Lena." His heart fluttered wildly as he spoke. "Of course I care."

"Then why haven't you said anything?"

"Because... it's hard?" It sounded so damn stupid to hear it aloud. Beyond stupid. It was humiliating. "I don't know."

She gaped at him.

"I'm sorry. You're the most important person in my life, Lena. I should've spoken up before now, I just... I didn't know how."

Lena looked like she was going to say something, but she stopped herself. Her imploring stare searched his eyes as she finally murmured, "I heard everything the demon said to you at the barn. All that stuff about me." A long, tense pause. "Was Bazolael telling the truth? Do you really feel that way about me?"

His heart was in his throat now, pounding away. He fought with all his might to keep his eyes fixed on Lena's. This wasn't the time to be timid. "Yes," he said. "Everything it said was true."

Her eyes sparkled in the moonlight as she studied him. Her lips parted, ever so slightly, as her gaze fleetingly dropped to his own mouth.

Suddenly emboldened, hoping he wasn't misreading her, Daniel reached over and cupped her cheek with his hand. Her damp skin felt smooth and warm against his palm.

He lingered for a second, waiting, giving Lena a chance to protest. When she did not, he slid his hand to the back of her neck, pulled her close to him, and kissed her.

The feeling of her soft, silky lips against his was dizzying. Electrifying. Fire flooded his chest, surging throughout his entire body as he leaned into her, deepening the kiss. He wound her hair around his fingers the way he'd been wanting to do since high school and drew her even closer.

Lena wasn't only unyielding, she was kissing him back. Hard.

Everything else dissolved into oblivion.

There was only them.

There was only now.

When Daniel finally pulled away, he didn't know how long they'd been kissing. Time didn't make sense anymore. He gawked at Lena. She was radiant, impossibly beautiful, tear-smeared mascara and all.

"I love you, Lena," he breathed, savoring the taste of her on his lips. "I always have." He felt a heavy pressure that he wasn't even aware of until now lift off his chest as he finally said those words aloud. "I wish to God I hadn't pulled you into all this, but... I'm also, selfishly, glad that I did, because you're here with me, now."

He paused to breathe. "You don't have to say anything, I just... I want you to know that I will always do whatever it takes to keep you safe. Always."

Lena smiled, reached for his hand, and interlocked her fingers with his. Daniel slung his free arm around her back, pulling her body against him. She rested her head on his shoulder as he held her, and everything felt right in the world.

The encounter with the demon in the gas station, Justin's senseless death, Bazolael's cryptic taunting in the barn, the threat of Abalaroth's impending return, Lena's nightmares and the journal pages she had destroyed, it all fell away.

They were here, together, safe at the Compound. The future was hazy, but they had each other, and that was all that mattered.

"I'm not letting you go back to Crofton," he said.

Lena huffed, but he could hear the smile in her voice when she said, "You're not 'letting' me?"

"Nope."

"I have to ask," she lifted her head from his shoulder and looked at him, "did you really only stay in Crofton because of me?"

"Yeah." It felt good to admit it. "I did."

She laughed, heartily. "I only took the job at the county hospital because it was close to you."

"Seriously?"

"Yep."

He thought his heart was going to burst with elation. He shook his head in disbelief and let himself laugh with her. "I'm glad we've finally cleared that up."

"Me too." She bit her lip, then reluctantly said, "I never told you this, but I actually got a crazy-good job offer from Vanderbilt. I was really considering it, but I finally turned it down because I didn't want to move to Nashville." She gave him a shy smile. "It was just too far away. From you."

"You turned down *Vanderbilt?*"

Lena shrugged dismissively. "I probably would've hated it anyway. Nashville traffic sucks butt."

"True."

As their voices grew quiet, Daniel imagined an alternate reality, one that possibly could have happened if this conversation had occurred a few months earlier. He pictured them in a little studio apartment downtown, Lena working nights at Vandy, Daniel employed at one of the many historical museums Nashville had to offer while he studied for the GRE. This version of them spent long, lazy Sunday mornings in bed together. Daniel made them omelets for brunch. They grabbed lattes from a trendy local coffee house run by mustachioed hipsters and spent the afternoon wandering the aisles of McKay's bookstore, hand in hand.

It was an impossible fantasy. Even with their feelings for one another out in the open now, a normal life together outside the Compound wouldn't happen.

But they could start over here. They could build a new life together on this side of the gate, where Abalaroth couldn't touch them, just like everyone else here had done.

There were loose ends back in Crofton that they would have to address somehow, and quickly, but there was now a shared understanding that all future trips to Crofton, Tennessee, would be temporary.

This was their home now.

Lena relaxed against Daniel and released a contented sigh.

They sat like this for some time, clinging to one another beneath the shimmering night sky.

A Note from the Author

Thank you so much for reading *The Compound.* If you would be so kind, please take a moment and head over to Amazon, Goodreads, BookBub, or anywhere you review books, and leave a rating and a short review. I'd love to hear your thoughts on the book, and your ratings and reviews greatly help other readers determine if *The Compound* duology is right for them.

If you'd like to receive updates about future books, visit my website, gwennamcallis.com, and sign up for my newsletter.

Thank you again, reader. It's been an honor and a lifelong dream to have you here.

About the Author

Gwenna McAllis grew up in the Deep South where she spent her free time as a kid reading and writing stories about the paranormal. Her love for writing eventually led her to the University of South Alabama, where she majored in English with a concentration in creative writing. Today, she writes supernatural suspense novels to make use of her otherwise useless B.A. in English. She resides in North Alabama with her husband, two young children, and an aging rescued pup.